# WAGING

## The Hounds of Zeus MC

## Book 1

## By Faith Gibson

Copyright © 2019 by Faith Gibson

Published by: Bramblerose Press LLC

Editor: Jagged Rose Wordsmithing

First edition: May 2019

Cover design: Jay Aheer, Simply Defined Art

Cover photography: RLS Model Images Photography

Cover model: Tyler Halligan

Back cover photo: Adobe Stock


ISBN:  978-1096436393

# Dedication

For Jennifer and Willow Jean

# Acknowledgements

This book has been a long time coming. Not just the fact that it's been so long since I got the last book out, but these characters have been on my radar for a long time, and here they are. I couldn't have done this without my tribe. Candy, Jennifer, Kendall, Kerstin, and Nikki, thank you for your support, whether it was helping with the book or keeping me sane during the last few months.

Thank you to all the beta readers. With this being a new series, I reached out to a bunch of you, and your feedback was both helpful and appreciated.

My girl Jen, thank you is never enough.

Jay, thanks for putting up with me and giving me another stellar cover.

To the man - Thank you for trying to keep the pup occupied so I could write. I love you.

*"Now hear another monstrous sight: Beware:*
*The sharp-beaked hounds of Zeus that never bark"*

*~ Aeschylus, "Prometheus Bound", 5th century BC*

# Prologue

THE SOLES OF her feet were bleeding. Slipping on the leaves, she grabbed hold of a tree branch to keep from falling, but she lost her grip. Landing against a sharp rock, she tried to suck in air when pain lanced her ribs and stomach. When no air was to be found, panic set in, but she pushed through it. She couldn't lie there when she needed to move. Her life depended on it. When she righted herself, she took a shallow breath and set off again.

Not long after she fled, her shoes had been sucked off her feet when she trudged through a mud hole. The pain had long since passed excruciating, and now her body was numb except for the tree branches scraping her face and slapping against her arms as she lurched through the dense brush. The woods were thick, and the rain only added to the darkness. How she wished her brain was numb, too.

Escaping into the forest had been her only option. She should have known someone would be watching. Known she was gone and come after her. The man noticed everything and everyone. He was the wolf in sheep's clothing she'd heard about in church all her life. Too bad the preacher failed to mention how to get away without the wolf's sharp teeth digging into your skin, ripping the flesh, and tearing through the marrow.

Now, she was running from the one she was supposed to trust. From one who was supposed to protect her from the sinners of the world. From one who touted God like he was on a first-name basis with Him. She didn't dare pray. Not if he was on God's payroll. She'd beg Satan himself for help before she trusted God again.

The barking grew louder, and her body shivered. Not from the rain, but from the thought of what those sharp teeth would do to her. She scrambled toward the sound of running water. When her feet went numb earlier, she'd been grateful, but now it was hindering her progress as she tried stepping on stones on the slimy creek bed. Slipping, she landed on her knees, jarring her wrists when they caught her on the rocks below. Frozen, she tried to get her body to budge. She had to move, or all the pain would be for nothing. It would get worse if she was caught. Her hair plastered to her face, stuck from the blood and tears mixing to form an adhesive the rain couldn't wash away.

The water rushing downstream hypnotized her. It was too dark to see what lurked beneath. That should have scared her. It didn't. It was the dog and the men chasing behind her that gripped her heart and lungs and twisted both until she couldn't breathe. Man, she was tired. So tired. If she let her arms collapse, she could succumb to the rushing water. She wouldn't have to worry about what he would do to her when she was dragged back to the place that was supposed to be a sanctuary. A haven. What a joke. Her freedom had been stolen. All because of a man. A sob tore through her chest, and in that moment, she saw the faces of her parents. God, her parents. She wouldn't do that to them.

After what felt like hours, she dragged herself across the shallow depths, digging into the silt beneath the water for leverage. Her fingernails were being torn and her knees cut with each rock she used for leverage. By the time she made it the short distance to the other side, her clothes were soaking wet, which made climbing from the embankment all the more difficult. Her bare feet did little to help, so she had no choice but to claw at the grass embankment until she was out of the water. Pushing her hair off her face with a muddy, bloody hand, she staggered to her feet and stumbled a few steps before she was able to move more steadily. A trail cut through the woods, and she decided moving along the path would be easier even if it gave those chasing her the same advantage.

Pain thrummed through her body, a steady beat clogging her ears. She was walking too slowly, but she couldn't see far enough ahead to move swiftly. Even if it had been daytime, she couldn't have moved any faster. She'd heard of adrenaline kicking in at times of dire need. Her situation was pretty damn dire, but her adrenaline had taken a pit stop somewhere along the way. She couldn't give up, though. She was in this mess because of a damn man, and she wouldn't give him the satisfaction of seeing her defeated. Her toe caught on a tree root, and she pitched forward, hitting the ground so hard her jaws clacked together. A growl cut through the darkness, and she scrambled to her feet. Sharp teeth snapped close to her ear.

"NO!"

# Chapter One

ONE WEEK OF freedom. As he strode with purpose trying to escape campus before a student sidelined him, Warryck let his mind wander to the future. He knew it was time to retire from teaching when he thought of spring break as freedom from his everyday life. Freedom from talking day in and day out about things he no longer tried to understand. Midway through college, Warryck had changed his major from criminal justice to psychology. He wanted to know what made people the way they were. Mostly the ones who had no qualms about taking the life of a young, pregnant woman. The mind was an ever-changing entity, and no two were the same. No matter how long he'd studied psychology, War still didn't grasp the intricacies of what made people tick. Or kill.

War and Harlow were in their second year of college when she was kidnapped. When she put up a fight against the men trying to take her, they didn't hesitate to beat her within an inch of her life. Harlow survived long enough to deliver their baby girl. Warryck lost more than his wife that day. He almost lost his will to live. Warryck couldn't look at the small child who lived while his precious woman didn't. Harlow's aunt and uncle, Vera and Lucius, took the baby into their home and even went so far as to adopt her on the condition he finish his college education. He really didn't have a choice considering he refused to let his own family raise the child. It was then he changed his direction in studies.

"Professor Lazlo, wait up." Warryck stopped walking, but he didn't have to turn to know who had called after him. The young woman had done everything except strip down in his office and offer to blow him. He had done everything except threaten to turn her in to the Dean of Students if she didn't stop with her failed attempts at getting him alone.

"Miss Perkins." War sighed and rubbed the bridge of his nose with his thumb and forefinger.

"I was hoping we could grab a coffee over spring break and discuss the latest assignment."

"Miss Perkins—"

"I've asked you to call me Ingrid," she said, running a sharp, fire-engine red nail down his arm.

Warryck took a couple steps back. "Miss Perkins, I've tried being subtle, but obviously that doesn't work for you, so here it is, plain and simple; I won't grab coffee. I won't do lunch. I won't have a conversation regarding anything with you, assignment or otherwise. There are plenty of students who understand the curriculum almost as well as I do who can discuss the assignment with you. I am not interested in you personally. Now if you'll excuse me, I have a meeting to attend." Warryck walked off, leaving Ingrid glaring. It wasn't a good look on her.

Ingrid Perkins wasn't the first student to come on to him. Both young women and men had tried to get the attention of the hardass psychology professor, but he wasn't going there. Warryck heard the whispers about his good looks. He ignored the digs at his less than chipper personality. Every year, it became a game of sorts with the students to see if any of them could break through the concrete walls of Professor Lazlo's stern exterior.

He wasn't homophobic by any means, but men didn't turn his head. Since his wife passed away twenty-four years ago, Warryck had taken women to bed but never for anything more than a one-night stand. He understood the physical need for sex. Hell, he craved it. Never did he meet up with anyone who knew who he was, which meant traveling out of town when the need became too much for something other than his hand.

When the school term ended, Warryck planned on taking a trip to get away from all things academic. He was burned out on teaching and had already turned in his resignation for the end of the school year. In a few months, he would be free from all responsibilities at the university, and he looked forward to packing a few clothes on his Harley and taking off across the country.

Over the years, Warryck had kept in touch with Maveryck. His twin never let him go long without at least calling and talking for a few minutes. He also never stopped encouraging Warryck to join the Hounds of Zeus. All his brothers were members of The Hounds Motorcycle Club. Mav just knew one day War, as his family called him, would get tired of teaching, and he'd been right. Warryck was over the daily grind, but that didn't mean he was ready to join the MC. He'd had enough rules and regulations to last a while.

Slipping into his hybrid SUV, Warryck drove on autopilot to the house he'd lived in for the last twelve years. Originally, he planned to rent until he was ready to move on, but when he realized he was going to be at the university a while, War finally broke down and bought a small house, considering it an investment. He didn't need much, just a couple bedrooms and a garage to house his car and Harley. One of those bedrooms he'd turned into an office. Never having company meant he didn't need the spare bedroom for its original purpose.

He'd just hit the garage door opener attached to his visor when his phone pinged with an incoming message, bringing on a four-year-old sense of déjà vu. War had been coming home for his gear, heading out on his bike for spring break...

*War sighed, praying it wasn't some last-minute crisis from the school. His bag was already packed and bungeed to the back of his bike. The weather had turned from several rainy days to clear and mild. Perfect riding weather. All he had to do was change out of his teaching attire into something suitable for a road trip on two wheels. He could already feel the wind blowing across his skin.*

*After placing his computer bag on the kitchen island, he fished his cellphone out of his blazer pocket and stared at the screen. An email from his twin wasn't unusual, but the subject matter was: Lucy. Warryck had kept his distance from his daughter all these years, but his family had taken it upon themselves to watch over the girl. She was family, and eventually, she was going to find out where she came from. Per his wishes, they only told him things about the daughter he abandoned if they were important. Opening the email, he read the message Mav deemed important enough to send. There were only two words along with an attachment. "Vera's gone."*

*"Gone where?" he pondered aloud until he opened the attachment to find an obituary. Both of Lucy's adoptive parents were dead, leaving the girl alone. It wouldn't matter that they had left her with an estate on the lake, cars, and a sizable bank account. His baby girl was alone except for the few friends she had at school. "Fuck," he muttered, raking a large hand down his scruffy face. He hadn't bothered shaving the last couple days, knowing he was taking off on his bike.*

*"Fuck," he said louder, his voice echoing in the small house. If Lucy got hold of Lucius's safety deposit box, she would find her birth certificate. Not the one stating who her adoptive parents were, but the one indicating her birth parents – him and Harlow. He didn't know Lucy, but if she was anything like her mother, she would come looking for answers.*

*Sending a response to Maveryck's email, he asked, "Does anyone have eyes on her?"*

*His phone pinged with an incoming text.* **You know we do.**

*Warryck went to the fridge and grabbed a beer, taking it to* his bedroom where he shed his khakis and dress shirt. Lucy wasn't his family's responsibility. She was his. But how did he explain to her why he left her with Harlow's family instead of raising her himself? Sure, his heart had been shredded from losing his wife, but a child wouldn't understand that unless they'd gone through the same kind of loss. She lost Lucius and Vera, but losing a parent wasn't the same as losing the other half of your heart.

When War returned to the kitchen, he grabbed another beer before sitting down in the recliner in his small living room. His jeans and boots were forgotten as he stretched out in a pair of sweat pants and a Henley. Torn between taking his road trip and staying put in case Lucy came looking for him. Was he ready for that? To face his daughter after all these years? No, he wasn't. Call him a coward, but he wasn't ready to admit the truth. With that realization, Warryck downed his beer and continued with his plan to hit the road. After taking a leak and washing his hands, he swapped out his sweats for a worn pair of jeans before sliding his feet into his boots. As he walked out to the garage, War did his best to drown out the voice chastising him for turning his back, once again, on his baby girl.

Instead of taking the direct route along Highway 7, War selected some backroads leading to Green Mountain in Vermont. It was rare he visited somewhere urban when he wanted to get away from his life, and this time was no different. Opting for an abandoned national park, he could become one with nature while indulging in his natural habitat. Preferring the eagle over the lion, War was more at home in the woods than anywhere, and he'd found a nice, secluded section of the Finger Lakes where he could camp out without anyone finding him.

Spring break only lasted a week, so War planned on spending every minute of those seven days relaxing with no one else around. He'd long ago tired of teaching. If he was honest, he'd never enjoyed it. When he applied for the position, he thought instructing others in the way the human brain worked was better than sitting in an office trying to help humans figure out why their mind was different. Why they were depressed. Why the voices spoke to them. As he guided his Harley along the pavement, *the doubts rose up as they always did when thinking he'd made a mistake.*

*It's never too late to make a change, War. It was something Maveryck said every time they spoke on the phone. He knew his brother was right, but did he want to sit in an office and listen to strangers talk about their mental health? Did he have it in him to give advice to people who were in pain when he himself was still going through the motions of living?*

*He didn't need the money. His plan when he retired from teaching was to get on his bike and go. He didn't have to work if he didn't want to, but War knew himself; he would get bored without a purpose. The rest of his family had a purpose. One he should be on board with. One he should be helping them with instead of staying away. Mav accused him of using the MC as an excuse to keep an arm's length from the family, but it wasn't an excuse.*

*Okay, maybe it was.*

*Growing up, he didn't have a problem with the club his father oversaw. War had always planned on being part of the group of men who gathered around the large, oak table each week to discuss how to make the world a better place. When they were little, he and Mav stayed up late talking about the bikes they would ride, and they would argue over who would be president. It wasn't until he met and fell in love with Harlow that his priorities, as well as loyalties, shifted. His mother accused War of allowing Harlow to influence him and convince him to turn his back on the family. He argued that wasn't the case, but now that he thought about it without the sting of Harlow's death clouding his judgment, he could see Rory had been right.*

*Harlow had come from a prestigious family. Her father and Lucius were brothers, both brilliant in their own right. Where Lucius spent his time holed up in a laboratory researching their kind, her father, Vincenzo, traveled the world making one business deal after another. Harlow spent as much time with Lucius and Vera as she did her own parents who thought it best to leave Harlow with Vera instead of dragging her across the globe. On one such trip, Harlow's mother, Beverly, got caught in the crossfire of a shooting. Even though the man who'd killed her* mother hadn't belonged to a motorcycle club, the fact that he rode a bike turned Harlow against the two-wheeled machines, and thus her hatred of all things chrome and metal was born.

Beverly had been in the wrong place at the wrong time, and Vincenzo never recovered mentally from the loss of his love. Gryphons didn't have fated mates the way other shifters did. Sure, most of them remained loyal to their mate once they fell in love, but if one of them passed on to the afterworld, it didn't mean the one left behind couldn't find love again if they chose to. Vincenzo chose not to. Instead, Harlow's father drank himself into a stupor daily, leaving Lucius and Vera to raise his only child.

Warryck's love for his wife had overshadowed everything. Her hatred of all things motorcycle hindered his plans to join his twin in sitting at the oak table wearing the colors of the Hounds. Instead, he married his love and followed her in going to college. With Harlow's family's money, neither of them wanted for anything. When they found out she was pregnant, Warryck had been scared. He hadn't planned on having kids, at least not before the two of them could graduate and become established in their jobs.

Fate had thrown War for a loop with impending fatherhood, and then again when it took Harlow from him. On her death bed, her last words to War were begging him to not raise their child in the MC world. He made his wife that promise, and he kept it. He allowed Vera and Lucius to convince him to finish his education, because it's what his wife would have wanted. Back then, he allowed Harlow, as well as her memory, to dictate how he lived and the decisions he made.

So twenty-one years later, why was he still doing that? Why was he allowing a memory to keep him away from his family? From the daughter he didn't know? Did Lucy even want to know him? Hiding out in a national forest was not the way to find out. With the mountains looming in the distance, War took the next exit and circled back toward home.

An hour later, he pulled into the driveway of his small house. He was both surprised and relieved there wasn't a strange car waiting on him. Did you really think she'd find you this quickly and be waiting for a family reunion? *The only mother Lucy had ever known had just been laid to rest. Hell, she might not have found her birth certificate yet. War's emotions were getting the better of him. He should have continued on to his camping trip. He needed the fresh air filling his lungs as he floated on the wind, stretching his wings. Feeling like a fool, he backed out of the driveway and once again turned his bike toward the forest, where he spent six days brooding.*

Warryck had waited, rather impatiently, for the day his daughter showed up at his door. He could have reached out to her and put them both out of their misery, but he didn't have the balls. Instead, he looked over his shoulder constantly. Every time the door opened to his office or someone called his name on campus, War expected to find his daughter standing there, ready to tear him a new one. It wasn't until several months later he came face to face with the ghost from his past. Now, their relationship was tenuous, at best, but he'd expected nothing less.

After reading the email from one of his colleagues, War let out a deep breath and stepped into his small house, striding to the bedroom where he changed clothes for the ride. His duffel was already secured to the back of his bike, so within ten minutes, he was back out the door. He'd made the same trip for the last few years. As he steered his Harley across the state line to the mountains, his thoughts always strayed to the same day all those years ago when Mav let him know Vera was gone.

# Chapter Two

"HEY, KERRI, GET me another beer, would ya?" Sam called from the other end of the bar.

"Yeah, *Kerri*, get me another beer," Dalton sneered in front of her.

Ignoring her boyfriend, Kerrigan poured a pint of Guinness and took it to Sam, one of the regulars at Harper's Point. She'd had a great life up until Dalton walked into the seaside tavern where Kerrigan tended bar. Her parents had migrated over from Ireland right before the world fell apart, and she'd been born in America. She took after both parents with her red hair and green eyes, and she'd picked up a bit of their Irish brogue. They'd started off in Maine, and Kerrigan loved it there. When her father's work dictated, her parents moved to South Carolina. Kerrigan opted to remain where she'd grown up, went to school, and made friends.

She'd started tending bar while going to college, and she found she loved her job of slinging pints of beer and pouring shots of whiskey while the patrons sat around, loudly conversing and laughing. So much so she dropped out of school and made a living behind the bar. Sure, it was hectic, and the grease from the kitchen clung to her long, curly red hair every night, but work was never boring.

Kerrigan had dated several men during college, but none had held her interest long. It had taken Dalton months to wear her down into going on a date. It had taken even longer for her to agree to have sex. Soon after, though, she agreed to move in with him. Each day was getting harder to bear. At first, Dalton had been perfect. Showering her with gifts and flowers. Telling her how much he loved her and wanted a life with her. Little by little, his true colors bled through until there was nothing but black covering the rainbow canvas. It had taken her a while to notice he'd alienated her from all her friends. Since he worked days, leaving his evenings free, Dalton sat on the same stool each night, glaring at every man who spoke to her, whether they were merely ordering a drink, or they were trying to carry on an innocent conversation. More than once, Brooks, her boss and owner of the tavern, had asked Dalton to leave, but whenever that happened, Kerri paid for it when she got home. His accusations were becoming more insistent, his tone harsher. More than once, he'd balled his fists until she did the only thing that calmed him down; Kerrigan shed her clothes wordlessly, offering herself to him.

"You need to get away from that man, Doll," Sam said low so Dalton wouldn't be able to hear.

"You need more pretzels?" Kerrigan asked, filling up the empty bowl instead of waiting on a reply. Sam wasn't the only one warning her about her boyfriend. On the nights Dalton didn't show, more than one regular approached her about getting out before it was too late. She knew they were right, and she'd been stashing money away in a savings account until she had enough to take off and go to her parents.

"There's my favorite girl!"

Kerrigan didn't have to look to know whose big voice boomed over all the noise. Ambrose Tucker, a large fisherman, strode into the bar, heading straight toward Kerrigan. The man was larger than life, and it had nothing to do with his six-foot-six frame. He owned several crabbing boats, and he'd made a name for himself around New Portland. Everyone who knew him knew he was married to the sea. They also knew his first stop once he made land was Harper's Point. Kerrigan put his age somewhere close to fifty. The sun and salty air gave the man a worn, hardened look, but it didn't detract from his handsome face. His bright, green eyes danced with mirth whenever he looked at her. *If only.*

Before he could make it to the open end of the bar, Dalton was there, hands fisted at his sides. "Who the fuck are you?" he demanded. The other bar patrons stopped talking. Stopped moving. Most had probably stopped breathing.

Ambrose smirked, cocking an eyebrow. "Ambrose Tucker. And you are?"

"I'm her boyfriend, you prick. I suggest you take a hike." Dalton punctuated his words by pointing toward the front door.

Kerrigan should have run at that point. Should have gone out the back door and headed south and never looked back, but she wouldn't leave Brooks without a bartender. Not on a night when every seat in the place was filled. "Dalton, stop."

"Why's that, *Kerri?* So you and Pops here can have a warm homecoming?" Dalton asked, never taking his eyes off the man who was twice as large as he was.

"Want me to take out the trash?" Ambrose asked Brooks, who was now standing next to Kerrigan.

"Nah, I'll handle it." Brooks came around the bar, grabbing Dalton's bicep. "Let's go," he said, dragging Dalton toward the door. "I warned you the last time. You're no longer welcome here."

Dalton jerked free. "Get your fucking hands off me. Come on, Kerrigan. You're quitting." He stood by the door, expecting her to go with him.

"I'm not leaving until my shift is over. I'll see you at home," she said, knowing this was it. This would be the breaking point, and she would have to leave New Portland that night.

"Fuck you," he spat before slamming the door open and stepping out into the dark.

Everyone turned to stare at her, but she waved her hand in the air. "Next round's on me," she called out. Most everyone went back to their drinks and conversations. Brooks and Ambrose did not. "I'm sorry, Brooks."

"You have nothing to be sorry for. Dalton's the one with the problem." Brooks stared at her, waiting. For what she didn't know, but she knew she had to be honest.

"I hate to do this to you, but I guess it's time I took off. You've been more than gracious dealing with him, but I won't let my troubles darken your doorstep any longer."

"Kerri, let me handle it," Ambrose offered. His soft words belied the darkness behind his eyes. "I need to know my favorite person in the world will be here when I come home." He didn't hesitate to pull her to him, wrapping his large arms around her shoulders. Kerrigan allowed herself a moment to be held. She tucked her arms between her chest and his stomach. She inhaled deeply, reciting to memory the way Ambrose made her feel. The way he smelled like sun, salt, and man. Kerrigan couldn't stop herself from sliding her hand up his chest to where the buttons were undone, touching his skin briefly. Ambrose kissed Kerrigan's curls and inhaled. It was like they both knew this was the last chance they would have to do so.

"Have a seat," she said, pulling away and returning to her place behind the bar. Kerrigan poured his favorite beer and shot of whiskey combination, setting both in front of him. She didn't linger, because if she did, she would ask him to take care of Dalton for her, and she couldn't have that on her conscience. She went about her job as she always did, smiling at every man and woman in the place, calling most of them by name. But tonight, she did more than that. She committed to memory every single one of them.

When closing time came around, only Brooks and

15

Ambrose were left. "What are you going to do?" Brooks asked.

"I'm going to stop by the bank and withdraw my savings. Then, in the morning after Dalton leaves for work, I'm going to pack my bags and go to my parents' place in South Carolina. I'm sorry to leave you like this, but I'd rather you have it rough for a few days without me than for this to happen again. Because it will happen again."

"Please don't," Ambrose said. "Don't let him win, honey. Come stay at my place while we figure something out."

"I appreciate the offer. I really do, but this is for the best. Me leaving isn't letting him win. Not really. But I can't ask either of you to risk your livelihoods for me."

"That's a risk we're both willing to take," Brooks said.

Kerrigan's heart broke. She knew both men would take care of her if she allowed it, but she couldn't. She was the one who'd gotten in bed, literally, with Dalton, and she was the one who'd get out of it. She would do that for them as well as herself.

"At least let me follow you," Ambrose offered.

"That I can do. Let me finish up here, and we'll go."

"I've got this. You go do what you have to. You have my number if you need me. Yeah?" Brooks said.

"Yeah. Thank you for everything. I'm going to miss you." Kerrigan hugged Brooks and kissed him on the cheek, not trying to keep her tears at bay. This had been her home for so long, and she was leaving a big part of herself behind.

Ambrose followed her to the bank and waited while she went in the glassed-off room at the front where the ATM machine was. She slid her card into the slot and punched in her PIN. *Insufficient Funds* popped up on the screen when she attempted to withdraw her money. She hit the "check balance" button, and when zeros appeared, Kerrigan had to grab onto the wall to keep from falling to her knees. The bastard had taken all her money. Taking a deep breath, she

16

walked out into the night, faking a smile.

"Everything okay?" Ambrose asked.

"Yes," she lied.

Ambrose pulled Kerrigan's hand up and placed something metal in it. "If you change your mind, or if you need somewhere safe, my place is secure. No strings attached."

Kerrigan opened her hand to find a house key. If she was smart, she'd use it. She'd take him up on his offer and hide out. But she knew that would only make things worse in the long run. Ambrose told her the address and waited while she put it as well as his number into her phone.

"Want me to follow you home?" Ambrose asked, pushing Kerrigan's hair off her shoulder.

She shook her head. "I'll be fine. We'll have words tonight like always, and in the morning, I'll take off."

Ambrose ghosted his fingers across her cheek while studying her face. When she thought he was going to pull back, he slid his hand underneath her hair and pulled her to him. The kiss was as soft as his fingers had been, but it was filled with so much emotion. She'd never allowed her feelings for this man to grow, because she knew there could never be anything between them. Still couldn't. His life was the sea, and hers...

"Maybe once this all blows over, I'll come back," she whispered.

"Nothing I'd like more," he returned. "You call me if you need me. If I'm on the water, it'll take a while to get back to you, but I will come for you."

"I know. You're a good man, Ambrose Tucker."

"And you're a better woman, Kerrigan O'Shea."

Ambrose kissed her again before opening her car door. She slid into the seat, not allowing herself to look at him again. She drove home on autopilot. When she reached the driveway, Dalton's truck wasn't there. She pulled out her phone and called her parents. Telling the truth of what happened was one of the hardest things she'd ever done in her life, but by the time they hung up, her dad had promised to wire money to a local Walmart. If she only knew where Dalton was, she'd pack her things right then and try to get away before he made it home. Headlights flashed in her rearview mirror. Too late. Drawing a deep breath, Kerrigan got out of her car and went inside so the neighbors wouldn't hear the fight she knew was coming.

The front door slammed behind her. When she turned around, Dalton was on her. Hand around her neck, he pushed her into the nearest wall, squeezing against her trachea. If he pushed much harder, he'd crush her windpipe. Kerrigan didn't fight him. She waited for the verbal lashing, and she didn't have to wait long.

"Looking for this?" Dalton held up a stack of money, flapping it in her face. "Think you're gonna just take our money and run off with that fishy-smelling bastard? Think again." Dalton shoved the money in his pocket before punching her hard in the stomach. With him still holding onto her neck, she couldn't double over from the pain, but she did bring one knee up in case he did it again. Dalton threw her to the ground, and before she could take a breath, he kicked her in the ribs.

"Dalton, please. I don't have feelings for anyone," she managed to cry out.

"Don't fucking lie to me! I saw you through the window, all cuddled up after I walked out. Then again when he followed you to the bank. What did you need money for, huh? I provide a house and food for you. I give you everything you need, yet you still whore yourself out behind my back." He kicked her again, and Kerrigan could do nothing to stop him. "Never again." Dalton crouched down beside her, running a finger over her cheek, gathering a tear. "Turnabout's fair play, *Kerri*. While I'm gone, I'd suggest you use your time to think about how you're going to act going forward." He patted her cheek hard before digging into her pocket for the key Ambrose had given her. Rummaging through her purse, he pulled out her cell phone, dropped it to the floor, and smashed it with his boot. Only then did he storm out of the house.

"Oh, God." Kerrigan couldn't breathe. Never had she felt such pain, but she had to get out of there. Crawling to the bedroom, she managed to pull herself to her feet. Instead of worrying about a suitcase, she shoved as many clothes as possible into her backpack. Without a phone, she couldn't call anyone, but she knew the address to her parents' place. If she could get to Walmart and to the money they were wiring in the morning, she'd be able to get a new phone then.

As she drove away from the small house where she'd lived the last few months, Kerrigan didn't look back. Walmart was about ten miles away, but she'd only gone about four when her car began acting up. Instead of keeping to the main roads, she'd taken the back route, and now she was on a dark road with no houses or businesses in the area. Kerrigan didn't want to pull over, especially having no phone, but when her car sputtered to its death, she had no choice. Putting on her emergency flashers, Kerrigan thought about her choices. She was in no shape to walk the half mile to where she would find life, but she didn't want to sit and wait on someone to possibly drive past. The weather was still chilly, and she only wore her leather jacket over her clothes. Whether she remained in her car or took off walking, she was going to be cold. Just as she made up her mind to walk, headlights shone in her rearview mirror. The car pulled to a stop, and Kerrigan watched as a man got out and walked to her window.

God, she was so screwed. The stranger was tall, well-built, and he could easily subdue her even if she wasn't hurt. The man smiled at her as she cracked her window. "Car trouble?"

"Yeah." She didn't want to admit she had no phone, but

19

what else was she going to do? "I forgot my phone, so if I could borrow yours, that'd be great." Kerrigan could hear the shakiness in her words, and the man didn't miss it.

"You're hurt. Are you running from someone?"

"I fell down the steps when I got home from work. I was just headed to the walk-in clinic."

"Young lady, the walk-in clinic is closed. Why don't you let me drive you to my brother's? He's a doctor. I'll call for a tow, and while you wait for the auto shop to open, we'll get you taken care of. I know you don't know me, but I wouldn't want my daughter out here with no one to help her if she were in your position."

The man seemed sincere, but Kerrigan's intuition told her not to trust him. What choice did she have? If she didn't go willingly, he could break the window and force her out. He seemed to notice her hesitation, because he pulled out his phone, tapped a few times at the screen before putting it to his ear.

"Yes, hello. My name is Stanley Carson. I'm on Johnson Road off Route 67, and my car is broken down. I'd like to request a tow. I have someone to take me home, so I'll leave the keys in the ignition. Great, thank you."

The man – Stanley – pocketed his phone. He hadn't mentioned her to the guy on the phone. "I didn't tell him your name because I didn't know it. Maybe we can rectify that?"

"Kerrigan. But you don't have to take me anywhere. I'll just wait on the tow truck and ride with them. You've been more than helpful."

"Nonsense. I can tell you're in great pain. Please let me take you to my brother."

It was getting harder for Kerrigan to breathe through the pain. She'd never passed out before, but she felt like she was close to doing so. If that happened, she was at his mercy anyway. At least if she went willingly, she might have a fighting chance if he tried something. Ignoring her backpack, Kerrigan grabbed her purse and unlocked the door, letting him help her out of the car. He got her seated in the sedan he was driving. While he was climbing into the driver's side, she hissed through the pain of reaching back over her shoulder for the seatbelt. Stanley gave her a cursory glance before pulling onto the road. Kerrigan fought to keep her eyes open. Just as her eyelids fluttered, she had a sinking feeling she'd made the wrong choice.

Again.

# Chapter Three

WARRYCK TOSSED ANOTHER piece of wood on the fire. Being a shifter, he didn't get cold, but there was something soothing about the flames as they danced in the dark. He returned to his spot on the ground and leaned back against the base of a large tree, stretching his long legs out in front of him, crossing them at the ankle. The night was quiet save the crackle from the fire. Warryck was the only animal awake, and it didn't suit him the way it used to. It had been too long since he'd spent any amount of downtime with another person. The closer he got to retiring, the less he appreciated the solitude. Twisting the cap off a bottle of whiskey, he took a long pull as he thought of all the people in his life who would probably love to take away the loneliness.

Maveryck was never far from his mind. War loved his whole family, but he missed the closeness he once shared with his twin. All the plans they made when they were younger were invading his thoughts often, begging for consideration instead of letting them remain as nothing but childhood dreams. Every time they spoke on the phone, Mav reminded him how much he still wanted them to ride side by side, even if War didn't patch into the club. Warryck knew it wasn't that simple. If he went back home, his brothers wouldn't stop hounding him until he took his rightful place at the table.

Having no plans after retirement other than hitting the open road, War found himself considering joining the family's mission in taking down every faction of the Ministry they could find. That mission was a noble one. More noble than teaching. More ambitious than riding cross-country alone. He was looking forward to traveling, but how long would that keep him satisfied? How long until the loneliness kicked in? War could always call Mav and ask him to accompany him, and he knew his twin would jump at the chance. The last time they rode together had been after he graduated college and they went after the ones responsible for Harlow's death. Their family had no problem taking out the trash.

The Ministry, a cult of religious fanatics, had caused the near-apocalypse some thirty years before. When the first child had successfully been cloned, they took it upon themselves to rid the world of the scientist who they claimed was playing God, all while doing the same by raining judgment on the man's clinic as well as the world. The bombs weren't only directed at the clinic where the doctor saw patients, but major cities all across the globe. According to the Ministry, they were doing God's bidding. Like with Sodom and Gomorrah, the great flood, and the plagues, they were purging the world of the sinners. Setting off a cataclysmic "storm" of epic proportions, the Ministry single-handedly brought the world to its knees. It took a while, but eventually, cities began to rebuild, with most adding "New" to the city's name, letting the world know they were doing their best to rise from the ashes.

Before the Ministry happened, the Hounds had spent their time protecting humans from the other dregs of society. Having charters across the world allowed the Gryphons to gather their kind under the guise of the club. Not all Gryphons were Hounds, but all Hounds were Gryphons. Each one who wore the kutte and swore the oath vowed to protect humans as well as other shifters. As with all motorcycle clubs, they made their own rules, policed their own, and lived by a code. It was a lifestyle Warryck had grown up in and one he wholeheartedly agreed with. That is until Harlow convinced him otherwise. Now, twenty-four years later, he found himself thinking more about doing his part.

Originally, the Hounds weren't mercenaries for hire. When the Ministry caused the chaos which ended life as the world knew it, military factions were stilted from lack of funding, and the Hounds stepped in, attempting to restore some facsimile of order to the world. When word got out there was a small group willing and able to rid the world of the scum the government failed to track and take down, the Hounds began taking on paid jobs.

If Warryck didn't join his family, he had no idea what he would do with his time once the school year was over, but one thing was certain – he no longer cared about being a psychologist, teacher or otherwise. Sitting there, staring into the flames, War decided he would definitely reach out to his twin and ask him to come along. Having one-on-one time with Mav would allow him to figure out his next steps as well as find out more about his daughter. Lucy was now entrenched deeply within the family, and for that he was thankful. They had welcomed her with open arms, just as they would have if he had let them raise her.

In getting pulled into the family, Lucy had been caught by the government hacking into computers. The GIA – Global Intelligence Agency – had given Lucy two options. One, come to work for them, or two, do jail time. Lucy chose to become a government agent, and now his baby girl traveled the world putting her computer skills to work for her country. Being a Gryphon, he shouldn't worry about her. She had the animal strength to protect herself, and now she had training in hand-to-hand combat as well as weaponry. He did worry, though.

War dug his cell phone out of his pocket and thumbed

open the photo app, pulling up the last picture Mav had sent of his daughter. Seeing Lucy's smile didn't hurt as much as it had in the beginning. She'd grown into a beautiful young woman, and he could now look at her without seeing her mother. That pain had eased over the years, but the guilt at letting Lucius and Vera raise his daughter was still there.

Maybe his family was right, and it was time to put the past where it belonged – in the past. Lucy being a government agent didn't leave much time for her to visit, but War needed to make an effort to get to know her better. Not the agent who traveled the world. Not the Gryphon who could take care of herself. But the daughter who looked up to Ryker as a father figure. Surprisingly, it had been his oldest brother who latched on to Lucy the most. The others loved her and doted on her, but it was the stoic man who had loss and pain of his own who always made sure Lucy's needs came first, even though she had to remind him of his past. If Ryker could overlook what happened all those years ago and let Lucy into his heart, Warryck should be able to do the same, especially considering she was his child.

He had no idea where Lucy was at the moment, but sending a text wouldn't disturb her if she was sleeping.

Warryck: *Hey, Lucy. I just wanted to reach out and ask how things are going. I didn't want to call in case you were asleep.*

Taking another long pull from the bottle, Warryck gripped his phone tightly in his other hand. It wasn't Lucy's fault she'd been born. Wasn't her fault her mother had been injured so badly she died while giving birth. Wasn't her fault he abided by Harlow's wishes to keep Lucy away from his family and the club. She had every right to ignore him. He hadn't immediately asked for forgiveness when he explained why he gave her up for adoption. War didn't feel he deserved it.

When his phone pinged, the sound echoed in the silence of the woods.

Lucy: *I'm currently in Norway, and it's morning here.*

Warryck: *On assignment or vacation?*

When Lucy set out to find him, she'd enlisted the help of a friend from college who was adept in computer manipulation. Lucy's words, not his. Lucy learned the basics of hacking and started helping the family track down the Ministry using her new skills. The government had been alerted. What Lucy had done didn't warrant being thrown in jail as far as he was concerned, but they saw it differently.

Lucy: *A little of both. I am taking a couple extra days to enjoy the town where I'm staying. It's a shifter town, and it feels nice to be around those who are different like us.*

Warryck: *It's a town of Gryphons?*

Lucy: *Gargoyles as far as I can tell. I've only seen one of them shift, but he has family here.*

Warryck: *I know you can handle yourself, but please be careful. We don't know enough about their kind.*

Lucy: *I will be. Now, what are you up to? How's the university?*

Warryck: *I'm sitting in the woods enjoying spring break. I turned in my notice, so I'm contemplating my future at the moment.*

Lucy: *Does your contemplation include joining the Hounds?*

Warryck answered honestly: *Maybe? I do miss riding with Mav. I still have a few weeks left in the year, and I'm going to be busy tying up a lot of loose ends. After that???*

Lucy: *I'm sure you'll figure it out. I hate to cut this short, but I gotta run. Thanks for reaching out. Talk again soon?*

Warryck: *Of course. Take care.*

Their conversation might not have been all that personal, but it made Warryck feel good. His daughter had answered immediately, and she even thanked him. That made him feel like shit. His own kid shouldn't have to thank him for texting her. Maybe next time he'd actually call.

Before the full week was out, Warryck was ready to go home. Go back to the land of the living where he wasn't

26

alone. That was when he knew he was truly ready for a change. Never before had he felt such a deep-seated need to be around others. Around his family. He'd spent the week trying to figure out why the sudden change. Maybe it was Lucy's presence. War was finally ready to get to know his daughter.

He'd never shared this spot with anyone, but now he wanted Mav there with him. When they set out on their journey, he figured this would be a good place to start. To show his twin the peaceful place he no longer felt the need to hide from others.

Dogs barking in the distance drew Warryck's attention away from the future and back to the present. In all the times he'd camped at that particular spot, he'd never heard dogs. Never ran into other campers or hikers anywhere close by. Gryphon senses were heightened, but unless they were in their animal form, they weren't extraordinary. War turned up the bottle and took another pull of whiskey. He didn't drink to numb himself. Not any longer. After Harlow passed away, War found himself drinking quite often. Now, he did it because he liked the taste of the smooth, amber liquid. It had been a long time since he felt the sadness that came with his wife's memory. Time did heal all wounds. Well, at least it had his. He couldn't say the same for Ryker.

His older brother's pain seemed to always thrum right below the surface. It made sense why he latched onto Lucy. It also made sense why Ryker had issues with War giving her up to Harlow's family. It had been over twenty years, and War still felt the contempt and judgment from his oldest brother. Being twins, War and Mav had a closer bond than with the others. The younger brothers, Hayden and Kyllian, were closer in age, so they had a bond as well, but Ryker was the loner. He cared for all of them in his own way, but it was always at an arm's length.

When the barking receded then ceased altogether, War put it out of his mind, choosing to focus on the upcoming

27

months. For the first time in as long as he could remember, War was looking forward to the future. He didn't know what it would bring, but he was ready for a change. Ready to spend time with Mav. With all his family. And that included getting to know Lucy better. He had already asked her forgiveness, which she'd said there was nothing to forgive. She understood his reasoning. Understood the promise he'd made to her mother.

Closing his eyes, War let the coolness of the night air wash over him. Instead of getting into his tent and sleeping, he remained seated against the tree. When he woke the next morning, his ass was numb, and his body was damp from where the dew had fallen overnight, but he felt alive. Ready for whatever the future held. Ready to go home and plan. Instead of remaining in the woods the whole week, he got to his feet, and after making sure the fire was extinguished, War packed his gear and headed home.

The weekend passed with War looking at websites, mapping out the first leg of his trip with Maveryck, even though it was several weeks away. The thought of not answering to anyone but himself was getting his adrenaline going. He needed to channel the fire into his last few weeks of school so the kids he was teaching didn't get a raw deal. He'd signed on to be a professor to make a difference, and he vowed he would do that, no matter how badly he was ready to be done with teaching. While he should have been going over notes for upcoming classes, he just couldn't stop himself from thinking about the future with Mav by his side.

# Chapter Four

KERRIGAN AWOKE TO a woman's voice singing what sounded like a hymn. It wasn't one she was familiar with, but the words spoke of pearly gates and streets of gold. Definitely not her type of music. Maybe the nurse at the emergency room was religious. Turning her head toward the sound, Kerrigan opened her eyes. The singing stopped, and plain, brown eyes set deep in a nondescript face stared back at her. Kerrigan then took in her surroundings. Definitely not a hospital. The dingy, gray room was devoid of anything on the walls, including windows. The only light came from an oil lamp sitting atop a small side table.

The pain in her ribs wasn't as bad as she expected when she pushed herself up to a seated position. When she threw the covers back so she could stand, a firm hand tugged the material the other way. "You need your rest," the young woman said.

"Who are you? Where am I, and how long have I been here?" There was the barest hint of pain from her ribs, but they wouldn't be nearly healed if she had only been there a few hours.

"You're somewhere safe. Brother Steven saved you when your car broke down."

The name Steven didn't ring a bell. The man who'd stopped had said his name was Stanley. "Saved me? He was supposed to take me to his brother who's a doctor. I need to go. My parents — "

"You're in no condition to leave. Brother Silas has tended to your wounds, and you are supposed to rest."

Kerrigan took in the woman's appearance. The clothing she wore was as drab as the room. A beige cotton tunic topped a long-sleeved, white T-shirt. Beige cotton pants matching the top completed her ensemble. Maybe they were scrubs, and she was a nurse. Her hair was braided down her back, and she wore no makeup as far as Kerrigan could tell. "What is this place?" She tried to sit up again, and again, the woman pushed her down. "I really wish you'd stop pushing me." Kerrigan was getting pissed, but she was in no condition to put up much of a fight. "Where am I?"

"Like I said, somewhere safe. I'm going to tell Brother Gideon you're awake."

"Wait. Who are you people?" Kerrigan had a bad feeling with all the "brothers" the woman had spoken of.

Ignoring her, the woman stepped out of the room and shut the door behind her. When the lock clicked from the outside, Kerri shivered. She pushed herself to sitting, hissing through the pain. Okay, maybe she was worse off than she originally thought. While she waited on the woman and this Gideon character to return, Kerrigan thought back to how she'd gotten there. Dalton beating her. Her car breaking down, and the man – Stanley – insisting he take her to his brother's. It sounded like he had lots of brothers.

"Kerri, you are a fool," she mumbled to herself. She didn't know what day it was or how long she'd been out of it. There were no windows to show whether the sun was shining or if it was still night. For all she knew, they could have drugged her for weeks.

The lock turned, and the door opened. A tall, well-built man stepped into her room. "Thank you, Agnes. That will be… all." He stared at Kerrigan like he'd seen a ghost. As quickly as his face had shuddered, he composed himself, standing taller with an air of importance. His black hair was slicked back from his face, and even though he smiled, his eyes told a different story. She'd seen the same look in Dalton's eyes. Cold. Calculating. "Hello, Kerrigan. I'm Brother Gideon. Agnes tells me you have questions."

Even though she was fully clothed, albeit in the same type of drabness Agnes had on, Kerrigan pulled the sheet up higher. "You're damn right I do. Where the hell am I for starters? I was supposed to be going to see a doctor."

"Foul language isn't tolerated here at The Sanctuary. You really should be more appreciative of our generosity. Brother Steven brought you here where we could help you recuperate from your injuries."

"I'm feeling pretty recuperated, so if you'll give me my clothes back, I'll be on my way."

"I'm afraid it isn't that simple." Gideon took a step closer, his hands clasping in front of his immaculate suit. "Your boyfriend is causing quite a stir looking for you, and we feel it's best for you to remain here where you will be safe."

Kerrigan didn't feel safe. In fact, she was terrified, but she did her best to keep that to herself. "I appreciate what you've done thus far, but I was supposed to have gone to my parents, and they're no doubt looking for me."

"We took the liberty of telling your family you were safe so they wouldn't worry about you."

"You did what?" Kerrigan threw back the covers and stood quickly. Her ribs protested, but she ignored the sting. "You had no right! And you cannot keep me here. That's kidnapping."

"Kidnapping is such a harsh accusation, Kerrigan. You flagged down Brother Steven for assistance. We only brought you here to help. Of course, you're free to go, but you should know, The Sanctuary isn't close to a town. Let's just say, we're off the beaten path, and if you were to leave, you'd be on your own."

Kerrigan was beyond frustrated. How had her life

31

gotten to that point? She would blame Dalton, but she'd been the one to agree to moving in with him. This was all on her. Why hadn't she let Ambrose take care of her? If only for one night? Then she could have gotten safely to Walmart and on to her parents. God, her parents. They thought she was safe. Nobody, save these crazies, knew where she was. She needed a plan. If what Gideon said about their location was the truth, she couldn't just take off. She'd end up lost and starved.

"I need to use the phone to call my parents."

"I have already assured your family we were taking care of you."

"How the hell do you know who my parents are?" Kerrigan, even more leery than before, wanted to hit the man, but she knew it wouldn't end well if she did. He was even larger and more imposing than Dalton. She needed time to think, and that meant she would have to bide her time and get to know the lay of the land. To do that, she would have to rein in her temper as well as her urge to take off running as soon as she was allowed outside. "Can I at least have my own clothes?"

"We are a simple people, Kerrigan. For your duration with us, you will need to dress as we do."

"You mean I'm stuck in the ugly uniform, or you're giving me a suit?" she asked, pointing to the clothes he was wearing.

Darkness flared briefly in his eyes. "No. The clothes you are wearing are the typical attire of our flock. Since I have important meetings, I dress for the occasion when it's necessary. Now, I will go fetch Agnes. She will be taking you to your new quarters."

"I'm not staying here?" she asked, looking around at the bland room. Moving to a new room might not be a bad thing.

"This is the infirmary, so no, you are not staying here. Your ribs are healing and will continue to do so in your new home. While you are among our people, you will adhere to the schedules and... customs as if you were one of our own. Who knows? You might find you like the peace and solitude enough you'll want to stay."

Kerrigan bit the inside of her mouth to keep from saying there was no way in Hell she would want to stay. Instead, she nodded, crossing her arms over her chest so she wouldn't fist her hands. Without another word, Gideon left the room. Kerrigan could hear him speaking in low tones to someone in the hallway, but she couldn't make out the words. Seconds later, Agnes reappeared, her face devoid of any emotion.

"I'm to escort you to your new housing. I'm also supposed to take you around and show you where everything is as well as inform you of our schedules." Without waiting, the woman turned on her heel and left the room. Kerrigan could either stay put or follow. If she were honest with herself, she was a little curious as to The Sanctuary and the other people who lived there. How many were there by choice, and how many had been brought there like she'd been?

As Kerrigan walked behind Agnes, she took in her surroundings, doing her best to remember every turn they made. Once outside, Kerrigan was surprised to see what she considered a compound of sorts. All the buildings were square, one-story structures with no discernable differences. Instead of entering any of them, Agnes continued on toward a tree line. They walked down a worn, dirt path for close to ten minutes. Kerrigan had to pause a few times to catch her breath. When they cleared the other side of the trees, more buildings came into view. These were the same bland concrete as the others had been only on a smaller scale. Kerrigan was noticing a pattern – everything, save Gideon, was plain and boring.

"The women's quarters are on the right and the men's on the left. Under no circumstances are you to ever enter the men's quarters. Here we are," Agnes said, stopping in front of the fourth building. Her new accommodations were sparse at best. Two bunkbeds lined the side walls, and one door was positioned on the far wall. At least there were long windows situated high above the beds. Other than oil lamps sitting atop two small tables, that was the only source of lighting. "That's the bathroom," Agnes said, pointing to the door. "You will sleep on the top bunk above me," she instructed, pointing to the beds on the left.

"Who sleeps in the others?" Kerrigan asked. There were no personal effects. No photos or any type of artwork adorning the walls. At the foot of each bed stood a small chest of drawers.

"Sisters Mary and Katherine. They are tending to the gardens at present. You will meet them at lights out."

"Gardens? Like flowers, or…?"

"Vegetables. The Sanctuary is self-sustaining in that we grow our own vegetables. What meat we eat comes from venison as well as the cattle and poultry we raise. We do have to have some items brought in from the outside, but it's bought and stored in bulk. You'll see all that when we head back to the square."

Kerrigan took the square to be the buildings they'd passed on the way to their room.

"All I saw were plain buildings. Where are the animals and gardens?"

"They're in the south."

"The south? Like, away from here?" Kerrigan still didn't know where "here" was.

"No, the southern acres. The Sanctuary is vast in its expanse."

"And where are we exactly?"

Agnes sighed. "I'm not supposed to tell you that. I will tell you we are in Vermont."

Shit! There was a state between her and home, and since she didn't know what part of Vermont she was in, it could be as much as nearly two states away. She'd foolishly thought she would be able to bide her time and make an escape, but considering she was in the middle of nowhere, Kerrigan was screwed. "Where are my things?"

Agnes stepped to the chest at the foot of their shared bed and pointed at the third drawer from the bottom. "Your purse and underwear are there, and your clothes are in the bottom drawer."

Kerrigan opened the bottom drawer expecting to find her own clothes. She should have known better. It was more of the same thing she currently had on. Opening the third drawer, she went to grab her purse but stopped when she saw the bras and panties. Pulling out the top bra, Kerrigan grimaced at the article she doubted her grandmother would wear. Tossing it back in, she removed her purse and dug inside for her wallet. What little money she had was still there, but her credit cards and driver's license were missing. With no money to speak of, no identification, and no phone, she was well and truly fucked.

"Gideon said I'm not a prisoner, but in taking all my possessions, that's how I feel. Does anyone ever get to leave once they're brought here?"

"No one wants to leave. Why would they? The Sanctuary is like heaven on earth." Agnes didn't address the part about people being brought there against their will.

"Right," Kerrigan muttered to herself. Instead of letting her disappointment show, she walked over to the bathroom door and opened it. Plain bottles lined the shelf in the shower. "What about soap, shampoo, and other toiletries?" She didn't see a bottle of Suave or a bar of Dial anywhere.

"We make those as well. Much better for us and the environment."

"And feminine products? It's almost time for my period."

Agnes blushed and pointed to the cabinet under the sink. "There are supplies in there."

Kerrigan didn't bother to look. She probably wouldn't like what she found. "So, if the men and women are separated, I take it there're no couples in The Sanctuary?"

"Oh, sure there are, but they reside in a different area."

Kerrigan closed the bathroom door. "Are you dating anyone?"

Agnes looked as though Kerrigan had slapped her with the question. "Brother Gideon hasn't chosen me yet." Agnes shrugged.

"Maybe you just haven't met the right man." Kerrigan didn't understand why Gideon would have to choose Agnes for a relationship, but the way the other woman curled around herself told Kerrigan it was a topic best left to a later date. They hadn't passed any of the others on their walk to their room. Kerrigan didn't know what else to call it. Quarters seemed too generous. "Speaking of men, where is everyone?"

"Everyone has a role to play. Much like where you are from, we all have jobs. Come on, I'll show you where everything you'll need is." When Kerrigan closed the door behind them, she went to lock it, but there was nothing but a plain knob.

"Uh, why isn't there a lock on the door?"

"We are a peaceful people. We don't need locks."

"So, anyone can just walk into our room whenever they want?"

Agnes shook her head. "It's against the rules, and everyone follows the rules."

Kerrigan understood there were nice people in the world, but she also knew there were those who weren't. She'd met both kinds, and she didn't believe not one single soul in this place wasn't at least less than honest. "Since I was a bartender back home, will I get to do the same type of work here?"

"Alcohol isn't allowed in The Sanctuary. It's considered a vice, and Brother Gideon teaches us vices can ruin

36

people."

No alcohol? How the hell was she going to get through her time there? Kerrigan wasn't a drunk, but working at Harper's Point had allowed her to join in with the regulars whenever they celebrated or just wanted her to have a shot with them. As she followed behind Agnes, Kerrigan thought back to Ambrose. Why hadn't she taken him up on his offer? If she'd gone home with the large fisherman, they would have no doubt fallen into his bed, and even though Dalton was a dick, Kerrigan wasn't a cheater. But looking back, it would have been worth it. He might not have stuck around for long, but she'd have been able to get safely to her parents. Now, they thought she was okay and wouldn't be looking for her. She'd told both Brooks and Ambrose she was going to South Carolina. Dalton might ask around, but not because he cared. He would be pissed she got away from him. No, he would give up, figuring she got to her folks' place. Her reality slammed into her chest, much like what she thought getting shot would feel like.

No one would come for her. Kerrigan had been taken to hell, and Gideon was the devil.

# Chapter Five

SITTING IN THE arena waiting for the graduation ceremony to commence, Warryck thought back to his own graduation. The pain had lessened over the years, but the memory wasn't among his happiest. Instead of celebrating with his wife, instead of tossing his cap into the air amidst the flurry of black mortarboards, Warryck pushed his way through the throng of his fellow graduates.

*War flung his graduation cap into the nearest garbage receptacle. The Bachelor of Science degree he'd been presented less than forty-five minutes prior was just another reminder of what he'd lost. Instead of walking across the stage immediately after the love of his life, he walked after some guy he'd never met. Some nameless face like all the other college students graduating that day. If it hadn't been for his wife's aunt and uncle pushing him to finish, pushing him to succeed, pushing him to live, he'd have gotten on his Harley and driven off into the proverbial sunset, never to return. But they had pushed. Lucius and Vera Ball had saved Warryck's life in more ways than one.*

*He'd done as they asked and graduated college with a degree, but now that he had the piece of paper, he had no interest in pursuing a career in psychology. No interest in becoming the man he'd dreamed of. Without his wife, Warryck had no interest in anything at all, and that included his six-month-old baby girl. Warryck couldn't see her little face and not see Harlow. He couldn't look at her and not think about the life he and his high school sweetheart were supposed to have. Maybe one day he would* look at his daughter and not feel the loss of his beloved, but that day wasn't today.

While the other graduates celebrated with their families, Warryck slipped into the men's restroom and removed the gown, stuffing it into the trash can before taking a piss. He didn't bother looking at his reflection in the mirror as he washed his hands. Warryck already knew what he'd see, and it wasn't the face of the happy man who should be standing there. The one who should be celebrating as both he and Harlow graduated together while their families looked on. In that man's place was the Gryphon that lived within, driving him to seek revenge for Harlow's death. Drying his hands, Warryck grabbed the fake diploma and headed for the exit.

"War," a deep voice growled, causing Warryck to release his talons. If he'd been paying attention instead of wallowing in self-pity, he would have noticed the man leaning against the truck parked next to his bike. Since his head was somewhere else, he had been caught off-guard.

"Fucking hell," he cursed, retracting his claws while looking around to see if anyone had caught his infraction. Seeing the coast was clear, Warryck turned his attention to the other man, taking in the changes since the last time he'd seen him. "What are you doing here, Mav?" Warryck asked his twin. Standing at six-four, Maveryck Lazlo was the same height as Warryck, but he had bulked up over the last few years, giving him at least thirty to forty pounds on Warryck. His twin did favor the lion over the eagle, so it only made sense he wouldn't be as lean as Warryck.

"Did you think I'd let you graduate alone?" Maveryck took a deep drag off his cigarette, blowing the smoke up and away from Warryck. "You might have abandoned the rest of us, but we didn't abandon you."

"I didn't abandon anyone. I made a choice, and that was Harlow."

"I get that, but just because you got married and went to school didn't mean you had to cut the rest of us out of your life. I'd like to have been there for you when my niece was born. Mom was pissed as hell about that. Still is."

"Yeah, well, I didn't have a lot of time to call family in." Warryck didn't want to talk about that night.

"I'm real sorry about Harlow. I liked her."

Maveryck's words, even though they surprised War, couldn't have hurt any more if he'd hauled off and punched Warryck in the gut. "How did you know?" he asked, his question barely more than a whisper.

"You think I didn't keep tabs on your ass when you left? You're my fucking twin, War. Besides that, I'm a Hound, for Zeus's sake. Just because you don't embrace your inner nature doesn't mean I don't."

The Hounds of Zeus were Gryphon shifters, created by the god to protect his human children. At least that was the story that had been passed down through all the generations.

"You don't know anything about me. Not anymore." Although it was the truth, it didn't sit well with War that he and his twin were no longer close. He knew it was his own fault, but he had chosen his wife over his family. That didn't sit well with his brothers, and it especially pissed off his mother.

"No? Are you gonna look me in the eye and tell me you aren't getting ready to run? That you aren't abandoning your baby girl as well as four years of education so you can go on a suicide mission alone? That you're gonna continue to act like you don't have a brotherhood ready to hit the road with you so they'll have your back? Look, I get the club isn't the life for you, but you're still one of us whether or not you wear a kutte."

Ignoring his brother's keen insight into exactly what Warryck had planned, he diverted the conversation. His twin's vest had patches depicting the name of their club, and War pointed at the one under Mav's biker name, Mayhem. "I see you're VP now. How does Ryker feel about that?"

"Seeing as he's now the Pres, he likes it just fine."

"Pres? What happened to Sutton?"

"Dear old Dad passed down the gavel. One of his old Army buddies tried to recruit him for a black ops mission, but Sutton told him he was retired. When his friend pressed the issue, Dad found out what the mission entailed and told his buddy he was in.

40

Dad came into Church, holding a special meeting to let us know about the mission and how he was going undercover. He filled us in on as much as he could, but the little he told us was some really sick shit."

"I thought he was retired from that life."

"You never retire, War. Sometimes you lay the gavel down. Sometimes you swap out the uniform for a different one, but you never truly get too far away from who you are deep down inside."

"Seems like you should've been the one to study psychology." Warryck unlatched the flap on his saddle bag and stuck the fake diploma inside. After refastening the clasp, he crossed his arms over his chest. Sutton Lazlo had been a lot of things in his long life, but chief among them was detective for the New Houston PD back before he relocated the family to upstate New York. If his father passed leadership of the Hounds of Zeus to their oldest brother, the mission he was investigating must have gone way beyond the pale.

"What does Rory think of all this?"

"You know Mom. She's got Sutton's back. And from what Dad told us of this mission, the rest of us were ready to ride along with him. He convinced us he could do it alone, so he passed the presidency down to Ryker."

He did know his mom. Aurora Rose Lazlo was a hell of a woman. She was as fierce as any of the men in their family, and that had nothing to do with the Gryphon side of her. If he wanted the MC life for his baby girl, he knew Rory would step up to help him out in a heartbeat. Since he didn't want that life for her – since Harlow didn't want that life for his baby girl – he turned to Vera, thus turning his back on Rory. At least that's the way his mother saw it, and when you pissed her off, it was nearly impossible to get back in her good graces.

"Sutton always did like to do things on his own."

"It hasn't been an hour since you graduated, yet here you are getting ready to straddle the horse and set out on your own. I guess you come by it honest, huh?"

Warryck couldn't miss the sadness in his brother's voice. The two of them had been inseparable growing up. Being Gryphons

41

meant they had to be careful who they friended, but being twins meant they had a built-in best friend. The two had been close until Warryck decided he wanted a life outside the MC. The Hounds of Zeus was more than a motorcycle club. The members were all shifters, and they were family, by blood or by choice. Not only that, but all the members were good men who lived their lives looking out for others. Warryck considered himself one of the good guys. At least he had until Harlow was taken from him. After that, all he could focus on was revenge. It was the main reason he had stayed away from Maveryck. He didn't want to bring his twin down to his level. Then again, the Hounds never hesitated to take out the evil of the world, so would Mav be doing something different by helping War?

"You're right. Some things never change, like my love for you. That's the very reason I have to do this alone. I'm going to find out who is responsible, and I'm going to make them pay. I won't have your blood on my hands should something happen."

"I think you're forgetting something; I'm just as powerful as you are. We're shifters, War. Hounds of Zeus. Not the club but the chosen. If you haven't noticed, the world has gone to shit, and we're needed now more than ever. The humans are dead-set on destroying this world, and there's no one else to save them from themselves but us. That's another reason why I'm here." Maveryck licked his fingers and crushed the cherry on his cigarette before putting the butt into the pocket of his worn jeans. "The ones you plan on going after? They're part of the mission Dad is investigating. We know who's responsible for Harlow's death. They're called the Ministry, and we want your help taking them down."

"You should have started with that. Let's go." Warryck straddled his bike, but before he could start it, Maveryck grabbed his wrist.

"What about your daughter?"

"She's fine with Lucius and Vera."

"You're going to leave her? Just like that?"

"Like I said, you don't know me anymore." Warryck pulled free from his twin's grip, ignoring the accusing glare. Firing up *his bike, he backed out of the parking space, not bothering to wait on Maveryck. It wasn't until his twin pulled up beside him that War noticed several more bikes behind them.*

*"We didn't turn our backs on you."*

"Professor Lazlo."

"What?" Warryck blinked, focusing on the man standing next to him.

"It's our turn." War's colleague and sometimes lunch partner motioned toward the front where the psychology students were waiting to be presented their awards. He'd gone on to receive his doctorate so he could teach, because after he had ridden with his family to get his revenge, War was still on the outside looking in.

Warryck made his way to the front where he spoke of things he no longer cared about and praised students he hoped he hadn't truly failed over the last year.

# Chapter Six

KERRIGAN HAD ONLY thought she was in hell when Agnes told her there was no alcohol allowed. Rules were a major part of living at The Sanctuary, and she found herself wanting to break every one of them. Meals were served at a set time, and she was only allowed to eat what was prepared. There were no snacks to be had just because you got hungry. The only drinks allowed were water, milk, and juice. Water was available at all hours during the day, but anything else was only available in the dining hall with meals. After breakfast, the single men went about their jobs, while the single women were assembled together for Bible study. Afterwards, Kerrigan and the others went to work, and the men had their own study group after lunch. Married couples studied together, and the children had their own area Agnes had only told Kerrigan about.

Kerrigan was never allowed to go anywhere alone. It was one of the rules Gideon had put in place for all newcomers. She knew it was so they wouldn't attempt to run away. With a shadow, it would be harder to sneak off. When she first toured the compound with Agnes, Kerrigan had inquired about what they did for fun. Agnes let her know quickly the only thing available for downtime was reading. When Agnes showed her the library, Kerrigan laughed when she perused the titles available to be checked out. All were religious themed. Whether historical or fictional, all books were deemed wholesome. She did find it odd, though, there were no Bibles among the reading material.

After the first week, Kerrigan didn't care if she had reading material or not. She was bone tired from working. Being new, she was considered on probation, thus given a job pulling weeds from the gardens. Maybe it was also punishment considering her ribs were still healing. Slinging drinks and working behind the bar, she was used to using her hands and being on her feet all day, but in her new job, she was down on her knees for hours at a time. Her only reprieve was she was allowed to use gloves. Her body ached, and at the end of each day, she was ready to climb onto the top bunk and crash. That, however, wasn't allowed. She had just enough time for a shower before supper, and skipping meals wasn't tolerated.

The next day when she entered the garden, she came across a young woman she'd never seen. The other women tended to make small talk amongst themselves, but they were ignoring the newcomer, much the way they avoided Kerrigan.

Squatting down a few feet away, Kerrigan glanced at the younger woman. Her auburn hair looked as though someone had chopped it off in a hurry. She appeared to be in her early twenties, but Kerrigan couldn't be sure. "Hello." She knew how it felt to be ostracized, so she opted to befriend the girl. "I'm Kerrigan."

"Yes, I know. Word gets around pretty quick when we have someone new show up. Especially someone who..." The girl shook her head. "I'm McKenzie. My friends call me Mac. Well, they used to. I don't have friends anymore." With her hands still in the dirt, she turned her face to Kerrigan.

Kerrigan couldn't help the gasp that left her lips, forgetting about the woman's abandoned comment. A jagged scar marred the otherwise pretty face staring back at her. She wanted to ask what happened, but she didn't want to be rude.

The girl – Mac – tentatively touched the pink mark. "Just a word of advice – don't go into the woods."

"Are there animals out there?"

The girl looked off in the distance, and Kerrigan followed her gaze. Gideon was walking out of one of the buildings, followed by four of his guards. One of the burly men looked their way, and Mac ducked her head. "There are animals everywhere."

Kerrigan concentrated on her own soil so she wouldn't be chastised for talking instead of working. She didn't want there to be any reason she and Mac were separated. Something about the younger woman called to Kerrigan. "How long have you been here?"

Mac kept her head down. "Nine years, but it seems like forever."

"I take it you don't like it then?" Kerrigan needed to be careful of their conversations. Then again, she didn't really care if word got back to Gideon that she wasn't happy. She'd tried to make that clear to anyone who would listen.

"Do you like it here?" Mac whispered, almost too low for Kerrigan to hear.

"Not at all."

"Maybe with time, you'll get used to it."

Mac wasn't wearing a wedding band, but that didn't mean she wasn't partnered with a man. None of the married couples wore rings, so it was hard to tell who was taken and who wasn't.

Kerrigan braved a glance toward the men. They had stopped walking, and Gideon was focused on her. Instead of locking eyes with her captor, Kerrigan bowed her head. She didn't want the man to single her out for any reason other than taking her away from the compound and back to civilization, but in her heart, she knew that would never happen. Kerrigan waited until the men were out of sight before she returned her focus to Mac. "I've never seen you before, you know, at Bible study or in the dining hall. Are you married?"

Mac bowed her head. Kerrigan thought the young woman might be praying, until she raised her head. Tears streaming down her cheeks. "I've been grieving the loss of my baby, and I was given a month to pull myself together. Now..." She shrugged.

"I'm so sorry, Mac." Kerrigan reached out to comfort the young woman, but Mac pulled away. "Don't. If they see you offering me comfort, they'll think we're friends."

"And we're not?"

"No. You don't want to be my friend, Kerrigan. Trust me." Mac gathered her things together. When she stood with her basket in hand, Kerrigan noticed the blood dripping from the young woman's fingertips.

"Mac, where are your gloves?"

The young woman's eyes were haunted. "Whores don't get gloves."

In the following days, Kerrigan caught sight of Mac during meals and Bible study, but she was always surrounded by a group of women. She'd wanted to talk to the young woman again. Kerrigan felt if anyone would tell her the truth of what really went on at the compound, it would be Mac.

The longer she was held prisoner, the more isolated she felt. Kerrigan tried making friends with others besides Agnes, but she could see the jealousy in each woman she spoke to. Other than Agnes, no one spoke to her, and she didn't understand why until one night she overheard their two roommates whispering about how Gideon was paying too much attention to Kerrigan. The next morning, she pulled Agnes aside to ask her about it.

Agnes scrunched her face. "Brother Gideon has singled you out, and it's not hard to see why."

"Because he likes redheads who curse too much?" Kerrigan had noticed Gideon watching her on more than one occasion, but she'd chalked it up to keeping his eye on his newest flock member. Unlike the other men, he was always dressed in slacks and a button-up shirt. The men who accompanied him wore black fatigues and T-shirts. They didn't have weapons on their person, at least none Kerrigan could see, but the way they carried themselves lent an air of military.

Agnes huffed. "One would think that would be a turnoff. Not your hair, but the way you insist on speaking what's on your mind. Women here are supposed to be seen and not heard. Tell me, Kerrigan. What has your punishment been?"

"Punishment? I don't—"

"Exactly. You break the rules. You curse. You wear your hair loose when it's supposed to be braided. You don't wear your head covering to meals. Meals which you have been late to on more than one occasion. You refuse to participate in Bible study. And still, Brother Gideon has yet to punish you for your discretions. The others have noticed, and it isn't fair."

"I figured weeding the gardens was my punishment. What exactly would my punishment be if he were to decide I needed it?" Kerrigan didn't really want to know. Then again, if it was something inhumane like whippings or canings, she'd do much better about towing the line.

"Everyone who comes to The Sanctuary starts off with the less-than-desirable jobs. If you do well and abide by Gideon's rules, you move up to better positions. Those who don't remain where they are. As for your transgressions, he could cut your hair or withhold meals. He could forbid you from speaking to anyone for as long as he deems fit. Those are minor."

"Compared to what? Does Gideon beat people? Does he break bones, or worse?"

"That's another thing. You refuse to call him by his title. You disrespect him at every turn."

"Where I come from, respect is earned. I didn't ask to be here, Agnes. My car broke down in the middle of the night when I was running from an abusive boyfriend. You saw me when I arrived. I was trying to get to my parents. *Gideon* sent my parents a message telling them not to worry. Well, they should be worried. I'm being kept here against my will."

"You can leave. He told you that."

"Yes, but he also told me it would be on foot. He took my identification and credit cards. What little money I have isn't enough to call an Uber even if I had a phone. I wouldn't make it very far without those things. Instead of doing the right thing and having someone drive me to civilization, I'm stuck here in a life I don't want. I want to go to my parents. I want to see the ocean. I want to go back to working at a bar where I'm allowed the choice of whether or not I drink. This place is nothing more than a cult, Agnes, and you've drowned in the Kool-Aid."

Agnes's eyes grew wide as she looked over Kerrigan's shoulder. Goosebumps rose on Kerrigan's arms. She didn't have to turn around to know Gideon was standing behind her. She could feel his presence.

"Agnes, you are going to be late to breakfast. I'll escort Kerrigan to the dining hall after she and I have a little chat."

Agnes didn't hesitate to leave their room, her eyes trained on the floor as she fled. Kerrigan turned to face Gideon, crossing her arms over her chest.

"I had hoped you would come to appreciate the simplicity of life we offer here, but I can see that hasn't happened. And Agnes is correct in my lack of punishment where you are concerned. I have been lenient given the circumstances under which you came to be with us. Your body, as well as your mind, needed time to heal." Gideon slid his gaze along Kerrigan's body, and she couldn't help but shiver. He reminded her, yet again, of Dalton in that moment. When he was once more looking at her face, he continued. "Brother Silas has assured me your outer wounds have healed. Perhaps it is time we focus on your mind." Looking over his shoulder, Gideon said, "Take Sister Kerrigan to the inner chamber."

"What's the inner chamber?" she asked.

"It's where you will spend some time in solitude, thinking about what you said to Agnes."

One of the guards motioned for her to follow, and Kerrigan knew she didn't have a choice. Gideon took a step back when Kerrigan walked past, but before she got out the door, he grabbed her wrist. "You could have a good life here. A really good life if you chose." She didn't miss the heat in his eyes or the intention of his words. She could have a good life *with him*. Kerrigan's definition of good wasn't in the same dictionary as Gideon's. He was a handsome man; she'd give him that. But he would never convince her he wasn't a modern-day Jim Jones or David Koresh.

Kerrigan wrenched her arm away from his grip and motioned for the guards to lead the way. She didn't feel as brave as she was letting on, but she refused to let Gideon see she was afraid. Everyone was already in the dining hall and didn't see her being escorted through the compound. The guards and Gideon were the only ones who knew where she was being taken, since Agnes had been sent on to eat without her. Agnes would know something happened when Kerrigan didn't show up to eat, but she wouldn't know what.

The inner chamber turned out to be a ground-level dungeon. The room was vacant of any furniture. There was a metal bucket in one corner, and she had a feeling she knew what that was to be used for. An old, musty blanket was tossed into the opposite corner, but she refused to use it. The guard hadn't shoved her into the room, but when she halted at the threshold, he did give her a nudge, but not until he leaned in and smelled her hair. *That wasn't creepy at all.* When the door closed behind her, that same guard remained at the small window, his eyes raking over her body. Kerrigan walked over to the wall farthest from the door and sat down. There were no windows save the one in the door, so time was hard to keep track of without the fading sunlight guiding her senses.

As badly as she wanted to stay awake, her aching muscles convinced her otherwise, and Kerrigan lay down on the cold concrete, using her arm as a pillow. When she awoke, there was a tray on the floor next to the door. At least they weren't starving her out. Yet. Stretching, she stood and walked over to see what had been brought. It bothered her she hadn't heard anyone come into the room, but she'd always been a heavy sleeper. A small bowl of plain oatmeal sat alongside a glass of milk. She'd always enjoyed oatmeal at home, but she'd doctored it up with lots of brown sugar and raisins. The stuff they served at the compound was something akin to mush. Still, it was better than nothing. She ate it slowly, knowing she wouldn't get anything else until lunch.

Her body still ached, but Kerrigan didn't sit back down. Instead, she chose to walk around the small enclosure, attempting to loosen the muscles in her legs. She'd never wondered how inmates felt being confined in jail cells. Now, she had a feeling she knew exactly how they felt. While she circled the room, Kerrigan remembered why she was imprisoned, and she pondered Agnes's words. Yes, Kerrigan tended to skirt the rules, but seeing how she wasn't there of her own choosing, why should she have to obey the rules? Why did she have to fall in line with the law Gideon had set down for The Sanctuary? He'd told her she was free to leave anytime she wanted, but he knew she was at his mercy considering how far away from civilization they were.

Or were they? She was going on the word of a kidnapper. It was entirely possible they weren't all that far from the nearest town. She'd been told, not shown, the property where The Sanctuary was located was vast. Agnes mentioned cattle, so it made sense there was a section large enough to accommodate the animals, but what if they only had a few cows and not a herd? They wouldn't need thousands of acres for twenty cows. Then again, she was only speculating. Kerrigan had never visited a farm or a ranch. It was possible Agnes didn't know how large the land was. Gideon, and probably his guards, knew the truth about the property, but he was keen on keeping his people under his control.

Kerrigan wanted to think everyone there had made the decision to live in such a way. Away from society. Away from what Gideon considered evil. His teachings were much more fire and brimstone than the Catholic mass she'd heard in her young days. Sure, the priests had talked about good versus evil, but it was nothing like Gideon spoke of during Bible study. She found it odd for their meetings to be called such, when the only Bible she could see during that time was the one atop the lectern. The one Gideon never bothered to open. He could be pulling the scriptures he quoted out of his ass for all she knew.

Gideon... she didn't know his last name... likened himself to God. He made the rules, telling his followers he knew what was best for all of them, and that included unions among his people. She didn't understand that either. If a man and woman fell in love, who was he to say they weren't good enough for each other? And poor Agnes. She said Gideon hadn't chosen her. Shouldn't it be the man she was interested in doing the choosing? That was just one of several reasons Kerrigan was convinced she was living among a cult. Now, how did she get away from it?

52

# Chapter Seven

WARRYCK'S PLANS TO hit the road immediately after the school year didn't go as planned. Lucy had gotten caught up in something sinister when her new boss wanted to use her studies of genetics at MIT as well as instruction under Lucius to carry on her great uncle's work. Ryker kept War apprised of the situation. War offered to leave school, even though there were only a few weeks left, but Lucy insisted War should finish out the school year. It didn't sit well with him, leaving his daughter's fate in the hands of his brothers or the Gargoyle she'd met recently. Ryker convinced War the family had it handled, so he remained where he was and completed the year.

The second school was over, War walked away from the university, having already cleaned out his office. He made arrangements with a neighbor to watch over his house while he was away, and he headed to his daughter's home. He didn't stay long, but it was long enough to hear what she'd been through as well as meet the Gargoyle who was her mate. Gargoyles had one mate for life, and Lucy happened to be Tamian St. Claire's. Not only was the male a shifter, he was heir to the Italian Gargoyle throne. His family and Clan welcomed Lucy with open arms, and the two of them were off to New Atlanta where one of the Gargoyles was going to instruct Lucy in computer infiltration.

After a brief visit with his parents and brothers – because that was all he could handle – War and Mav set out. When studying the map and figuring out where they wanted to start, they agreed on heading east to Maine and working their way across the States as far as they could, stopping at parks and campgrounds. Thirty years prior, when the Ministry attempted to take civilization back to the dawn of time, another canyon had been formed in the middle of the country, making travel by land harder to navigate, but they figured they'd head as far west as possible and traverse around the deep gorge when the time came.

They didn't take their time getting to Maine, only stopping for fuel, food, and a couple hours sleep. When they arrived on the coast, they decided to get a hotel room for the night to recharge before they started back the other way. War was happier than he'd been in years, and Maveryck was like a kid in a candy store, energy thrumming through his body now they were together again. It hit War hard how much he'd missed his twin.

It was fairly early when they entered Harper's Point, a local tavern. The bar had more patrons than Warryck had expected for the time of day. "Just pick a table," the bartender called out.

War let Maveryck choose where to sit, and he picked a table well away from the other customers. When they were settled, a pretty blonde came over to take their order. She eyed them both, but it was Maveryck who flirted with the young woman. War couldn't help but grin as his twin bantered with the waitress. The male could charm the habit off a nun. They were similar in height and hair color, and they both had the same dark blue eyes, but Mav had more tattoos than War. His hair was longer and his blond beard fuller. Now that War didn't have to look somewhat presentable as a professor, he planned to not worry about such things. After spring break, he stopped cutting his hair, and it was already touching his collar. The tattoos he had were mostly hidden by his clothes, but he could see that changing as well.

"Ever think of settling down?" War asked after taking a long pull of his beer.

"I tried that with Jenna. Even bought her a ring, but one day things were perfect, and the next... She just took off. Sent me a fucking text saying she needed to find herself, whatever the fuck that meant. Three years together, and she was the same the day she left as the day we met. I thought things were great, but they obviously weren't."

"She never contacted you afterwards?" War never knew how badly Jenna's leaving affected Maveryck. Why would he? He hadn't been around to see the two interact.

"Nope. It's been four years, and you would think that shit gets easier, but I still miss her. Well, maybe not her specifically, but being with one person you enjoy coming home to every day. She knew all about us, and she never once batted an eyelash when I had to do work for the family."

Not all Hounds told their significant other the truth as to their inner selves. Harlow had known because she was also a Gryphon. What she hadn't known about was the family business, only about the MC. She didn't want Lucy raised by bikers. If she'd known they were mercenaries, she'd have probably never agreed to marry Warryck. If a Gryphon told their mate about their true nature and the mate couldn't handle it, Gryphons had the ability to alter their mate's mind so they forgot.

"Weren't you worried she'd tell someone about us?"

"Not really. As far as I know, she didn't have any proof. It wasn't like I shifted and lay around the house as a lion. Although there was one time we were in bed, and she kneed me in the balls. I might have nipped her shoulder with my beak in retaliation."

"How long has it been since you fully shifted?"

"Four years. It was the day I got the text, and I may or may not have gone off the rails temporarily. How about you?"

"Twenty-four years. It was the day I took out Obadiah. I'm looking forward to getting out and—"

"Brooks? Is Brooks here?" An older woman with an Irish accent rushed into the bar. She was pretty with fading red hair, and the man with her was probably her husband.

"I'm Brooks. You must be Kerri's parents." Brooks had been tending bar, but when the woman called out for him, he came around to greet them.

"Is Kerrigan here?" her father asked in a deeper Irish brogue, shaking Brooks's hand.

"I haven't seen Kerri since she quit a couple months back. She was supposed to be coming to visit you. Please tell me she made it," Brooks pled.

"No. She called us asking for money. Said Dalton had wiped out her savings. She asked us to wire her some money, but it was never picked up. We received a text from a random number saying she was safe and had decided to stay here. When we try calling, her phone doesn't even go to voicemail, and all messages we've sent have gone unanswered."

"That sonofabitch!" A large man stood from his stool at the bar and stalked over to where the others were talking. "It all makes sense now."

"What makes sense, Ambrose?" Brooks asked.

The large man – Ambrose – shook with rage. "I followed her to the ATM. Damnit! She didn't tell me the money wasn't there. She told me everything was fine. Still, I gave her a key to my place and told her she was welcome to stay if she needed to. When I noticed things moved around at home, I just thought she was coming in when I wasn't there. If he took her money, then he probably found the key."

Brooks rubbed his eyes with his fingertips. "I'd seen

56

Dalton being a jerk before, but after I kicked him out of here that night, he was beyond livid. If he took her money, he... It could have been him texting you saying she was safe."

"Oh, God," the mother cried, gripping her husband's arm with one hand while covering her mouth with the other.

Maveryck made a move to stand, but War stopped him. "What are you doing?"

"We made a vow to protect humans. If this Kerrigan is in trouble, we should use our abilities to help find her. Can you sit here and tell me you honestly don't care?"

War shook his head. "Of course I care, but what are you going to say? 'Hey, we're shifters, and ours is a family of mercenaries. We'll find your daughter then take out the bastard who did this to her?' They don't know for certain what happened to her."

"We can leave out what we are, but we can offer our help." Mav crossed his tattooed arms over his chest and glared at War.

"I'm with you on this, but I think we should help a little more discreetly. Don't you? I know I'm only a professor and not part of the family the same as you, but let's sit and listen before we do anything rash."

Mav relaxed back in his seat, and they drank their beer in silence while keeping their ears open. Ambrose put one of his large hands on Brooks's shoulder. "I have a friend in the New Portland PD. I'll give him a call. I promise, we'll find Kerrigan."

Brooks sighed. "Thank you, Ambrose." When the man walked off to make the call, Brooks turned to the parents. "Why don't you come sit down? Can I get you something to eat or drink?"

"A Guinness would be nice," the father said.

When Brooks looked at the mother, she surprised War. "I'll have one too, but would you please add a shot of Jameson?"

57

"Coming right up." Brooks led them to a table next to War and Mav before heading behind the bar. The other patrons went back to their own drinks, but talk was muted as they whispered among themselves while catching glimpses of the parents.

"I'm so sorry I didn't listen to you sooner, Enya." The father took his wife's – Enya's – hand. Their discussion was interrupted when Brooks returned with their drinks. The place was getting busier, so he returned to his place behind the bar.

War ordered another round of drinks, and once the waitress had moved away, he leaned closer to his twin. "I'm interested in what the cop has to say. If nobody knew the woman was missing, he's probably not going to be much help."

Maveryck was the more laid back of the two. At least he had been when they were growing up. War took a good look at his brother, noticing the lines creasing his forehead. War had his own lines, but his were from years of worrying about himself and the classes he taught, not the fate of others. Warryck wasn't trained in search and rescue. Not the way his twin was. His family might not search for individuals, but they did rescue humans from the hands of those who took them and kept them locked away inside their cults.

While they waited on the cop, they eavesdropped on the parents as Enya and Shawn did their best not to blame the other for not checking on their daughter sooner. Warryck's guilt reared its ugly head. This couple was torn apart with their adult daughter's disappearance, while he'd gone his own daughter's whole life without worrying about her. Sure, the family kept him updated on her well-being, but if they didn't call, he hadn't given her much thought. He was a shitty being.

When the cop showed up, he didn't move the parents to a back room to speak quietly. He was dressed in civilian clothes, and he drank the offered beer. His questions and mannerisms belied his off-duty appearance. Mav busied himself, typing away on his phone, but Warryck knew his twin was taking notes on everything being discussed at the next table over. War had to admit he was also interested in the conversation. Brooks's description of Kerrigan's boyfriend didn't surprise War. He knew there were men who felt the need to control their partners, and when that control slipped, so did their tempers. He felt bad for the parents, but it was Ambrose, the large sailor, who was beating himself up the most for not following Kerrigan home that night.

By the time the cop was done gathering information, the date of her disappearance had been established as well as all the information they had on her boyfriend, Dalton Watkins. Some of the bar patrons who had gathered around admitted to seeing Dalton around town at other bars. None mentioned seeing him with another woman, but it didn't mean he hadn't moved on. It also didn't mean he had anything to do with her disappearance, although he was the last one to see her.

It was apparent Kerrigan O'Shea was a woman who was well-loved by more than just her parents. The other customers still standing close by offered to help find their daughter. If the young woman took after her mother, she would be gorgeous. Not that it mattered to War. He knew from dealing with his students over the years that beauty came from the inside.

Maveryck waited until the crowd had dispersed from around the next table to speak. "I just sent all the information to Lucy. I figured since she's in New Atlanta with the Gargoyles' computer expert, they could lend a hand."

Lucy's mate, Tamian St. Claire, was a half-blood Gargoyle, and even though he was heir to the Italian throne once his father stepped down, he still claimed the North

American Clan as his own. They had been instrumental in saving Lucy during her ordeal a few weeks back. Now, she was living in New Atlanta and learning from what Lucy called one of the best computer information specialists in the world. The equipment the Stone Society had at their disposal, along with Julian Stone's brain, enabled them to find almost anyone at any time.

"So, what's our plan? Are we going to hang around until we know what happened to the girl and then hand the information over?" War asked.

"No. We can't exactly share where the information comes from. If you don't want to go after the woman, Lucy can send an anonymous tip to the New Portland police."

For some reason, that didn't sit well with Warryck. He felt an unexplainable need to follow through on this themselves. "How long will it take Lucy and Julian to find what we need?"

"Depends on—" Maveryck's phone pinged with an incoming text. "Huh. About that long." He scooted closer to War so they could both see the text that came through. After reading the information, they were only marginally closer to knowing what happened to Kerrigan O'Shea. Traffic cameras showed her car leaving the area of her home and was lost when she'd taken to some back roads. It was picked back up being towed approximately an hour later. Kerrigan hadn't been with the tow truck. The only other vehicle shown in the vicinity at the same time was an older model sedan. "It's possible she caught a ride with the driver."

"Or, they could have taken her."

Maveryck leaned back. "Are we going to have Lucy send this information to the police or…?"

"Not yet. I think we need to pay a visit to the tow truck driver." War couldn't walk away from this mystery. As a matter of fact, his adrenaline was coursing at the thought of having a new purpose. While he'd been camping, he'd vowed to himself to make a difference in some way. He

60

wasn't ready to join the MC, but this was something he and his twin could do together.

# Chapter Eight

THE LAPS AROUND the small room had Kerrigan warmed up. Needing to stretch out her muscles, she put one hand on the wall, and with the other, grabbed an ankle, pulling it up towards her butt. She did the same with the other leg, and when both were sufficiently loose, Kerrigan bent over to touch her toes. She'd been facing the back wall, so in her current position, she was able to look backward between her legs. Gideon was watching her through the door, his eyes fixated on her ass. If the man didn't creep her out, she might have remained where she was so he could get an extra eyeful. Since he did make her skin crawl, she stood and turned toward the door, crossing her arms over her chest. She gave him her best scowl. The same one she used on drunks at the bar when they hit on her.

Seemingly unphased, Gideon unlocked the door and entered, stopping just inside. "Good morning, Kerrigan. I hope you've had time to clear your mind."

Clear it? Oh, no. She'd filled it with ways to get the hell out of the compound. "It's obvious I don't have a choice in the matter. You kidnapped me, and now I'm at your mercy. If I'm willing to give your way of living a chance, will you show me some mercy?"

Gideon's eyebrows shot up. "I'm not sure I understand."

"It's simple, really. I don't want to be here. Didn't ask to be here, because, you know... kidnapping."

"Again, we did not kidnap you. Your injuries were so extensive that your memory of the night's events is skewed. You flagged down Brother Stanley. He brought you here because our healer was better suited to taking care of you than a walk-in clinic."

"We'll have to agree to disagree on that. But since I'm stuck here and have no way of getting back to the real world, I'm asking for leniency until I become more accustomed to the way things are done. You see, where I come from, I had liberties to make my own decisions. Like the type of clothes I wore. How I did my hair. Makeup really isn't that big a deal, but I had freedom to choose whether or not I put it on. I could eat when and where I wanted. I didn't have to eat oatmeal every day for breakfast if I would rather have pancakes. I didn't have to curb my language for fear of offending someone's delicate sensibilities. Your drastic way of ruling might be okay for all the sheep of your flock, but they choose to live this way. It's not my choice. Even my parents allowed me to make my own decisions starting when I was a teenager."

"So, you're saying you want what? Free rein? To do as you please when no one else has to?"

"Not at all, because I know someone like you won't abide that."

"Someone like me?" Gideon took a step closer. "How exactly do you see me, Kerrigan?"

"As a man who likes complete control. Hell, you even decide who in your flock can date each other. Well, date is the wrong word since there isn't anything around here to do that would be considered going on a date, unless you milk the cows together, or maybe gather eggs. Tell me, Gideon. Do you watch when a couple has sex to make sure they're doing it the right way? Do you have rules about that as well?" Kerrigan knew she should shut up while she was ahead, but she was curious.

63

When Gideon took two more steps, he was so close Kerrigan could smell his cologne. His eyes darkened, and his nostrils flared. His breath, when he spoke his next words, was fresh with mint, reminding her she hadn't brushed her own teeth since the morning before.

"Would you like for me to watch you having sex? Would you strip down for your partner knowing I was seeing what they were going to do to you? Is that the type of woman you are, Kerrigan? Is that why you showed up battered and bruised?" Gideon ran his fingertip down her jaw, ghosting the proof of where Dalton had marked her.

Kerrigan wanted to smack his hand away. "No. I don't like to be watched, and I definitely don't cheat. I was beaten because someone else wanted complete control over me as well."

"And we see how that went for you."

"Exactly. So, forgive me if I'm a little skeptical of what you're asking of me."

Gideon pushed Kerrigan's hair behind her ear. If he had been anyone else, the gesture would have been sweet or romantic. Since it was Gideon, Kerrigan wanted to go take a shower and wash his touch off her body. "And you believe it's fair I should show partiality to you because you don't want to follow the rules of our society?"

"I think you should give me a break because you freaking kidnapped me." Gideon opened his mouth to argue the point, and Kerrigan held up her hand. "You claim I was brought here to have my wounds tended, but I was still taken away from my world. If I had come here willingly, then yes, I would expect to do as you say. But I didn't ask for any of this. If you would take me to the nearest town, my not wanting to follow your ways wouldn't be an issue. Hell, even blindfold me so I don't know where *this* is."

"Why is our way of living so offensive to you? The outside world has laws as well. Are you telling me you

64

don't obey them?"

"Laws, yes. Archaic rules, no. It's called free will. Why won't you — ?" Kerrigan's brain had a sudden clarifying moment. He wouldn't let her go because he was afraid she would tell someone about them. Even if he blindfolded her, she would be able to contact the police stating she'd been kidnapped. She knew that's how she'd ended up at The Sanctuary, and Gideon knew it as well. She was never getting out of there.

"I think another twenty-four hours of thinking is in order." Gideon turned to go, and Kerrigan let him. It really was too bad the man was an egotistical psycho. In another lifetime, another world, she could see how he could charm his way into her life. *Yeah, and look how well that turned out with Dalton.*

Kerrigan returned to her spot by the far wall and sat down, pulling her knees up and resting her chin there. She had no illusions about being kidnapped, no matter how fiercely Gideon protested otherwise. She had been in pain, but it hadn't affected her memories of that night as he tried to convince her. If she was able to make it out of there and contact the authorities, Gideon's little hideout could be exposed.

As the day progressed, a guard brought her lunch and then supper. She'd finally given in to using the bucket to pee in when she could no longer hold her bladder. She'd moved the container to the corner next to the door for privacy. They'd not bothered to leave toilet paper, so Kerrigan had to drip dry. If she had to do more than pee, she would be in trouble.

No, she would be at their mercy to ask to leave the room, and that wouldn't happen until she agreed to Gideon's terms. She'd never considered lack of basic personal hygiene to be a form of torture. She now knew better. Then again, if she wanted to risk the man's ire, she could rip her pants and use the cloth to wipe with. Closing her eyes, she leaned her head back against the wall.

Were her parents looking for her yet? Gideon had told them she was fine, but she spoke with them at least once a week. When she didn't check in, would they get worried? If they did, would they show up at her – Dalton's – house, demanding to know where she was? Even he didn't know what happened to her. Had he tossed all her belongings? Or was he smug enough to think she'd come crawling back? So many questions ran through her brain until she had a headache. Another night of sleeping on the cold concrete wouldn't help, so she needed to at least get out of the inner chamber and back to her bunk. It was the lesser of two evils. The better of two shitty situations.

Every which way Kerrigan thought of making her escape always brought her back to the same conclusion – she was going to have to play a game. One in which she bided her time and made Gideon believe she'd had a change of heart. She couldn't seem too eager, because that would be too obvious. No, Kerrigan had to make it seem like she was still opposed to being held against her will while agreeing to his terms. She just prayed she was strong enough for whatever he threw her way.

Her breakfast was brought in by a different guard. One who didn't even look at her. He dropped the tray on the floor and picked up the empty one from her supper. Kerrigan was almost afraid to eat the slop. Her stomach had rumbled during the night, but she'd been able to avoid using the bucket. If she ate the oatmeal, she was afraid she wouldn't have a choice. Then again, she'd made the decision to get out of her prison as soon as Gideon came to see her so she could at least use a proper bathroom.

The man didn't come to her until what she figured was a couple hours after the guard brought her morning meal. She'd tried to keep track of the minutes so she'd know the approximate time of day, but memories of her former life, her parents, the bar, Brooks, Ambrose, even her time with

Dalton, interrupted, making her lose count.

Gideon was once again alone when he unlocked the door and stepped through. He was dressed down from the ways she'd seen him since she'd been brought to the compound, but he still wore khaki pants and a button-up shirt. He was no less imposing just because his clothes were more casual. There was nothing casual about the way he carried himself. "I've given consideration to your request for leniency."

"You have?" Kerrigan pushed up from where she was seated but remained against the wall.

"Yes. You have two options. One, you can go back to your job in the garden and living among the others as you were. If that is what you decide to do, you will be expected to abide by the rules as they are given. You will receive no reprieve for disobeying, and if you do not behave as expected, you will find yourself back here in this room for an extended period of time."

"And option two?" Kerrigan had a feeling she didn't want to know what option two was.

Gideon remained close to the door, his eyes raking in her appearance. "Option two is that you become one of the chosen."

"Chosen for what?"

"For tending to my needs."

"Like a harem? No, thank you." Kerrigan had no intention of being his whore. Agnes had mentioned being chosen, but Kerrigan assumed that was how Gideon decided who among them deserved to have a partner. Agnes had wanted to be Gideon's mistress.

"Harem?" Gideon laughed, and his normally dark eyes lit up with mirth. He was nice-looking when he was serious, but he was extraordinary when his features softened. "I do not believe in polygamy. The sharing of bodies is a sacred act, and I do not allow those who live here in The Sanctuary to engage in random sex. It is why I am involved in the process of two people becoming a couple. It is important for the man and woman to get to know one another on a platonic level. If they aren't compatible in the long run, then they haven't sullied themselves with rutting around like animals."

The way Gideon eyed Kerrigan's body was at odds with his words. There was no way a man so virile was a virgin. "If not a harem, then what? Are the chosen your personal house maidens?"

"Something like that. I have a select few I allow in my personal quarters so I can spend time getting to know them better. If, after a time, they do not meet my expectations, I release them back to the population and choose a replacement. I have yet to find the one who I wish to take as a wife. In all the years I've searched, no one ever held my attention long enough to want to give myself over to her for the rest of my life."

Kerrigan swallowed hard. Agnes's words about how Gideon let Kerrigan slide in breaking the rules came rushing back. Had Kerrigan been correct when she joked it was because Gideon liked mouthy redheads? The way he licked his lips had her considering she had been right. Kerrigan gave his strong body a once-over, hoping she wasn't making the third biggest mistake of her life.

Kerrigan released a deep breath. "I'll take option two."

# Chapter Nine

AFTER TAKING ADVANTAGE of the continental breakfast at the hotel, War and Mav headed out to Sully's Garage. New Portland was intriguing with its brick roadways, breweries, and large cathedrals. As he followed his twin, War took a deep breath of salty air. He missed flying in his eagle form over large bodies of water, dipping down, dragging his talons through the waves, as he eyed fish he could easily catch in his beak. It had been too long since he'd enjoyed the majesty of humpback whales as they rose from the depths, arching in the air, only to splash down and do it again. War envied animals their freedom to live in their skin, hides, and feathers. Maybe he would sell his home and look into buying land with plenty of acreage where he could let both sides of the Gryphon loose.

Sully's was surprisingly neat for a garage. Several cars were parked along the side of the lot, and the bay doors were open, even though the temperatures were still in the forties. An older man stepped out of the first bay, wiping his hands on a grease rag. He stopped just outside the door, watching as War and Mav climbed off their bikes.

"I don't work on bikes, if that's what you're here for," he said when they closed the distance.

War stood behind his twin, letting him take lead. "We're not looking for a mechanic. We're actually looking for a car."

The man frowned. "This isn't a car lot. It's a garage."

"Not to purchase. We are looking for a specific car that was towed here on April seventeenth at approximately two a.m."

"I remember that one. Charlie got the call." He turned around and yelled into the bay, "Hey, Charlie. Come out here a minute."

Warryck was surprised to see a younger woman striding out of the building. Wearing blue coveralls, her long brown hair was pulled back in a ponytail. "What's up, Dad?" She slowed her steps when she got a look at the twins. Standing well over six feet and dressed in all leather, they made most people take a good look. With Mav's visible tattoos, he made people take more than one look and usually a step back.

"They're here about the abandoned car. Tell them about the call." A loud bell rang, and the man said, "Excuse me," before heading back inside.

Charlie wiped her hands on a grease rag, same as her father had done. It appeared the woman was both mechanic and tow truck driver. "Some guy named Stanley, if I remember correctly. Asked for it to be brought here specifically. Thing is, when we tried to call him later about the needed repairs, the phone had been disconnected. I checked the glove box, but all the paperwork had been removed. It sat on the lot over there" — she pointed to where the other cars were lined up — "for about a week, and then Dad called the police. They ran the plates, and the owner came back as being a woman, definitely not a Stanley. They sent it to the impound lot since we didn't want it taking up needed space."

"Was there anything at all in the car?" Mav asked.

"Just a backpack stuffed full of women's clothes. Do you know the owner? Is that what this is about?"

War sighed, running a hand through his short beard. "The owner of the car is missing. We were hired by her

70

parents to see if we can find her." It wasn't exactly the truth, but the deeper they got into this mystery, the more determined Warryck was in finding out what happened to her.

"Do you have a record of the call so we can get the man's name who phoned it in?" Maveryck asked.

"I gave that to the police, but I still have a copy in the office. Hang on."

When Charlie walked back into the building, War said, "We need to find her."

Mav grinned. "What about our road trip? I thought we were supposed to be bonding."

"We can bond while we do a little snooping, asshole." War shoved his twin's arm and grinned back.

"Here it is. I made a copy for you." Charlie handed War a sheet of paper. It was the service order detailing all the issues with the car as well as the time it was brought in and the man's name and phone number. Seeing all the needed repairs had War's hackles going up. The woman shouldn't have been driving something so unreliable. He already knew Dalton Watkins was a piece of shit, but this added to his list of sins.

"Thank you for your help," War said as he and Mav turned toward their bikes.

"I hope you find her," Charlie called after them.

"Yeah, me too," Warryck muttered.

"We need to find the other car Lucy noticed on the road that night. If we can locate it, I bet we find Kerrigan." Maveryck pulled his phone out of his saddle bag and typed off a text to Lucy with the man's name and phone number, even though it had been disconnected.

"Is Julian's computer really that good?"

"According to Lucy it is, as well as the male using it. But if the police have this same information, wouldn't they have run the plates and gone to her house and questioned the boyfriend?"

War shrugged. "You would think so. It didn't sound like the cop at the bar last night had heard anything about that."

They both leaned against their bikes, waiting to see if Lucy could get any information quickly. "What're we going to do if we don't get any solid information?" Maveryck asked.

"I guess we continue on with our original plan." War rubbed his short beard again, still getting used to the feel of it. Maveryck's was quite a bit longer, but it suited him, as did all the ink and piercings. They weren't identical in the first place, and all Mav's enhancements only added to their differences. War was okay with that. They didn't have to be mirror images to feel a bond.

Mav's phone vibrated and he answered. "Lucy, you're on speaker. Whatcha got?"

"Hey, Mav. Hey, Dad. The good news is we were able to track the car as far as New Conway in New Hampshire. The bad news is it disappeared once it entered the White Mountain forest on 302. Either they stopped somewhere among all the trees, or they switched vehicles. The tag was renewed six months ago, but the car is registered to a Clara Orr, only she's been dead for several years. We're looking into all relatives, but so far that's come up empty. I also searched for stolen vehicles in that area, but that turned out to be a dead end."

"What about the boyfriend? Did the police speak with him at all?" Mav asked.

"Julian tapped into the New Portland PD's system, but they never opened a case since nobody filed a missing person's report on Kerrigan. I went ahead and gathered his information for you, and I've sent it to your email. Are you guys going to continue looking into this? I know you were supposed to be riding cross-country."

"As long as you keep feeding us pertinent information, it won't hurt to continue looking for a while. I remember what it was like when you went missing, and I'd hate to think there hadn't been anyone looking for you," Warryck said. "I'm just sorry it wasn't me."

"Water under the bridge, Dad. We've discussed this." Warryck's heart warmed every time Lucy called him Dad. And they had discussed what happened to her as well as why he wasn't there along with the Hounds. She was much more forgiving of him than he was of himself. He had a lot of ground to make up for.

Mav clamped a hand down on his shoulder, squeezing. War cleared his throat and said, "We'll start with the boyfriend, and if we don't get anything out of him, we'll head toward the forest. Maybe camp out and stretch our wings. See if we can find something that way."

"I'll continue to search on this end, and if I come up with anything, I'll let you know."

"Appreciate it, Luce," Mav said at the same time War responded with, "Thank you, Lucy."

Maveryck disconnected then plugged the directions to the boyfriend's place into the GPS before setting the phone into the holder attached to the handlebars. "Let's go talk to this asshole."

Traffic was light considering it was before noon and most people were at work. According to the information Lucy dug up, Dalton Watkins had lost his job soon after Kerrigan went missing. There were no employment records since. If he wasn't working, how was he paying rent on the two-bedroom house he'd shared with Kerrigan? He had taken all her savings out of the bank, so maybe he was living off that.

There were two cars in the driveway when Warryck pulled up to the curb behind Maveryck. After shutting of their motors, both males angled off their rides, and together they strode toward the front door. A crash came from inside, followed by yelling. Before they could knock, the door flew open and a redhead stepped through.

73

"You're not leaving me, Kerrigan!"

The woman balled her hands into fists and turned on the man. "I am not Kerrigan! No matter how many times you call me by her name, I'll never be her. Wouldn't want to be her!"

"Tasha, wait. I'm sorry. Please." Dalton rushed through the door, but when he noticed the two large males standing there, he froze. "What the hell do you want?"

Tasha had also stopped when she caught sight of Warryck and Maveryck.

"Are you okay?" Warryck took a step closer when he noticed the bruise forming on her cheek. "Did you hit her?" He turned his attention to Dalton who was backing into the house. Before he could close the door in their faces, Maveryck stuck a large boot in the way and shoved, knocking Dalton backwards.

War left his twin to tend with the human while he remained with the female. "Did he do this to you?"

"Yes, but it's the last time. I can't help that I'm not his precious Kerrigan. The man is obsessed. I should have listened to my gut."

"What can you tell me about Kerrigan?"

The woman rolled her eyes. "Other than she was prettier than me? Taller, smarter, a better cook? When I met Dalton, he was nice. Charming. The first time he called me by the wrong name, I chalked it up to an honest mistake, but when he continued to do so, I got pissed. At first, he apologized, explaining how I reminded him of his dead wife. Then he'd get drunk and tell me all the ways I was lacking compared to her. I hated this woman I'd never met. Earlier today, I went into the spare bedroom. I was going to move his wife's clothes out of the closet in the master so I'd have more room for mine. I mean, it's not like I was giving them to charity. I was just trying to find somewhere else to put them. That's when I found a shrine hidden away in the spare bedroom closet. I confronted Dalton, and he told me

74

how she was his high school sweetheart, and he'd been devastated when she passed. He assured me I wasn't a replacement for her, but I knew better. We're too similar."

"Is that when he hit you?"

Tasha nodded, wrapping her arms around her middle. "I told him I couldn't live in her shadow any longer."

"Did he tell you how Kerrigan died? Or how long ago?" Red flags were going up all over the place, but if Tasha knew what happened to the other woman, they might be able to bring closure to her parents.

"He said it was a car accident several years ago." Tasha narrowed her eyes. "Who are you exactly?"

"I'm a private investigator. Kerrigan's parents hired my brother and me to find their daughter. Tasha, Kerrigan wasn't Dalton's wife. They lived together up until she disappeared a couple months ago."

"What? No. He was with me then. We've been dating for close to five months. I mean, we'd only see each other a couple nights a week and always at my apartment. Then out of the blue, he was begging me to move in with him. That bastard. Do you think he had something to do with her disappearance?"

"That's what we're trying to find out. He took all Kerrigan's money the night she disappeared, so I'd say you dodged a bullet. You might want to go to the police and file charges. Stop him from hurting anyone else."

"All my things are in that house. I need to get them back and find somewhere else to live." Tasha's eyes welled up, but she blinked the tears away.

"Do you have anyone you can call?"

"My sister. She's going to give me hell, because she thought I moved in with him too quickly. I guess she was right."

"Why don't you give her a call and have her go with you to the police station? Give them your statement and ask them to escort you back here to get your things. My brother

75

and I will make sure Dalton doesn't leave before you get back."

"Yeah, okay." Tasha narrowed her eyes. "Are you going to hurt him?"

"We only want answers." War didn't expound on how they would get those answers, and he couldn't promise they wouldn't rough the bastard up a bit. Give him a taste of his own medicine. He waited outside with Tasha while she called her sister. Only when she got in her car and drove away did he head inside.

When War walked into the house, Dalton was duct-taped to a chair. Mav was leaning against the sofa, arms crossed over his chest. "Is she okay?"

"She will be. Tasha is headed to the police precinct to press charges." War walked over to Dalton. If looks could kill, War would be incinerated on the spot. Too bad Dalton Watkins had no idea who – and what – he was dealing with.

# Chapter Ten

KERRIGAN FOLLOWED GIDEON out of the building and into the sunlight. She slowed her steps and basked in the warmth for a few seconds. When he realized she wasn't right behind him, he stopped and turned. The look he gave her was odd. He didn't look mad, more like he was... curious. She didn't apologize, but she did catch up to him. When they stopped in front of her sleeping quarters, she was confused.

"What are we doing here?"

"This is your cabin, and I assumed you would want to freshen up."

Kerrigan wanted to scoff. Cabin was a generous term for the block building. "I'm going to continue living here?" Kerrigan thumbed over her shoulder at the small structure.

"No, but I need to make certain arrangements. I will have someone transfer your things to my quarters. You have thirty minutes to take a shower and change." Gideon fisted his hands before shoving them in his pockets. Was the conversation upsetting him? If so, why? He was the one who wanted her to live with him.

Kerrigan could carry all her belongings in her arms, so him making arrangements didn't make much sense, but she wasn't going to argue. She was going to appreciate the next half hour of solitude. Nodding, Kerrigan slid past her captor so she could get busy with a shower and brushing her teeth.

Once inside, she grabbed a fresh set of clothes and took them with her into the small bathroom, closing the door behind her. There was no lock on the door, but Agnes had assured Kerrigan everyone who lived at The Sanctuary was honorable. Kerrigan thought they were all naïve if they believed that. Stripping out of her dirty uniform, she stepped into the small cubicle and closed her eyes, letting the spray rinse away the soreness from sleeping on the floor. The water pressure wasn't what she was used to, but it did the job in washing away the grit. She bathed and washed her hair quickly, not wanting to get caught naked by whomever Gideon was sending for her things.

After she was dressed, Kerrigan brushed the tangles out of her wet hair. Gideon had stated if she chose option one, she would have to abide by the rules. He didn't mention any rules for option two, but she wasn't willing to rock the boat. Not yet. She had a plan, and for it to work, she had to gain his trust. So instead of leaving her locks loose to dry, Kerrigan plaited her hair and covered it with the plain beige scarf. She hadn't noticed any of the other women dressed differently, so she figured the chosen had to wear the same drab uniform everyone else did.

Kerrigan removed her handful of garments and her purse from the chest of drawers. She clutched them to her chest as she waited for someone to come take her to Gideon's quarters. Her plan was risky, and it went against everything she was, but it was the only way she saw of getting out of her predicament. She'd had to do things she didn't want living with Dalton, and while she'd chosen to live with him, those things hadn't been her choice. This was. She prayed she could go through with it.

When the door opened, Kerrigan expected to see one of the guards. Instead, a pretty woman stormed in, her arms full of her own things. "Which drawers were yours?" She didn't make eye contact while she waited for Kerrigan to answer.

Kerrigan stood and pointed at the bottom two drawers with her foot. "Those two." The woman shoved her clothes into the drawers and slammed them shut before holding her arms out for Kerrigan's clothes.

"I can carry my stuff." The woman reached out, snatching the items, and turned around without speaking. Kerrigan picked her purse off the floor where it had fallen when the rude ass had grabbed her things. As she followed along, Kerrigan got the feeling she was being watched. Since the living quarters didn't have windows, she knew that wasn't the case. They were headed toward the woods and the trail which led back to the square. Kerrigan's legs were longer, but she still had to walk quickly to keep up. Once they made it to the other end of the trail, the woman slowed, and her demeanor changed.

As soon as they took a step out of the woods, Kerrigan understood why. Gideon was walking across the compound toward the building which housed the library, accompanied by two guards and two women. When he looked their way, Gideon ignored the other woman, but he inclined his head to Kerrigan. She nodded once in return. When they arrived at their destination, Kerrigan was led around the back of a square building just like all the others they'd passed. The other woman didn't bother stopping when they entered a warm kitchen. She didn't stop when they walked through a large living area filled with comfortable-looking furniture. She continued until they came to the last door on the right at the end of the hall. The woman flung the door open but didn't step inside. "I hope you're happy." She thrust Kerrigan's clothes at her chest before stomping back down the hallway and disappearing around the corner.

"Don't mind Sister Margaret." Kerrigan turned toward a soft voice. A pretty girl was peeking out the door across from her own. "She hasn't been here very long, and she felt Brother Gideon didn't give her enough of a chance. I'm Sparrow." She held out her hands to help with Kerrigan's belongings. "Here. Let's get you settled." Sparrow was a tiny slip of a young woman. Her blonde hair was longer than Kerrigan's, and her smile reached pale green eyes.

"She hasn't been at The Sanctuary long?" Kerrigan took in her new bedroom – yes, it was a bedroom all to herself – while Sparrow stored the clothes in an antique armoire.

"No, she hasn't been here at Brother Gideon's long. But it doesn't matter. He wasn't happy with her, and now here you are."

"So, this was her room? No wonder she was pissed at me."

Sparrow giggled. The woman couldn't be more than nineteen or twenty. She had a youthful look about her as well as a smile that lit up the room. "We've heard about you and your language."

"Who's we?" Kerrigan sat down on her bed, bouncing a few times. Oh yes. It was going to be heaven compared to sleeping on the top bunk.

"The other chosen. There are usually four of us living here. When Brother Gideon decides one of us isn't to his liking any longer, we are replaced with someone new." Sparrow looked away, but Kerrigan didn't miss the blush.

"How long have you been here?"

"Eleven months. I think Brother Gideon keeps me because he likes the way I cook. I figure if he hasn't asked me to marry him by now, he never will."

"Is that something you want?" Kerrigan had so many questions, like when did Sparrow cook for the man? Didn't they eat in the dining hall with everyone else?

"It would be an honor to be asked, but if I am not what he's looking for, I will be happy for him to find someone compatible." Sparrow reached up and removed the scarf from around Kerrigan's hair. "You don't have to wear this as long as you're in the house."

"What else is different? You said you cooked for Gid... Brother Gideon. Is that only for him, or do we eat here as

80

well?"

"We take our meals here with Brother Gideon. If he asks us to accompany him outside the house, he will tell us how he wants us to present ourselves. We are expected to cover our hair when we attend Bible study, but other than that, we just do what he asks and stay as quiet as possible when he's here."

"You keep saying we. Who are the others?"

"That's the strange thing. He came in earlier and told Margaret to take her things to your cabin and escort you here. As soon as she was gone, he gathered Emily and Muriel and told them he had suitors in mind for both of them."

"Why is that strange?" Kerrigan felt like she had hit the jackpot with Sparrow. The girl was friendly, warm, and chatty. If she could befriend the young woman, she might get useful information from her.

Sparrow leaned in closer. "Brother Gideon took them and not Margaret. Whenever he tires of the chosen, he usually finds them a husband. He didn't with Margaret. He —" A door slammed, and Sparrow jumped away from Kerrigan. "Come on. I will show you the rest of the house."

Kerrigan followed Sparrow through the small space. Four bedrooms and a shared bathroom were on one end, with Gideon's bedroom and office at the other. In between were the kitchen and living area. A laundry room was hidden by the back door, which surprised Kerrigan, since everyone had to wash their clothes by hand. There was no garage, so Kerrigan had to wonder where his car was. She had no doubt he had a vehicle somewhere on the compound. They had to have a way to get to the nearest town for things like kidnapping their next flock member.

Gideon stood at the kitchen counter, pouring a cup of coffee. *What the hell?* "Sparrow, I'll expect lunch as usual, but it will just be the three of us. Without Emily and Muriel, I'll need you to help Kerrigan with their duties. I have a meeting after we eat, so I will leave the two of you to sort out who does what."

"Yes, Brother Gideon. Kerrigan and I can handle everything."

"I have no doubts." After draining his coffee, Gideon rinsed his cup and put it in the dish drainer. Kerrigan had expected him to leave it for them to take care of. "I'll see you back here at noon." Gideon didn't look at either one of them before striding out the back door.

"He drinks coffee?"

Sparrow laughed. "At least a pot a day. We can have it with our breakfast if we want. Things are a lot more relaxed here in his house. Come on. I'll show you where all the cleaning supplies are. Since there were four of us, there wasn't that much for any one of us to handle. I usually only cooked and took care of the kitchen with the others doing the cleaning and laundry. I'll help you with everything since I can only clean the oven so many times."

"Can I ask you a question?"

Sparrow stopped in front of a closet and pulled the door open. "Of course. Depending on what it is, I may not answer."

"How long have you been here? Not at Brother Gideon's but at The Sanctuary."

"I came with my parents when I was about ten, so nine years ago? We lost our house when my daddy got laid off from his job, and Brother Gideon offered us a place to stay until my parents could get back on their feet. We never left."

"Your parents liked it here that much?"

"Sure. At least I guess they did. I didn't have a choice, but it wasn't so bad. It was nice not having to worry if there was going to be enough water or if the lights were going to be turned off."

"That's part of all this that confuses me." Kerrigan reached in the closet and pulled out a broom and dust pan. "I understand being self-sustaining, but the things like

82

water and electricity. Those have to be paid for somehow."

"The water comes from a system hooked up to a couple of deep wells. The whole town is set up on some large generators or something. That's how my daddy explained it. I never questioned it, because everything always works."

"But the generators need fuel. The items that aren't produced here, like paper products, have to be bought. Where does the money come from?"

"Like I said, I never questioned anything, because everything I need, I have."

"If you came here as a child, were you around other children? And if so, are there kids here now? Where are they? Agnes told me there's a separate area for them, but I haven't seen any."

Sparrow grabbed a dust rag and an unmarked bottle. "Yes, there are children. Brother Gideon thinks they should all be raised in the same manner. If a child has parents, they remain with them until they are old enough to go to school, then they move to their side of the community."

"What do you mean, if they have parents?"

"Some children are brought here when they need somewhere to stay. Like a big foster family."

"And when they are no longer school age? What happens then?"

"They are given a job and a place to sleep."

"So, the kids are raised by someone who isn't their parents? Why?"

"Well, I didn't understand it until I was older. The way Brother Gideon explained it, he is the only one who has a clear understanding of the Word. If he allowed someone else to share the message, their interpretation might not be as exact as Gideon's. The women who teach the children have to adhere to strict guidelines and never talk about the Bible. While the adults work, the kids go to school during the day. They have their own Bible study mixed in with their school lessons, but it's Gideon who leads those classes.

It's no different than a regular city, really."

"Except you have Brother Gideon deciding every facet of your lives as opposed to having a democracy."

"And how well does your democracy work? Aren't all the people in political offices corrupt on some level? Gideon only wants what's best for The Sanctuary. He isn't out lying to people for his own gain."

"No, but for those who don't choose to live here, isn't that his own form of corruption?"

"I don't see it that way. Living here under his protection, I never worried about being hungry or if one of the kids at school was going to turn a gun on me. I'm sure for someone like you who came from the city where you had all the bright lights and cars and clubs, things probably seem so boring, but when you grow up this way, it's sort of comforting knowing there's no crime."

"I miss my home, Sparrow. I miss having the choice to work in a bar or date whomever I want. I miss the busyness of downtown. I miss my parents. I would gladly take the threat of being mugged just for the chance to see them again." Kerrigan wanted to take Sparrow by the shoulders and shake some sense into her. The young girl had been raised among the sheep, so she wouldn't see how Gideon's form of ruling his little kingdom was the definition of a cult. Instead of trying to reason with her, Kerrigan changed the subject. "Okay, tell me what needs to be done so you can get to making lunch."

As she went about tidying up the already clean house, Kerrigan thought about everything she knew and what she didn't. She needed to figure out where Gideon got his money. Where they kept the vehicles. Where they went when they needed supplies like fuel for the generators. She was glad the other two women had been taken to find husbands or whatever it was Gideon had done with them. The less people she had to interact with, the better. And she liked Sparrow, even if the girl was brainwashed. She was sweet, and that made it easy to like her and want to get to know her better. Kerrigan was curious as to how Gideon behaved at home when he wasn't standing in front of the others teaching about right and wrong.

When Sparrow came to get her a little while later to eat lunch, Kerrigan got her first glimpse of a different side of her captor. After eating one of the most delicious meals she'd ever put in her mouth, Kerrigan now understood why everyone at the compound wanted to stay there. This wasn't the man spouting scripture and talking about the evils of the world. This Gideon was funny. He was kind toward Kerrigan. He was complimentary of Sparrow's cooking. He asked Kerrigan about her childhood, and he listened with rapt attention. He wanted to know about Ireland and her parents as if he genuinely cared. She knew better. After living with Dalton, Kerrigan knew a master manipulator when she saw one. Gideon's caring nature worked where his flock was concerned. He was going to have to dig a lot deeper and make the Kool-Aid a different flavor to convince her he wasn't the big bad wolf she knew he was.

# Chapter Eleven

WAR STRODE OVER and ripped the tape off Dalton's mouth.

"Son of a bitch! What do you want?" Dalton rocked the chair back and forth, trying to loosen the tape binding his hands together.

"We want to talk to you about Kerrigan." Mav stood and joined War. Shoulder to shoulder, they glared down at the human.

"Kerrigan? What about her? Bitch ran off and left me with a ton of debt. She's probably with that old bastard."

"From what we hear, you took all her money out of her savings account. You gone through all that already?" Warryck asked.

"That was as much my money as it was hers. I caught her swapping spit with the old man, and I knew she was getting ready to bolt. She wasn't leaving me high and dry, not after all I did for her."

"All you did for her? Did you beat her like you did Tasha? Something must have made her leave in the middle of the night."

"Nah, man. It ain't like that. She was fine last time I saw her." Dalton's eyes were dilated, and he licked his lips after every sentence. Warryck had studied enough psychology to know the man was lying.

Maveryck slapped Dalton hard across the face, the man's head jerking to the side. "Just like you're going to be fine when I get done with you. Now, you can either tell us the truth, or you'll end up worse off than Tasha was just now. A lot worse. Now fucking tell me what you know about Kerrigan."

"I'm telling you. I haven't seen her since that night."

Maveryck hit Dalton in the stomach. It had been years, but Warryck had been punched by a Gryphon, so he knew how it felt. This man was a decent-sized human, but that didn't mean he would be able to withstand being on the wrong end of a Gryphon's ire. "You better tell us what we want to know. I'm not gonna stop my brother until you do."

"I swear man. I haven't seen her since the night she took off. Yeah, I might have gotten a little rough with her, but the bitch was cheating on me. When I got home, she was gone. I figured she either went to the old guy's house, or she ended up at her folks' place."

Maveryck tossed a right hook across Dalton's face. "Does that feel a little rough to you?"

Dalton spit blood onto the carpet but didn't answer. While Maveryck continued questioning the man, War took a look around the rest of the house, careful not to touch too much. No need in leaving fingerprints just in case Dalton decided to rat them out to the cops. It didn't take long to find the shrine Tasha mentioned. The closet door was ajar, and War flipped the switch on the wall outside the small room. The clothes on the far rack had been pushed apart, revealing row after row of photos stuck to the sheetrock with pushpins.

War's breath caught in his chest. Tasha was a pretty woman with her long red hair and light green eyes, but she had absolutely nothing on Kerrigan O'Shea. Her hair was long and curly, and a deeper shade of red. Her eyes sparkled like emeralds. Bright and soulful. No wonder Dalton was so fixated on his ex. She was the most stunning woman War had ever seen. As much as he'd loved Harlow, even she couldn't hold a candle to the woman in these

87

photos. All the pictures were candid. Dalton must have hidden out with a telephoto lens, capturing Kerrigan's essence when she didn't know he was around.

The sound of fists meeting flesh reminded War what was taking place in the living room. He pulled one of the photos down, rubbing his thumb across her smile before placing it in his back pocket, telling himself it was to help him and Mav be able to identify her better. *Right.*

Mav kicked Dalton whose chair was on its side. Blood flowed from the man's nose, and his lips were cracked open. His left eye was swollen shut. "I think he's telling the truth." Mav kicked him again before striding into the kitchen to wash the blood off his knuckles. When he returned, he was drying his hands on a towel. He shoved it in his back pocket and then leaned against the chair, crossing his arms over his chest.

War knew what his family did. He was aware they got bloody. Knew they got violent when the need arose. Being mercenaries was a dirty business but a necessary one. There were people in the world who governments couldn't touch. Wouldn't touch. There were factions and cults, families and leaders who only wanted power, and they would do anything to gain more of it. Then there were pieces of shit, like Dalton Watkins, who were nothing more than bullies who liked to beat on women.

Warryck might not be a member of the Hounds of Zeus motorcycle club, but he was a Hound in the truest sense – one of the Gryphons created by the god himself to protect humans, and he had no qualms with the way Maveryck gave Dalton a taste of his own medicine. Did the human beating on women warrant a death sentence? No, and that was why they walked out the door leaving him alive, if badly broken.

Before following his twin, War knelt down so he had the man's attention. "If you ever put your hands on another woman in anger, we will end you." Dalton grunted, whether in agreement or as a "fuck you." War pulled the door closed using the tail of his T-shirt. Tasha could describe them to the police, but it was better to leave no fingerprints behind.

Mav was leaning against his bike, lighting a cigarette, his face pinched in anger. War asked, "Did you get anything useful out of him?" while tucking his tee back in. "He admitted to using the key he found in Kerrigan's pockets to search Ambrose Tucker's place, so that's one mystery solved, but it doesn't help us find her." Mav pulled the red-tinged towel out of his back pocket and stored it in his saddle bag. "What's next?"

"I say we head to White Mountain Forest and search for the missing car. Since Lucy didn't see them leaving via any of the routes coming out of the area, my bet is they're still there. As vast as the forest is, that gives whoever took Kerrigan plenty of places to hide. I've camped in several spots over the years, all of them different."

"If it's as vast as you say, it will take us a while to search the whole forest."

War grinned. "Do you have anywhere else to be?"

Mav took one last drag on his cigarette before crushing it under his boot. He picked up the butt and stuck it in his pocket. "Can't say that I do. The next few weeks were meant to be about bonding more than riding, so as long as you and I are together? That's a win in my book."

War couldn't agree more. They straddled their bikes, and after setting the GPS, Mav led the way. It was a two-hour ride to the forest. The area around White Mountain fell on desperate times when the world collapsed thirty years ago. What had once been a thriving mecca for snow skiing was now small towns where only the toughest could survive. There were no thriving malls. No big box stores selling everything one would need to survive the harsh winters.

The ski slopes still stood tall among the valleys

surrounding them, but the lifts hung overhead, swaying in the wind. It was one of the reasons War had chosen the area to camp in. Abandoned meant less people to run into and more freedom to shift into his lion. It wasn't odd seeing an eagle flying overhead, even if said eagle was larger than most. But a lion? That was out of the norm for North America unless one escaped from a zoo.

Finding an abandoned car would prove difficult considering how many had already been left to become one with the vegetation of tree-covered graveyards. Their only saving grace would be the white car wouldn't have had time to blend in to its surroundings. It had been several years since War had visited this particular area. During spring break, he opted to stay closer to home. In the past few summers, he had ventured west, looking for new places to relax.

As soon as they entered the forest where Lucy had last been able to track the vehicle, Mav pulled over on the shoulder so they could decide their next steps. Maveryck was the experienced mercenary, but Warryck was the seasoned camper. He better knew the areas to set up camp so they were both hidden as well as able to have a campfire without burning down the land around them.

Warryck pulled his helmet off and placed it over the mirror on the handlebar. He raked his hands through his hair as he looked around. "I think the first thing to do is find a camping spot where we can hide the bikes. Then we split the area into a grid with each of us taking a quadrant. We'll meet back at the campsite after searching each if we haven't spotted the vehicle." The Hounds had small packs they used to store their clothes and phones that were the right size to carry in their talons. Since they were naked when they shifted back, they needed a way to carry clothes with them in case they had to shift back unexpectedly. "If we find the car before we meet back, we'll shift and use our phones, assuming we can get a signal."

"Sounds good. Do you have an idea where you want to set up camp?" Mav lit a cigarette and inhaled deeply.

It had been a long time since Warryck had joined his brother with a smoke, and the smell brought back lots of memories. Ones that gripped his heart and twisted. They had been so close when they were younger, and being there with Mav was reminding him of how things could have been for the last twenty-something years. Climbing off his bike, he strode over to Mav and held out his hand. Maveryck cocked an eyebrow but silently handed over his cigarette. After taking a long drag, War held the smoke in his lungs before expelling back into the air.

"If you'll stay here with the bikes, I'm going to shift and take a look around. It shouldn't take too long." He reached into his saddle bag and removed the pouch for his clothes. Just in case.

"Sounds good. I'm gonna reach out to Ryker and check in. He was sending Hayden and Kyllian out on a run, and I want to see how it went."

Warryck shouldn't be jealous his brothers had a life without him. One in which they were all connected. He had made the decision to get married and go to college. Even if he hadn't gotten married, Warryck had intended to study criminology and become a police officer like Sutton had done. There was no better man – Gryphon – than Sutton Lazlo, in War's opinion. His father had been many things in his life, from husband to father, from soldier to cop, and all-around badass. Sutton was fierce in his love and even fiercer in his duty as a Hound.

War had wanted to be just like his dad, but he'd failed miserably. Not because he fell in love with Harlow, but because he'd allowed her to dictate how he should live his life. He'd thought giving her what she demanded was showing his love. All these years later, he had a feeling Harlow had been selfish in her ultimatums. His parents had the perfect marriage. Both Sutton and Rory did a lot of give

91

and take, but at the end of the day, they compromised in what was best for the family. For the Hounds. Rory might not be in the MC, but Sutton never kept anything from her. They had a true partnership. War had wanted that with Harlow, and during the quiet hours of the morning when he lie awake wishing there was someone at his side, he still wanted it.

After walking several yards into the trees, War stripped down and folded his clothes before placing them in the pouch. He called on his eagle, and the change was instantaneous. Gripping the strap in his right talon, War launched upward so he could scan the area. He searched for the perfect spot to set up camp while keeping his eyes open for an abandoned car. He didn't find the car, but he did find a spot next to a small creek. After returning to where Mav was waiting, Warryck shifted and dressed, walking barefoot to his bike. Mav was right where he left him, smoking another cigarette.

"I found a spot about a mile in. There's an old path we can take the bikes on. It'll be rough, but it's passable." He grabbed his boots and shoved his feet in.

"I do like it rough." Mav grinned and winked, leaving War with his brows furrowed. He didn't need to hear about his twin's sexual preferences.

Warryck led the way, since he knew where the trail was. He hadn't been kidding. The path was rough for two wheels, but their bikes were sturdy. Several of the Hounds were skilled in building machines from the ground up, and they made sure the motorcycles for the club were durable as well as comfortable. Well, as comfortable as two wheels could be traversing land less than suitable for a four-wheel drive. Warryck might not be a Hound, but he was a Lazlo, and as such, he was kitted with the same bikes as his brothers, thanks to Sutton.

The more he thought about his family, and the more time he spent with his twin, War's future was becoming clearer. There just might be one less spot at the oak table once his vacation was up.

# Chapter Twelve

THINGS WERE CERTAINLY different now that Kerrigan was living with Gideon and Sparrow. She still had to attend Bible study. Her clothes remained the drab cotton uniform. There was no alcohol, music, or television. What Kerrigan had once taken for granted would now be considered a luxury. But she no longer had to work outdoors on her hands and knees every day, even though she missed the chance at seeing Mac. She'd hoped to become friends with the other woman.

Kerrigan spent her time cleaning, even though there was only so much cleaning one house needed. She convinced Sparrow to stick with the cooking, and Kerrigan took care of the rest. She didn't mind, because if she let Sparrow help with the other chores, Kerrigan would have lost her mind from boredom.

Kerrigan got a better insight into the workings of The Sanctuary, or rather into how Gideon ruled his little world. He held meetings with the leaders of the cult in the chapel, but when he dismissed her and Sparrow to their bedrooms, she found out he also met with other men in his study, away from the members of his community. Men dressed in military gear. Men dressed in suits. Men who looked like they were from the city and not living off the land. Since Gideon's house was set back away from the other living quarters, he was able to entertain strangers with no one being the wiser. No one but Kerrigan and Sparrow, and probably the other women who'd lived there as chosen ones.

When Gideon insisted she and Sparrow remain in their rooms until his business was concluded, she grew suspicious. Did he not know the two of them were aware of these men? Or did he think they couldn't figure out there was more to the visits than dealing with sermons and living a simple life? Maybe Sparrow couldn't figure it out. Maybe the girl had been there so long she thought it was how things had to be so the community ran smoothly.

Kerrigan knew better. And if these men were coming to the property, they had to have come in using vehicles. Kerrigan climbed atop her bed, balanced precariously on the headboard so she could peek out the small window situated near the top of the wall. There were no cars in sight. When the men left, she didn't hear vehicles either. That meant they walked to the house. But from where? Just because they visited didn't mean they were close to a town. The men could have traveled from miles away.

A few weeks after Kerrigan had moved in, a man came calling unannounced. Before Gideon could get out of his office and command her to her room, Kerrigan opened the door to find a man who resembled Gideon standing in a charcoal suit.

"Kerrigan, go to your room." Gideon strode to the door, pushing her body behind his. The man smirked and leaned against the doorframe. "What are you doing here, Josiah?"

"Can I not pay my baby brother a visit?"

"Not without calling first. You know the rules."

Josiah took a step toward his brother, and when Gideon stepped backwards, he ran into Kerrigan. "I told you to go to your room," he snapped.

"You know, if she were mine, I'd want to keep her around," Josiah said, entering the house, followed by several men. Kerrigan was curious as to what the

95

unscheduled meeting was about, but she wasn't about to hang around to find out. When Kerrigan turned to go, Josiah tugged at her wrist, halting her steps. "Stay," he commanded, and she froze. Kerrigan looked between the two men, not wanting to make Gideon mad, but his brother held on tightly to her wrist.

"Take your hands off her." Gideon's eyes were colder than Kerrigan had ever seen, but his brother wasn't fazed by the look or his command.

Instead, Josiah raised her hand to his lips and gently kissed her knuckles. "It was a pleasure to finally meet you. I hope to see you again very soon." When he released his grip, Kerrigan hurried from the room. Climbing onto the bed, she sank back against the pillows, biting her bottom lip as she considered what the visit meant. These men weren't members of Gideon's flock. His leaders weren't part of this secret gathering, so it seemed Gideon kept secrets from his people. If that were true, what did he have to hide? The way Kerrigan saw it, if the man was keeping things from his own community, he wasn't a good man. Not that she had thought he was. He'd allowed her to be kidnapped, and when she arrived, he didn't offer to get her home. He lauded Steven for bringing her to the compound. No, Gideon Talbert wasn't a good man. She only knew his last name because she overheard one of the men in military gear greet him as such before she got her bedroom door closed.

Not that she'd snooped, but whenever Kerrigan straightened up in Gideon's office, there were no papers lying around with his name on them. He didn't have a computer that she saw. There were no photos on the walls or framed certificates giving any indication who the man was. She'd never seen a cell phone, but he had to have had some way of communicating with the outside world. He'd admitted to contacting her parents, unless that had been a lie. She almost hoped he had lied about it. Then her parents would be looking for her. Hopefully, they were looking for her anyway, since she hadn't checked in with them. She spoke to her parents at least once a week.

The bedroom door opened, and Gideon stuck his head in. Kerrigan shrank back, fully expecting him to rail at her for what happened earlier. Instead, his eyes heated as he took in Kerrigan on her bed. After clearing his throat, he said, "Come with me." When Kerrigan swung her legs over the side of the bed, he turned and crossed the hall to Sparrow's room, telling her the same thing. When the three of them were in the living area, Gideon pointed to the sofa. "Sit." She and Sparrow sat next to one another. Sparrow remained on the edge with her hands clasped in her lap, but Kerrigan leaned back and crossed her arms. "I will be away from the house for a few days. While I'm gone, you will remain here. There will be no Bible study, and no one is allowed into the house other than Brothers John and James. They will check in with you every morning to see if you need anything. I expect you to behave as if I were here."

"Why can't you take me with you?" Kerrigan knew the answer, but she still had to ask.

"Back to that, are you?" Gideon almost looked hurt. "I had hoped you would be happy here with me."

Sparrow gasped, and Kerrigan looked at the girl. Sparrow's eyes were downcast, but Kerrigan felt the young woman tremble. She'd said she knew Gideon wasn't going to choose her, but it was obvious she'd not given up hope until that moment.

Kerrigan didn't want to alienate Sparrow, but she had her own agenda where Gideon was concerned. Taking a chance, Kerrigan stood and closed the distance between her and her captor. "I am happy here, but I've gotten used to having you around. I'm going to miss you. That's why I wanted to go with you." Kerrigan stretched her hand toward Gideon, but at the last second, she pulled away, as if unsure he would welcome her touch. She wasn't like the virginal women who'd been vying for a shot at being

Gideon's wife, and he knew that.

Gideon grabbed her hand before she could move away from him and held it gently. "Do you mean that?"

Kerrigan lowered her eyes and nodded. She'd learned how to be submissive while living with Dalton. Being quiet and pretending to be shy went against everything she was, but it had kept her from his wrath on more than one occasion. Gideon placed a finger under her chin, lifting her face to look at him. With narrowed eyes, he studied her. Kerrigan did her best to keep her face void of emotion. She couldn't pull off happy, because she wasn't. She couldn't pretend to want the man, because thinking of him touching her sexually made her want to throw up. Still, she licked her lips, drawing his attention away from her eyes. With a tenderness she didn't expect, Gideon pulled her fingers to his lips and kissed them.

"I will be back before you know it, and then, you and I will have all the time in the world."

Kerrigan looked up at him and smiled. "Okay. I can wait."

Gideon squeezed her hand before releasing it. "Good. Sparrow, I will talk to you when I get back. Until then, you two ladies enjoy a few lazy days."

Sparrow didn't move until Gideon had left the house. She stood and headed toward her bedroom. After a couple steps, she stopped and looked back at Kerrigan. "Well, I guess that's that. I knew I didn't stand a chance, but... Congratulations."

"I'm sorry, Sparrow." And she was. Kerrigan didn't have any intentions of being Gideon's wife, but she had to get him to lower his guard where she was concerned. With him out of the house, she had a few days to figure out how to get away.

# Chapter Thirteen

WARRYCK FELT LIKE he'd traveled back in time. He'd forgotten how much he loved spending time with his twin, and now, he knew he wouldn't let anything stand between them ever again. The two of them spent their days in eagle form, flying over the vast forest, searching for any sign of the vehicle in which Kerrigan O'Shea might have been taken. At night, they sat around a fire, eating and drinking, reminiscing, and talking about things in their lives they'd encountered over the many years they'd been apart.

After a couple days of searching and coming up empty, they packed up, got on their bikes, and moved their campsite up the road. At the end of the first week, there was no sign of the car. Warryck returned to the campsite after bathing in a nearby creek and sat down across from Mav who was cooking a couple rabbits over the fire. "It pains me to say this, but I think we need to give up the search." And it did pain him. War had felt an instant connection with Kerrigan when he saw her photo, and giving up on her felt like he was giving up on finding a part of himself.

Mav left the rabbits to roast and grabbed a bottle of whiskey. "It doesn't make sense. If Lucy is right and that car came through the forest, it has to be somewhere."

"Truth, but she could have missed seeing it leave the other side. We're not even sure Kerrigan was in that car. She could have left her own vehicle and taken off on foot. If her injuries were as bad as her parents believe, she could already be dead."

"If that's the case, wouldn't someone have found her body after all this time? Surely the cops have searched the area where her car was picked up by the tow truck."

"You would think so, but we both know not all cops are as good as Dad was. Is there a Hounds chapter in that area?"

"What are you thinking?" Maveryck passed the bottle over while he turned the rabbits.

"I think we should have someone we trust search the area. I know you have a life to get back to, and I don't want to waste our time together on this more than we already have. Don't get me wrong. I hope the woman turns up, but we've spent over a week looking for her. Hell, she might not be in the country. Whoever took her could have managed to get her on a plane and sold her to the highest bidder in Russia."

"Russia, huh?" Mav grinned. "The Hounds don't deal with a lot of human trafficking, but there is always that possibility.

"No, but you do deal with all the cults. Isn't the Ministry sort of like human trafficking? They take good people and brainwash them. Who knows what they do with them once they're under the influence, so to speak."

"We've been going after these bastards a long time, and not all the compounds we find follow the rules set by the Ministry. For the most part, we've found the people living in those places want to be there. If they aren't breaking any laws, we leave them alone. It's the ones who are recruiting militant types and going after good people who don't subscribe to a lifestyle they agree with that we target. The Ministry is strict in the way they run their communities. Children are raised from birth to conform to the ways of the leaders. The adults have to adhere to strict guidelines and have no say in how the kids are raised. The teachings are archaic with women treated no better than slaves. If a man is found to be weak, he's escorted off the property and never heard from again." Mav reached for the whiskey bottle and took a couple sips, wiping his mouth with the back of his hand after setting it back down between the two of them.

"Then there are the ones who fall somewhere in the middle. They are a commune who live off the land, raising their families away from society, but they aren't without a cause. We know this because people get tired of having no say in the way they live their lives, and they run. From what we've been told, most people just go along with the rules, but those who don't are made to suffer if they try to leave, and that deters the others from trying to escape." Mav removed the rabbits from the spit and handed one over to War.

War took a bite of his supper. When Mav laughed, War looked up. "What?" he asked around a mouthful of meat.

"I know we're Gryphons, but we do have utensils. Would you like a knife and fork?"

"Nah. Less to clean up this way." Warryck's true self had been smothered for too long, and being out in nature for a week solid had reminded him of that. "Unless you prefer me to use my indoor manners while we're out in the middle of nowhere?"

"Nah. We're good." Maveryck laughed again and picked up his own rabbit, forgoing a plate as well.

"So, back to the ones in the middle. If they aren't peaceable but aren't building armies, what is their endgame?"

"It isn't so much an endgame as it's them bucking the system. They want to live in a community free of those who aren't like them. No gays. No one who isn't white. No religious beliefs other than what they preach. No women in power. They don't go out looking to eradicate the different kinds from the world, but they make sure no one can come in and tell them what they're doing is wrong, either. They own their land but refuse to pay taxes on it. They make it so the government can't come in and arrest them for not paying those taxes. Sort of shoot first, ask questions later."

"So, the Hounds leave those groups alone and only go after the Ministry?" Warryck had been involved early on in going after the men who tried kidnapping Harlow. If she hadn't been a Gryphon, they would have succeeded in killing her when she fought back. Then again, the only reason she'd been able to fight at all was because she was a Gryphon. After that, Warryck left the family to take a teaching job and never again got involved in what they did. Until now.

"Yes. There are too many of the Ministry out there for us to focus on those groups that aren't actually harming other humans physically. I know we're just riding together for a couple weeks, but have you given any thought into what you're going to do next? Maybe…"

War finished off his rabbit before answering, and Mav didn't push him. When War had picked the bones clean, he tossed them in the fire and took a long swig of whiskey to wash it down. "Maybe finally take my seat at the table? Yeah, I've thought about it. I've been doing the same thing for over twenty years, and I want to take some more time off before committing to anything full-time."

"I get that, but you have to understand. The club isn't full-time, and it doesn't make us any money. We do that because it's our calling. Ridding the world of those who wish to harm humans. The merc jobs are where we make money." Mav tossed his own bones into the fire and wiped his fingers on his jeans. "Owning your own company has its benefits. We get paid well for the jobs we take, and with being some of the best in the business, we can pick and choose which jobs we do or don't take. If we need time off for hunting Ministry or going on road trips with our twin, we have that luxury. You could join us on jobs and see how you like it. It's a far cry from teaching."

"Of that I have no doubt. And we'll see." War stood, stretching his arms toward the sky. "For now, I want us to continue our ride, getting as much road time in before you have to get back to the club."

"So, we're definitely abandoning our search for the woman?"

Warryck wanted to say no, but how did he explain to his twin it was the last thing he wanted? They were supposed to be spending this time getting reacquainted, and he hated to ask Mav to continue helping him. "Unless Lucy and the Gargoyle find something else to go on, I think we're wasting our time searching around here. If they happen to come up with something to check out, I can always backtrack. I think you should call in your Brothers in the area where she was last seen and ask them to search for a body, just in case."

Mav pulled out his phone and called Ryker, filling him in on what was going on and asking him to get in touch with the Hounds chapter closest to New Portland. They talked for a few minutes, and the one-sided conversation bothered Warryck. He waited until his twin hung up to find out what was going on. "What was that about? I know if it's club business, you can't discuss it, but it sounded like you were worried about Ryker."

"I don't worry about our big brother when he's taking jobs. He's the baddest of the bad; you know that. He's sending Hayden out, and that pisses me off. The kid's never done a solo before. Ryker said it was an in and out, but that doesn't make me worry any less."

Warryck wanted to laugh at his twin calling their baby brother a kid, but he was the youngest, and everyone in the family refused to let him grow up, even if he was almost thirty. "Ryker trained him, right?"

"Yes, fuck." Maveryck ran his hands through his beard as he stared up at the stars. "It's hard thinking about Hayden and Lucy being old enough to handle themselves.

103

After that shit went down with her job, I'm telling you, War, I wanted to kidnap Lucy myself and take her where no one could find her."

"But her mate did that for her. I can't believe my baby's mated, and to a Gargoyle no less. At least she's studied their kind for years."

"And his sister Tessa's hot as fuck. You should see her, War. Long red hair and an attitude that goes on for days. Plus, she rides a Harley like nobody's business. Makes me hard just thinking about her. Too bad she's got a mate already."

"TM-fucking-I, Brother." War shook his head, but he was laughing when he did it. He knew how Maveryck felt about women, and getting a hard-on for this Tessa was merely Mav appreciating her beauty. After Jenna walked out one day and never looked back, Maveryck gave up on anything but one-night stands. War was just glad their two youngest brothers had yet to deal with heartache.

Maveryck picked up the whiskey. "Here's to redheads."

When he passed the bottle, War raised it in the air. "To redheads."

After they polished off the liquor, War made sure the fire was banked before the two of them bedded down for the rest of the night. When the sun first broke, they got up and packed everything on their bikes. Before hitting the road, War called Lucy on the off chance she had found any more information. When she told him she hadn't, he informed her he and Mav were taking off on the rest of their trip, but for her to call if she found anything which would help find Kerrigan.

For the next week, the two of them enjoyed winding roads through small towns. They stopped and ate at out-of-the-way diners instead of hitting cities with chain restaurants. The longer they were together, the more Warryck knew he would join his brothers in one capacity if not both. He wasn't sure he was cut out for mercenary

104

work, but he would at least get Ryker to train him in case they ever needed backup.

Instead of traveling as far west as they'd planned, Ryker called Maveryck and asked him to take a job over in Ohio. War offered to go with him, but Maveryck insisted War continue on with his vacation. Since War wasn't trained, he agreed, because he didn't want to get in the way, possibly getting Maveryck hurt. Just because they were Gryphons didn't mean they couldn't be killed with a bullet.

"This job should only take a day, two at most, if everything goes to plan, and if I don't have another one lined up, I'll come meet you wherever you are, and we can spend some more time together," Mav said when they were ready to split up.

"That's a deal. By that time, I should have made a decision on what I want to do going forward."

The two brothers hugged, and Maveryck gripped him tightly. "I've missed you, Brother, and I'm not letting you go this time."

War had to blink back the tears. He'd hurt his twin's heart when he chose Harlow over the family, but he had no reason to be apart from them now. He knew forgiveness had already been given, and they would readily accept him back into the fold. He was looking forward to it.

Wanting to enjoy the rest of his vacation, War decided to head to the one place he found the most peace, and that was his usual camping spot in the Green Mountains. It would take him closer to home, so when he was ready with his decision, he could pack up his small house and put it up for sale. He had no illusions where his future was concerned. He would be moving closer to Mav.

# Chapter Fourteen

SURPRISINGLY, SPARROW WAS her normal chipper self within minutes. "I don't know how to have lazy days, but I'm looking forward to giving it a go."

"Come, let's sit and talk." Kerrigan took Sparrow by the hand and led her to the sofa. "Tell me about your life here."

"Can I ask you a question instead?" Sparrow rubbed her hands down her pants, not looking at Kerrigan.

"Of course."

"Why did you lie to Brother Gideon?"

"Lie? What did I lie about?" Kerrigan held her breath.

"You hate it here. You don't like Brother Gideon, yet you pretended to be excited at the prospect of being his chosen. Why?"

Kerrigan stood from the sofa, giving herself time to come up with a believable answer. When she turned back, she smiled. "I learned a long time ago that sometimes you have to make the best of a bad situation. I don't like the circumstances under which I came to be here. But I know I'm not going to be allowed to leave. Instead of making things hard on myself, I figure it's best to go with the flow, so to speak. If I have to remain here, why wouldn't I want to be here where I'm afforded a few luxuries? That may sound selfish, but I would much rather clean house for Gideon than toil on my hands and knees pulling weeds."

"That makes sense. I just wonder what will happen to me."

Kerrigan returned to sit next to Sparrow. "Do you think if I asked him to, Gideon would allow you to remain here with us? I can't cook for shit, and besides that, I'm rather fond of you." Kerrigan wanted Sparrow to talk freely with her, but what she'd said was the truth. She could cook well enough, but it was nowhere near what the young girl was capable of, and she cared about Sparrow.

"You'd do that?"

"Yes. I don't have any friends here other than you, and a lifetime spent without friends is a lonely one. I had hoped to befriend a young woman named McKenzie, but after talking with her in the gardens one day, it was like we were separated on purpose."

"You met Mac?" Sparrow's eyes glistened with tears.

"Yes. You know her?"

"She's my sister. How was she? We... I'm not supposed to talk about her, but I miss her so much."

"Why aren't you supposed to talk about her?" Kerrigan was surprised they were sisters. The two looked nothing alike.

Sparrow wiped at her cheeks. "She's a disgrace."

Kerrigan gasped. "Why would you think that? Is it because of her face? Sparrow—"

Sparrow jumped up and turned, hands fisted at her sides. "I don't think that. She fell in love, but it wasn't a sanctioned coupling. When the elders found out, they took... They took the man away, and Mac tried to go after him. She ran away, and, well, you saw her. Saw what happened to her. They took her from our cabin after that, and then I was brought here. I haven't seen her since. How was she?"

"I only met her one time, but she seemed... broken. Said she'd lost her baby and had been given a month to grieve. That doesn't sound like a lot of time, if you ask me."

"Baby? Oh no. Oh, no, no, no. That's so much worse."

"I have to agree losing a child is about as bad as things

could be." Kerrigan wasn't one who thought you had to be married to have a child, but she always thought if she was going to be a mom, she'd want to at least have a loving partner. Since she'd never had a long-term relationship, she'd long given up thoughts to having a baby. Before she met Dalton, she'd been happy with her single life.

"I've been so caught up in my own selfishness, I didn't even think about what Mac was going through."

"Sparrow, why are people who are unhappy here not allowed to leave? Why would your parents make McKenzie live this kind of life?"

"Because it's better than living on the outside."

Kerrigan didn't want to argue that topic again. Sparrow was young and obviously had bought into what she'd been told, so Kerrigan took a different route in getting answers.

"Agnes said that newcomers were given the worst jobs, and the longer they did as they were told, they moved into better positions. I was stuck weeding the gardens. My roommates also worked in the gardens. Are they new here, too?"

"No, the gardens aren't where new residents usually start out. You should have been given a cleaning job or working in the kitchen. I wonder why that is?"

Kerrigan knew the answer to that. Agnes said Gideon had been playing favorites with her. "Was weeding what Mac did before she fell from grace? Or was that always her job?"

Sparrow shook her head. "She worked with the animals. She always wanted to be a veterinarian when she was little, so it was the closest thing available when she aged out."

"Aged out? You mean when she finished her education?"

"Yes. Unlike on the outside, kids don't need jobs here because there isn't anything to spend money on. We don't work until we turn eighteen. We're given a job closely related to where our interests lie if at all possible. I worked in the library until I was brought to live with Gideon. Mac wanted to be a vet, so she was allowed to work raising the cows and chickens."

Working with the animals they raised for food was a far cry from becoming a doctor to keep them alive, but Kerrigan wasn't going to mention that.

"If I hadn't been chosen to live with Gideon, where would I have ended up? Since there isn't a bar here on the compound, would I have remained in the garden?"

"You probably would have been put to work in the kitchen or dining hall."

Kerrigan shuddered at the thought. Slinging drinks for a small crowd was one thing, but serving the masses was something she didn't want to contemplate. She'd rather work with the animals or toil in the sun on her knees all day in the garden where she was alone with her thoughts and not surrounded by people who probably considered her a disgrace as well. "Let's take a walk," she suggested, needing a bit of fresh air.

"We really shouldn't."

"Why not? Gideon told us to relax, and a little fresh air goes a long way in relaxing me. Besides, you'd be doing me a favor. I've not seen all of the property, and who better to show me around than someone who's lived here a long time? If I go wandering off alone, I'll just get into trouble somehow."

Sparrow bit her lip, her eyes narrowed at Kerrigan. Slowly, she smiled then nodded enthusiastically. "Yeah, okay." After grabbing their plain cardigan sweaters and their head coverings, they walked out the back door. "Where would you like to go?"

"I'd love to see the cows." Kerrigan looped her arm through Sparrow's and sighed loudly. "Back in Ireland, my mom was raised on a farm, and at night, instead of reading me bedtime stories, she would regale me with memories of being a little girl and helping her da." Kerrigan was going to Hell for lying, but she needed Sparrow's help these next few days while Gideon was gone.

"You sound sad."

"I am. I miss my parents fiercely, but there's nothing I can do about that, is there?"

Sparrow didn't answer. Instead, she pointed out things on their walk Kerrigan would never have noticed. Mainly because she was aware of the man following them. She'd caught sight of him as soon as they stepped out of the house, but he was keeping his distance. Of course, Gideon hadn't trusted her not to wander off. Sparrow named the different types of plants that were used to make medicine in the infirmary. Kerrigan barely paid attention as her housemate rambled on about things Kerrigan wasn't concerned with. Instead, she paid attention to the lay of the land. To the various paths they walked on and everything beyond. They walked until they came to a field. Wide open acres stretched out until they ended with another tree line.

Kerrigan approached the split-rail fence, and leaned her forearms on the top rail, taking in her surroundings. The barn was a typical wooden structure you'd expect to see on any farm. Another building, equally as big, was set farther back. A large, double door was fixed into one end. Big enough for vehicles to drive through. "What's that other building over there?" Kerrigan pointed to the massive structure.

"That's the garage where they keep the tractors, trucks, and other farm equipment. At least that's what Mac told me."

Kerrigan had no doubt that's where the cars Gideon used were kept. If she could get her hands on the keys, she might be able to get away from the compound. She wondered why Mac hadn't tried that since she worked so close to the building. Maybe she had, or maybe the keys weren't kept with the vehicles. Kerrigan thought back to the younger woman's warning about the woods. Looking into the distance, Kerrigan noticed a couple different breaks in the trees, which possibly meant trails leading away from the compound. She needed to talk to Sparrow's sister again.

"Is it against the rules for you to talk to Mac?"

"Not if she's back at work. But now that I'm at Gideon's, I don't have a chance to see her." Sparrow's tone was sad.

"What about Bible study? Can you not talk to her for a few minutes afterwards?" Kerrigan could only imagine what it would be like to have a sister who was hurting but she couldn't see her. Growing up an only child, she'd only had her friends from school to hang out with, but that couldn't compare to having a sibling around all the time. She'd often wished for a brother or sister, but her mom had a hard time delivering Kerrigan, and her parents wouldn't risk another pregnancy.

Before Sparrow could answer, a strong hand clamped down on Kerrigan's shoulder. She jerked then turned to face the man who'd been following them. She recognized him as one of the guards who'd been present with Gideon the day she met Mac.

"You ladies need to return to the house. It's going to rain, and you don't want to get caught in it."

Sparrow gasped, her eyes widening. She silently reached for Kerrigan's hand, grasping it tightly. Squeezing back, Kerrigan placed herself between the girl and the guard. "He's right. We don't want to get drenched." As she tugged Sparrow back toward the trail leading to the house, she wrapped her arm around Sparrow's shoulder. After turning to see where the guard was, Kerrigan asked, "Are you okay?"

Sparrow was shivering, but Kerrigan didn't think it was from the chill in the air. "I'm fine." When Mac had seen the group of men, she had tensed much the same way. Something snapped behind them, and Kerrigan tightened

111

her grip. When they reached the house, Sparrow rushed inside, not stopping until she was safely inside her bedroom. Kerrigan paused in the doorway.

"Sparrow, who is that man?"

The girl wrapped her arms around her waist, not trying to stop the tears rolling down her cheeks. "I think he's the father of Mac's baby."

"I thought you said her boyfriend was taken away from here."

Sparrow hiccupped out a breath. "I did. Elijah also worked with the animals. He and Mac spent every day together, and they fell in love. But Mac had been promised to Lewis. That's the guard who was following us."

"Promised? As in one of those sanctioned relationships?"

"Yes, but Mac hated Lewis. Said if it wasn't for him, she and Eli could have been together."

"But I thought Gideon oversaw all the couples to make sure they were compatible."

"Compatible from the man's perspective. You've heard Gideon speak about relationships during Bible study. The woman is to submit to the man."

Kerrigan had heard him say those words, and they'd pissed her off. They weren't living in the Stone Age, for fuck's sake. "So, the women who live here don't have a say in who they end up with? Sparrow, please tell me you don't agree with that."

"It doesn't matter whether I do or not; it's just the way things are."

"I'm confused. Brother Gideon also teaches about abstinence before marriage. If Lewis was the baby's father, why is Mac the one who is considered a disgrace? He broke the rules too."

"Yes, but he's a guard, and nobody goes against them any more than they go against Brother Gideon. The only time an unmarried couple can spend time together is when they're being watched over by Brother Gideon. Eli and Mac would never have had the opportunity to have sex."

"So, you're saying what exactly?"

Even though they were alone, Sparrow lowered her voice. "I think Lewis had sex with Mac, and Brother Gideon okayed it."

In other words, Gideon gave permission for the guard to rape Sparrow's sister. "She warned me about staying out of the woods. Is that where she was attacked? When she tried to run away?"

Sparrow nodded, swiping at the tears on her cheeks.

"Will you tell me about it?"

"I only know the details because our parents thought I was asleep. When Mac went missing, I was pulled from our cabin and taken to my parents', because they thought I might know where she was. It took half an hour to convince them I knew nothing about her disappearance. Mac had confided in me about Elijah, but after they took him away, she became sullen and refused to talk to even me. Finally, the guards stopped interrogating me, and I curled up on the sofa. When Brother Gideon came back, he told them Mac had run through the woods behind the cattle enclosure. She had received some injuries, but they were treating her in the infirmary. He refused to allow my parents to see her, saying she had disgraced the family, and as part of her punishment, Mac wasn't allowed to speak to anyone.

"When the room was silent, I thought he'd left, so I sat up. When he noticed I was awake, Brother Gideon bade me come with him. He brought me back here, sending one of the chosen back to her cabin. I didn't see Mac again until a couple months later on my way to Bible study. She was walking with Brother Gideon and Lewis. I called out to her, and that's when I saw the scar. I still don't know what happened to cause it. I… I know better than to ask. I just wish she and Elijah could have been together, then none of this would be happening."

113

"I really don't understand why you would want this life for her. How can you think she's better off here than living out in the world where she can be with the man she loves?"

Sparrow turned her eyes up to Kerrigan. "Because if she's not here, Gideon will give me to Lewis."

# Chapter Fifteen

THE CLOSER WARRYCK got to Green Mountain the stronger his Gryphon urged him to hurry. It wasn't that he never listened to his animal side. It had just been a long time since the Gryphon tried to take over, and he was surprised at the inner voice so loud in his head. The last time the voice had demanded War listen was when he and Harlow were together. His animal had fought with him to tell her no when she wanted to separate him from his family. When War wouldn't give in, it was like his Gryphon had retreated so deep War could barely feel it.

Sure, War called on his eagle when he felt the need to shift and free his baser nature for a few moments, but it wasn't the same as having his full Gryphon front and center. The eagle was always eager to spread its wings and soar. That was easier than letting the lion loose. Eagles didn't draw attention when floating along the clouds. A lion, however, wasn't something one normally saw outside a zoo or in their native habitat. Allowing the Gryphon to take over? That was the stuff fantasy novels were made of. If an unaware human caught sight of one, the Gryphon would have to use their powers to erase the memory.

Ever since hitting the road with Mav, the Gryphon had felt more alive inside. In rekindling his relationship with his twin, he was in a sense doing the same with the other part of himself. It had been so long – twenty-four years – since the

Gryphon was fully formed. That long since it had spoken inside War's head. He couldn't remember such an urgency from the animal. He knew his family didn't have a problem listening to their own animal, especially his parents. Since they were both over a century old, they had more experience and time acknowledging what they were and giving in to that side of themselves. As far as he knew, neither one had ever fought with their Gryphon.

Having studied psychology for so long, War understood the workings of the brain better than most, yet he still didn't understand it enough. Over the years, he'd read hundreds of books. Thousands of studies. The more he read, the more he realized he would never fully comprehend the human brain. He wasn't human, and even though he had some fundamental knowledge of his studies, it didn't help him to grasp why he suddenly felt so out of control.

Maybe the Gryphon was just ready to get back to that special place where War could be alone with his thoughts. Where he usually felt most comfortable. Or maybe there was something else going on the Gryphon was aware of. If that was the case, War had no idea what it could be. He'd heard some of his family speak of such things, but he'd never encountered it for himself. Having lived over half his life without his animal front and center like the others had, he wasn't surprised. On more than one occasion, Maveryck had talked about how without his Gryphon, he wouldn't have been able to do his job as well as he did. The sixth sense he'd gleaned from within had been paramount in his success.

War wanted that, he realized, as he wound his Harley through the backroads leading back to Green Mountain. He wanted something more out of his life. He already figured that much out, but until his Gryphon decided to wake up and talk to him, War had forgotten what he'd been missing – the rest of his soul. If Harlow had lived, would that have

116

happened? He never let himself think about that. About continuing on and becoming a cop. About living with his wife and raising their daughter together. Lucy still wouldn't have known the family, because Harlow hadn't wanted anything to do with them, so things probably wouldn't have been much different. Except he'd have known love. From both his girls.

Maybe.

And it was that maybe that had War refusing to consider what his past could have been like, because if he did, he would have to think about how his wife had been selfish. It was her who kept Lucy away from the Hounds. It was her who wanted War to abandon his family's MC. How long would their marriage have lasted if Harlow continued to be selfish, and how much more of his life would she have asked him to give up? She never wanted him to go into law enforcement. She tried more than a few times to steer him away from his criminal justice classes into something more mundane and safer. In the end, she got her wish. Had that been a subconscious decision on War's part because he knew it's what she wanted?

He hated thinking of Harlow in such a negative light, and this was why he never allowed himself to revisit the past. So why now? Was it because he was considering doing exactly the opposite of what she wanted? Probably, but he was okay with that. She was gone. Had been for years, so it was time to start living his life for himself and not her. Lucy had broken free from the bonds her mother had set for her at birth, and she was finally living her life as she chose. Warryck wanted to get to know his daughter. Needed to make up for all the lost time spent away from her. Inhaling the fresh, cool air, War felt freer than he had since he was a teen. Being a Gryphon, he had hundreds of years ahead of him, and he intended to start living his life again. One that didn't involve regrets.

Rain usually didn't bother Warryck, but the torrential

117

downpour had him pulling off at a small hotel instead of sleeping in the woods. A hot shower and a meal he didn't catch himself sounded pretty good in his head. After retrieving his small overnight bag, he paid for a room and was glad to be able to change out of his drenched clothes. Before he could get a shower, his cell phone rang, and Lucy's name flashed on the screen.

"Hello?"

"Hey, Dad. How's your trip going?"

"Mav had to take a detour for a job, so right now, it's just me. Did you find something on the missing O'Shea woman?"

"I think so, but it could be nothing."

"Or it could be something. What is it?"

"Well, it really bothered me that I couldn't track the car after it entered the forest, and then on top of that, you and Mav couldn't find it anywhere. So, I started looking at all the vehicles leaving the forest soon after the car entered. There was a large vehicle, like a moving van, that left the area about an hour after the car entered."

"Are you thinking the car was in the van?"

"Yes. I did some digging, and the van was registered under the same name as the car. I never stopped researching the woman's name or next of kin. I finally found something. The woman was never married, and according to everything I found, she never had any children. I was finally able to find a relative – a nephew. His name is Steven Pinion. The odd thing about that is he was abandoned by his mother, Clara's sister, when he was a teen. He went to live with Clara, but she disappeared and was presumed dead several years later. Steven married a woman named Maren Talbert. When I searched her name, nothing alarming came up until I got to her brother, Gideon."

"What's so special about Gideon?"

"I had to dig deep. Really deep, but what I found wasn't good. He has ties to the Ministry."

"Holy shit. If they got their hands on Kerrigan, she could be hidden away at one of their compounds."

"I'm afraid so. I know those places are bad enough for kids taken against their will, but at least they haven't lived full lives where they understand everything they're losing by being held with those nutjobs. Kerrigan, even though she was abused by her boyfriend, has parents who love her, and from what you and Mav said about the people at the bar, they love her too. I know all about being taken, and I bet dollars to donuts Kerrigan isn't happy where she is."

"Were you able to follow the truck?"

"For a distance, and then I lost it again when it got deep into Vermont where there were no traffic cameras. Julian has offered to trace it using satellite, but that's risky. If the government happens to find out Julian hacked into the satellite... Well, you know what happens when the government gets their hands on people doing what they aren't supposed to."

"How far into Vermont could you follow, and what direction was it headed? I'm on my way to Green Mountain, and I have nothing but time on my hands. I don't want you or Julian risking yourselves for this. I want Kerrigan to be found and safe, but you're my priority now, Lucy."

"I'll text you everything I have, if you want to follow-up."

"Like I said. I have nothing but time, so I'm willing to continue looking. Now, other than learning from Julian, how are things in New Atlanta?"

"Really good. Tamian's clan is wonderful. They're a little more civilized than the Hounds, but I like them anyway."

Warryck laughed at his daughter. He knew she loved their family as much as he did, but she wasn't wrong about his brothers being less than civilized. At least the two younger ones. "That's great, honey. I'm glad it's not a case of you dreading the in-laws. How's your mate treating you?

119

Do I need to head south and make an appearance?"

Lucy giggled. "Not for the reason you're asking, but you're always welcome to come see us. Tamian's great. Treats me like a queen." The love for her mate poured through the phone.

"Well, you will be queen one day." Warryck still couldn't get over the fact that his baby girl would be queen over the Italian Gargoyles. If anyone could handle the job, it was her.

"Yes, but not anytime soon. I'm still getting used to my new life. Having the freedom to do what I want is wonderful, and I'm happier than I've ever been. How about you? Are you enjoying your own freedom?"

"I really am. Nothing like seeing the country on two wheels at my own pace."

"So, do you have any plans, or are you going to be a nomad the rest of your life?"

"Well, I have been thinking."

"Don't hurt yourself."

"Hey! That's enough out of you." War laughed along with Lucy, and his heart swelled with so much love for his daughter. "Riding with Mav has made me realize how much I miss my twin. I'm thinking I may join the family. I didn't join him on his current job because I haven't been trained. I'm thinking of working with Ryker so I can at least go in as backup if one of the Hounds needs me."

"That's great. I know Ryker will be glad to have you back. He's missed you. All the family has.

What about the club? Are you finally going to patch in?"

"Probably. That's something else I'll need to talk to Ryker about. Mav seems to think all I'll have to do is say the word and Ryker will give me a kutte already kitted with rockers, but I don't want that. I want to go through the process of being a prospect first. I don't want the patch handed to me because I'm their brother. I want to earn it."

"If this was a normal club, I think that's exactly what would happen, but Dad… This is the Hounds. You're already one of them. It won't surprise me at all if Ryker already has a kutte waiting on you."

If it were anyone other than his older brother, Warryck would agree with his daughter, but Ryker had hardened over the years, and he still held a grudge against War for letting Lucy be raised outside their family. "We'll see. For now, I'm going to shower, grab something to eat, and get a good night's sleep. I'll take up the search for Kerrigan in the morning."

"Okay. Keep me posted. I really hope you can find this woman. She has to be scared out of her mind."

"I'm going to do my best. I'll talk to you soon."

"Bye, Dad."

The call disconnected, and War leaned his hip against the dresser where the television sat. Twisting the phone in his hand, he imagined the brothers welcoming him into the MC with open arms. He didn't deserve for it to be that easy. Even if Ryker surprised him, War wouldn't accept anything more than a prospect patch. He had a lot of years to make up for, and he was going to do it the right way. But before he called his older brother, he was going to do his level best to find Kerrigan O'Shea. With that decision made, his Gryphon pushed against his mind.

*We need to go.*

"It's pouring fucking rain. I'll get something to eat and a good night's sleep. We'll head that way in the morning."

*No. We need to go now.*

"What the fuck is so urgent we need to go out in this shit?" His Gryphon didn't answer. It continued to push against his mind, urging him to leave and head toward the state park. "Fine, but if I wreck because of this weather, it's on you." Grumbling, Warryck took one longing look at the bathroom where the shower wasn't happening and grabbed his things. He might not be spending the night in the dry

121

room, but by Zeus, he was getting some fucking food.

# Chapter Sixteen

"Excuse me?" Surely Kerrigan had misheard Sparrow. "What do you mean, he'll give you to Lewis? I thought his process of putting people together was to find those most compatible."

"Who told you that?"

"Gideon did. He said it was important for him to interact with all the couples so he could determine if they would be a good match for the long haul."

Sparrow stared at her like she had three heads. "That's... uh."

"That's what? If he lied to me, I'd like to know. Why would you be given to Lewis just because he and Mac didn't work out?"

"I want to take a nap. If you'll close the door behind you, I'd appreciate it."

Kerrigan hated the defeated look on Sparrow's face, but more than that, she hated the thought of Lewis getting anywhere near the young girl. Of course, Gideon had lied to her. Had anything he said been the truth? Had he contacted her parents, or were they out there searching for her? Had Dalton truly been losing his shit when she ran away? How the hell had they known about Dalton anyway? And how, without her phone, had he known who her parents were? If they were as simple a people as they portrayed themselves to be with no televisions or computers, how did they know anything about her other than her name and address? Hell, her address on her driver's license wasn't accurate. She'd never gotten a new one when she moved in with Dalton.

Those realizations put a screeching halt to Kerrigan's plan to get closer to Gideon. The kinder, gentler man she'd come to know in his home was just another layer to his already multi-tiered façade. But how the hell did she get away from him? If she rebelled at being his chosen, he'd send her back out into the masses where more people had eyes on her. Less freedom to figure out how to get away from The Sanctuary. Was that even possible? She recalled the intense scar on Mac's face from her attempt at running. Who or what had marred the young woman's face? There were too many questions and not enough answers. Kerrigan needed to bide her time in her own attempt to get away, but what better time than when Gideon was away?

If she waited until he returned, she had no idea how long it would be until he left again. And when he came home, what would he expect of her? She'd all but convinced him she wanted to be with him. If the rumors were true, and Gideon had been lenient with her because he wanted her, things would more than likely progress in ways Kerrigan wasn't ready for. She'd lived with an abusive, controlling man for months, and Dalton had been child's play to what she knew in her heart Gideon was capable of.

With Sparrow holed up in her room, Kerrigan took a chance and padded to the other side of the house to Gideon's bedroom. She'd never had the chance to look deeply into the man's sacred space. A cursory glance was all she'd managed when cleaning. Now, with him gone and Sparrow behind her closed door, Kerrigan slipped into the room. She didn't close the door in case Sparrow decided her self-imposed timeout was over. Like the rest of the house, this room was more like a normal home, instead of the bland walls of the cabin where she'd first been put. The bed was king-sized, covered with a billowy, navy comforter.

That she already knew.

She wasn't surprised to find the closet was a large walk-in. What did surprise her were the rows of military-style outfits lining the left side. Either Gideon had been promoted from guard when taking over as leader of his little cult, or it was a position he still filled, just not at their compound. It made sense he had a military background with the way he ruled his kingdom. He moved with unguarded precision. Not seeing anything else of interest, she closed the doors and skipped over the dresser. She already knew what those drawers contained, as she did his laundry.

The bedside table held an oil lamp and a well-worn Bible. She pulled open the top drawer and paused. A handful of condoms was scattered across the bottom. Well, well, well. It seemed abstinence was good for the goose but not the gander. Several neatly folded handkerchiefs filled the rest of the space. The bottom drawer held an intricately carved wooden box. Kerrigan withdrew the small chest and placed it atop the table. Holding her breath, she opened the hinged lid.

"Oh, my god." Kerrigan looked behind her, making sure she was truly alone. When she turned back, she touched the top object. A photo of a redhead – a very naked and bound woman – stared back at Kerrigan. It was almost as if she were peering in the mirror. The woman could have been her sister. Pushing aside the photo, Kerrigan found more pictures of the same woman. A woman with eyes the same color and shape as Mac's. "Holy shit." Had Gideon been involved with Mac's mother?

When she dug farther in the box, Kerrigan found her driver's license and credit cards. Her heart raced, tattooing rapidly against her chest. Closing the box, Kerrigan returned it to the drawer and rushed out of the room, back to the kitchen. She poured herself a tall glass of water and downed it. What the actual fuck was going on?

Gideon's attraction to her made sense, if the photos

were any indication of the type of woman he was attracted to. There had been no indication he'd taken the pictures. Maybe he just had a kink for bondage and had found those particular photos to his liking. Regardless, the similarity between the woman and herself was uncanny. And she didn't like it. Not one bit. She had to get out of there before she found herself tied to his bed. The thought of leaving Sparrow alone with Gideon didn't feel right, but if he hadn't taken the younger woman to bed before now, he more than likely wasn't going to.

But what if he took his frustrations out on Sparrow? What if her leaving set into motion something worse than Gideon keeping Kerrigan for himself? No. She couldn't stay. She would get out of there and get help. From whom, she had no idea, but there had to be someone out there willing to rescue those at The Sanctuary who didn't want to be there. Those like Mac. Sparrow's sister might be the only one who wanted to escape that life, but what if she wasn't? What if there were more like Kerrigan who'd been brought there against their will? She had to do it for them.

But how? She wouldn't ask Sparrow to cover for her. She wasn't strong enough or brave enough to go up against Gideon or someone like Lewis. A diversion would be best, but there was no one she could ask for help. She didn't trust anyone. Mac would be the only one who might possibly agree to it, but Kerrigan had no idea where the girl's cabin was. Even if she did, Mac was surrounded by others who would definitely be against Kerrigan leaving and threatening their solitary way of living. No, this was something she'd have to do on her own. If only Mac had elaborated on her own attempt, Kerrigan might have a better understanding of how the girl had managed to get as far as she had.

*"Just a word of advice – don't go into the woods."* Mac's words floated through Kerrigan's brain as she stared out the window. Lewis had been right about the rain. Sheets poured

from the sky, tapping against the side of the house. She couldn't see far at all. If she couldn't see more than five feet in front of her, then nobody would be able to see her either. And with twilight setting in, what better time to make a run for it? Kerrigan wished she had darker clothes to help camouflage herself. *Camouflage.* Gideon had a closet full of it. Granted, the pants would be too large, but at least she could swipe one of his black T-shirts. There was nothing to be done about her flimsy shoes, though.

After making certain Sparrow's door was still closed, Kerrigan returned to Gideon's closet and removed the last black tee from its hanger. Stopping at his bed, she once again opened the wooden box where her things were hidden beneath the photos of the mysterious redhead. She grabbed her license, leaving her credit cards where they were, and stuck it into her bra. With no pockets on her clothes, it was the best she could do. After slipping the black T-shirt over her head, Kerrigan went to the back door and peeked out the window. She couldn't see anyone, but that didn't mean someone wasn't out there waiting. Watching. Shoving against the rain, she opened the door and slipped into the wet evening.

Kerrigan set out toward the pastures where the cows were kept. If Mac had attempted to escape through the trees on the far side, hopefully the woman had known where she'd been heading. Kerrigan had no idea what lie in wait within the woods, but it had to lead somewhere. Getting there was slow going. She kept to the shadows, using the rain as cover. When she made it to the fence, she had to decide whether to risk climbing the fence and making a straight line toward the path she'd seen earlier, or taking more time going around. Valuable time she doubted she had.

Going around took her closer to the barn and the other building where someone could walk out at any moment, so she climbed the fence and ran through the pasture. The ground was unstable where hooves had dug into the wet grass and mud, but she ran hunched over and moved as quickly as possible. When she reached the opposite fence, she climbed over, falling to her knees when her pants caught on a stray nail sticking out of the wood. Kerrigan picked herself up and took off toward the break in the trees.

"Stop, Kerrigan!" Lewis's deep voice called out.

Shit! How had she been spotted so soon? Adrenaline kicked in, and Kerrigan dashed into the woods with her arms in front of her face, pushing away the low-hanging branches. She had a head start, but not enough of one. It had been a long time since she'd done any amount of running, and her legs were already trembling with the exertion. Still, she had to push through the pain, because whoever had seen her would have already alerted others to her running. When she landed in a deep mud hole and pulled her feet out of the muck, her shoes were sucked off in the process. She didn't have time to dig around for them, and even if she did, they'd be too wet to do any good.

Kerrigan pushed on barefooted, and not too much later, the soles of her feet were bleeding, cut from the rough ground she trampled over. Slipping on the leaves, she grabbed hold of a tree branch to keep from falling, but she lost her grip. Landing against a sharp rock, she tried to suck in air when pain lanced her ribs and stomach. When no air was to be found, panic set in, but Kerrigan pushed through it. She couldn't lie there when she needed to move. Her life depended on it. When she righted herself, she took a shallow breath and set off again.

The pain had long since passed excruciating, and now her body was numb except for the tree branches scraping her face and slapping against her arms as she lurched through the dense brush. The woods were thick, and the lack of moonlight only added to the darkness. How she wished her brain was numb, too.

Escaping into the forest had been her only option.

Kerrigan should have known someone would be watching. Known she was gone and come after her. Gideon noticed everything and everyone. He was the wolf in sheep's clothing she'd heard about in church all her life. Too bad the preacher failed to mention how to get away without the wolf's sharp teeth digging into your skin, ripping the flesh, and tearing through the marrow, metaphorically speaking. If she was caught, it would be literal. *Just look at Mac.*

Now, she was running from the one she was supposed to trust. From one who was supposed to protect his flock from the sinners of the world. From one who touted God like he was on a first-name basis with Him. Kerrigan didn't dare pray. Not if Gideon was on God's payroll. She'd beg Satan himself for help before she trusted God again.

And where had a dog come from? She'd never seen a domestic animal at the compound. The barking grew louder, and her body shivered. Not from the rain, but from the thought of what those sharp teeth would do to her. At some point since she hit the woods, the rain had stopped, and she was better able to hear the voices, which were getting closer by the second.

Kerrigan scrambled toward the sound of running water. When her feet went numb earlier, she'd been grateful, but now it was hindering her progress as she tried stepping on stones on the slimy creek bed. More than once, Kerrigan landed on her ass or her knees. Frozen on her hands and shins, she tried to get her body to move. She had to move, or all the pain would be for nothing. It would get worse if she was caught. Her hair plastered to her face, stuck from the blood and tears mixing to form an adhesive the rain couldn't wash away.

As Kerrigan lay there night after night on the hard mattress in the small room she shared with three other women, she thought about how the world was desensitized to things like cults and psychopaths. Rarely did she watch documentaries regarding men like Gideon. It didn't pertain to her, so why bother? If she had bothered, maybe she would have been given a clue as to how to escape without him unleashing the dog. Thinking of dogs, the barking was getting louder.

The water rushing across her legs hypnotized her. It was too dark to see what lurked beneath. That should have scared her. It didn't. It was the dog and the men chasing behind her that gripped her heart and lungs and twisted both until she couldn't breathe. God, she was tired. So tired. If she let her arms collapse, she could succumb to the rushing water. She wouldn't have to worry about what he would do to her when she was dragged back to the place that was supposed to be a sanctuary. A haven. What a joke. Her freedom had been stolen. All because of a man. A sob tore through her chest, and in that moment, Kerrigan saw the faces of her parents. God, her parents. She wouldn't do that to them.

After what felt like hours, she dragged herself across the shallow depths, digging into the silt beneath the water for leverage. Her fingernails were being torn and her knees cut with each rock she used for leverage. By the time she made it the short distance to the other side, her clothes were soaking wet, which made climbing from the embankment all the more difficult. Her bare feet did little to help, so she had no choice but to claw at the grass embankment until she was out of the water. Pushing her hair off her face with muddy, blood-soaked fingers, she staggered to her feet and stumbled a few steps before she was able to move more steadily. A wide trail cut through the woods, and she decided moving along the path would be easier even if it gave those chasing her the same advantage.

Pain thrummed through her body, a steady beat clogging her ears. She was walking too slowly, but she couldn't see far enough ahead to move swiftly. Even if it had been daytime, she couldn't have moved any faster. She'd heard of adrenaline kicking in at times of dire need.

Her situation was pretty damn dire, but her adrenaline had taken a pitstop somewhere along the way. Kerrigan couldn't give up, though. She was in this mess because of a damn man, and she wouldn't give him the satisfaction of seeing her defeated. Her toe caught on a tree root, and she pitched forward, hitting the ground so hard her jaws clacked together. A growl cut through the darkness, and she scrambled to her feet. Sharp teeth snapped close to her ear.

"NO!" Her throat closed on her, refusing to take in the needed air to scream. She wasn't ready to die. Not like this. She hadn't heard the dog closing in on her. Her ankle twisted, and she fell, face first, sucking the muddy water of a puddle into her lungs. Coughing and sputtering, she turned as the growl snarled in her ear. It was too late. Kerrigan closed her eyes and waited for the pain to come.

# Chapter Seventeen

By THE TIME War hit the entrance to the park, his Gryphon was pushing him to set up camp. Thankfully, the rain had stopped, but the area was a muddy mess. When the last stake was driven into the ground, he was urged to get his bag unrolled inside.

"Now what?" War was agitated at not knowing what was so fucking urgent.

*Take off toward the creek in our eagle. You need to find her.*

War shook his head but did as instructed. "Her who?" He stripped out of his clothes, tossing them inside the tent in case the rain started again.

*You need to hurry.*

War let the change take over as he shifted from human to bird. As bones reformed and feathers replaced skin, he breathed through the pain. It hurt less since he'd been shifting lately. Once he was transformed, he gave over to his animal's senses. The sound of a dog barking mixed with human voices yelling. He homed in on the sounds and flew faster until he saw the scene playing out below. The trees were dense, but his eagle's vision allowed him to cut through the branches. There below, a woman was being tracked by beast and man.

*Hurry!*

War didn't need any further encouragement. The dog was too close to the woman. She stumbled, and the large hound was almost on her. With seconds to spare, Warryck swooped down, clasping the woman's clothing in his talons, lifting her off the ground right before the dog's jaws latched onto her neck. The dog growled, jumping into the air, trying to get hold of its prey. His barks continued as War flew higher, doing his level best not to cause any more damage to the female than had already been done.

*Take her back to camp.*

Why the hell would they do that? His tent was too close to where they were.

*She's injured, wet, and probably going into shock. Get her into the tent and deal with the men.*

Fuck! War's grip on the woman was slipping, as the tattered clothing started ripping. He found an open spot in the trees and set her down before shifting back to his human form. He lifted the woman as gently as possible and took off running. When he got to his tent, he placed her on the sleeping bag, giving a cursory glance to her body, checking for wounds. When he pushed back a clump of muddy hair, his breath caught in his chest. "Kerrigan."

*Get dressed. They're coming.*

Warryck scrambled to put his clothes on and get outside before the men chasing Kerrigan reached his campsite. He had just opened his bottle of whiskey and sat down on an overturned log when two large men dressed in military gear burst through the wood, led by the hound that almost got his jaws on Kerrigan. War opened his mind and glared at the animal. As soon as it got its eyes on War, the dog dropped to its haunches, whining. *"That's right, fucker. I'm the Alpha Hound here."*

The men stopped short when they caught sight of War,

133

sitting on a log, drinking whiskey. He raised the bottle to them and took a swig. "Can I help you fellas with somethin'?" War called on his Texas roots and drawled out the words.

They looked at one another, then one of them stepped forward. "This park is closed. You're trespassing." War sensed something malevolent coming from the man.

"I've been campin' here for the last ten years, and I ain't seen another soul until you two. You gonna arrest me?" Warryck wished he'd had time to talk to Kerrigan and find out where she'd been and who'd taken her, but he knew by looking at the two men standing before him, they weren't law enforcement.

The one who was obviously the leader cocked his head to the side. "Ten years, you say?"

"Yep. What I said." War was deliberately obtuse. He didn't see a gun on either of them, and he knew he could easily take both of them in a fight. Rising from the log, he pulled to his full height. He wasn't much taller than either man, but they both looked him over, assessing his threat level. He wasn't dressed like someone who would be camping in the woods. He looked like someone who'd just gotten off a motorcycle and walked into a bar to get out of the rain. Before the man could respond, Kerrigan moaned from inside the tent.

Both men narrowed their eyes, and the leader pointed toward the tent. "Who's in there?"

"Just my girlfriend. I wore that ass out good." War grabbed his crotch, giving it a good squeeze. He hated saying anything crass about any woman, but he was playing a part. "You fellas out doin' trainin' missions or somethin'?" He pointed at their clothes.

"Something like that." Kerrigan moaned again, and the one doing the talking took a step toward the tent. "You sure your girlfriend's okay in there? She doesn't sound too good."

134

War stepped toward the tent, putting himself between it and the men. "Yeah, she's probably just takin' care of business since my dick's out here. You know how they get when they're on the rag. Horny as a dog with two peckers. If you don't mind, I need to get back in there before she pulls out Big John."

"Big John?" the man who'd yet to do any talking asked.

"Yeah. It's the biggest dildo I ever saw. Bigger'n my fist. I'm all for a woman tendin' to their needs if they ain't got a dick around, but I'd rather be fillin' her up and gettin' somethin' out of it instead of just watchin'." War rubbed his hand over his crotch again, hoping the men would get the message. He prayed they weren't the kind of men who'd like a show, because even if what he was saying was the truth and it was his woman in the tent, he wasn't into exhibitionism.

The leader scowled and took a step back. "We'll let you tend to your woman's needs, but you should probably head out in the morning. It's not safe in these woods for civilians. You never know when training bullets will start flying. Come on, Lewis."

"Good ta know. I'll just go give her another poundin', and after a good night's sleep, we'll head out. You fellas take care now. Ya hear?" War put the bottle to his lips and took a long pull of alcohol, never taking his eyes off either man. They turned and headed back the way they came, but the dog ambled over to War and plopped down at his feet. Warryck leaned over, scratching the dog between the ears, giving him a mental pep talk. He hated when humans used animals to do their dirty work.

"What the fuck?" Lewis scowled at the dog.

"Language." The leader scowled, and the other man bowed his head. "Duke, heel," the man commanded the dog. It looked up at War for permission, which he silently gave. If he'd had his car instead of his bike, he'd have taken the dog with him. After silent persuasion, the hound rose to

135

his feet and trotted to his master an[...] g at his side. Both men turned back to [...] a[...] w[...] before disappearing into the woods.

War waited until they were out of earshot before slipping into the tent. He didn't trust them not to return since they'd been following Kerrigan and she'd disappeared into thin air. When he got a look at Kerrigan, his heart broke.

"P-Please, don't hurt me," she stuttered quietly.

"I promise I won't, Kerrigan."

"B-but, I heard what you said to Lewis." Her eyes were wide and filled with tears. "Wait. How do you know my name?"

"I had to make them believe I had someone besides you in here. My name is Warryck, and I'm here because your parents miss you."

"My parents? They sent you after me?"

War figured the truth, at least most of it, was for the better. "I overheard them asking about you when my brother and I were eating at Harper's Point. You have some special people back home who care about you. How bad are your injuries? I didn't get a chance to look before those men showed up."

"Just some scrapes and bruises. I'll be okay."

"Do you think you can ride a motorcycle? We need to get out of here before they come back."

"I..." Kerrigan swallowed hard, her eyes taking in War's large frame.

"I promise I'm not going to hurt you. You have no reason to believe me, but here." War pulled the phone out of his pocket. "Why don't you call your parents and let them know you're alive. Tell them we're in the Green Mountain state park, and I'll take you to the Twin Ridges Inn about twenty miles south in New Woodland. They can come get you there if you don't feel comfortable with me. I'll either need to take you there on my bike, or we can call the police to come get you. Whichever way you feel safest."

"I've never been on a motorcycle, but I could probably hold on long enough to get to the hotel."

"Good. Now..."

*They're back. Do something.*

War put his fingers to Kerrigan's lips and leaned close. "Please trust me, Sweetheart." He pushed her down onto her back and covered her body with his. Kerrigan trembled beneath him, and not in a good way. He kissed her forehead then winked at her, hoping to convey how sorry he was for his next words. "Oh, yeah, baby. That's it. You suck my cock so good. Just like that. Fuck, your mouth. Fuck yeahhhhh. God, Donna. You could suck a tennis ball through a tail pipe. Damn, baby. Uh..." War had never talked dirty in his life, and he felt like an idiot, but he kept it up until his Gryphon nudged him.

*Okay, they're gone. That was close. Too close.*

"Sorry about that. The men came back, and I had to make it sound legitimate. They're gone now."

When he rose off Kerrigan's chest, her eyes were wide, but the crinkles at the edges let him know she wasn't scared. "A tennis ball? Seriously? Damn, I've got mad skills."

Warryck barked out a laugh. "Too much?"

"Hell no. That was brilliant. And what's up with that southern twang?"

"My family is originally from Texas. It just popped out when those jokers came sniffing around. I want to hear all about them and where they've been keeping you, but for now, I need to make sure they're really gone this time so we can pack up and get out of here.

"How did you know they were back?"

"I heard the branches snapping underneath their boots. My family, we're... trackers of a fashion, and we're trained to notice things like that." It was a terrible lie, but a necessary one. Granted, his brothers' business was all about tracking and finding people, but he wasn't part of it. Not yet, at least. And there was no way he could tell this stranger about his shifter, no matter how badly he wanted to. And wasn't that just fucked up?

"What can I do to help?"

Warryck took a good look at the beautiful woman who'd been chased through Hell but was now joking with him and offering to help. "Just relax. You've been through enough by the looks of it. Here." War grabbed his bag and handed it to her. "I've got clean clothes in there. They'll be way too big, but at least they're dry. Help yourself to whatever you want." War balled his hands into fists to keep from reaching out and touching her. He already knew she was stunning from seeing her pictures, but seeing her up close was a temptation he was having a hard time ignoring. He couldn't put his finger on why he was so drawn to her. She smelled like dirt and rain, and she looked like hell. Her spirit was strong, that he knew. Maybe it was the reason he felt the need to protect her with his life. "Stay in here until I tell you it's safe to come out."

"Okay. And Warryck? Thank you. If you... Wait. Last thing I remember, the dog was closing in on me. How did you get me away from it?"

War doubted she remembered what happened, but while he'd been bringing her back, he'd used his powers to alter her memory of being saved by an eagle. He pushed an image of him carrying her in human form into her mind. That was all he changed, though. He didn't want to mess with too much of what she remembered. He needed to find out who was after her and where they'd kept her so he and Mav could go back and take care of the men.

"The dog wasn't as close as you probably thought it was. I heard the barking and men shouting after you, so I went to investigate. I was able to pick you up and get you away before they got too close. I need to check to make sure we're alone. Change clothes and call your parents." War crawled out of the tent before he could do something stupid

138

like kiss her, or before she could ask any more questions. He hated lying to her, but he didn't know her.

*You want to know her.*

His Gryphon wasn't wrong. He wanted nothing more than to keep her there in the woods in his tent and get to know everything about the strong woman, but he didn't understand why. Why was he so drawn to her? It wasn't like Gryphons had fated mates. Zeus had given them free will when it came to who they loved and let into their lives. So why did Kerrigan O'Shea have War wanting to whisk her off and hide her out until he knew everything about her, both inside and out? Shaking his head, he searched the area. If she wasn't there, War would take to the sky once again and follow the men. But he couldn't risk her seeing him that way. Couldn't risk losing her to the truth. *Losing her? You don't get to keep her.* And the truth of that made his heart ache. No, he didn't get to keep her. He had to get her safely back to her parents and get on with his life.

# Chapter Eighteen

As Kerrigan dug around in Warryck's bag, she was mentally chastising herself. She knew better than to trust a stranger, but there was something about the man that called to her on a level she'd never felt before. Not even with Ambrose. She'd admired the man from afar, knowing she could never have anything long-term with him. She still adored him, and always would. He'd been hurt when she moved in with Dalton, but he told her he understood. Then Dalton had turned on her. She'd given in to his constant badgering more from him finally wearing her down than being in love with him. She had settled. Now, here she was, her body aching and her mind foggy all because she'd given in. She couldn't do that again, no matter how her heart beat a little faster when he was near.

She didn't know Warryck…? She didn't even know his last name. Knew nothing about him other than he was there and had rescued her. That didn't automatically make him one of the good guys. Steven had claimed to want to help her, and look how that turned out. Still, she was thankful he'd come along when he did, or she'd be on her way back to The Sanctuary and probably back in the inner chamber for more than a couple of days. Warryck left his phone with her so she could call her parents, and that alone helped her trust him, at least for the time being.

After choosing a T-shirt from Warryck's bag, she

removed the ruined one she'd borrowed from Gideon's closet, noticing her driver's license had managed to stay put in the granny bra she'd been forced to wear. Not wanting to risk losing it, she dropped it into Warryck's duffel. She slipped Warryck's borrowed shirt over her head then pulled her long hair out of the back, her hands coming away wet and muddy. The blood on her fingers had dried, and the ripped nails stung. She dug around in his bag looking for wipes but came up short. She'd just have to deal with being dirty until they got to the hotel.

She picked up the phone and punched in her mother's cell phone number. Her heart hammered in her chest as it rang, and when it went to voicemail, it calmed back down. "Mom, it's me. Kerrigan. I'm safe. I'm using the phone of the man who found me. We're at the Green Mountain park, and he's taking me to the Twin Ridges Inn, a hotel about twenty miles south of here in New Woodland, Vermont. I'll wait for you and Dad there. Call me back on this number when you get the message. I love you."

After she hung up, she repacked the duffel before rolling up the sleeping bag. She was ready to get on the road. She'd never ridden a motorcycle, and the thought was both daunting and thrilling. She certainly wasn't dressed for it, and if Gideon had men riding around looking for her, she'd be easily spotted.

Warryck stuck his head into the tent. "It's safe for now, but we need to move."

She stood, having to bow her head inside the tent. "Here's your phone. I called my mom, but I had to leave a voice message."

Warryck slid the phone into his back pocket. "Did you tell her where to meet us?"

"Yes. Depending on when she listens to the message, it'll take her a while to reach me. She'll have to catch a flight, and I'm not sure where the nearest airport is to here, since I don't exactly know where here is. I know you said we're in

Vermont, but that could be anywhere."

"We're in the southwest corner. New Albany is probably the closest major hub, but don't worry. I'll keep you safe until they get here. I would offer to fly you home, but you're pretty banged up, and I'd rather get you to a doctor while we're waiting."

Kerrigan stiffened at the mention of him taking her to a doctor. She'd fallen for that line with Stanley – Steven – and that hadn't turned out so well. But Warryck was different. She felt it all the way to her soul.

"You okay? You look like you're ready to run."

"I... Honestly? No, I'm not okay, because the last time someone offered to take me to a doctor, I ended up in a cult."

"Kerrigan, I—

"No. Warryck. For whatever reason, I trust you, but no doctors. Okay?" And she meant it, but she couldn't help remembering what she'd been through.

Warryck was angry. Shouldn't her words have eased his mind?

"Okay, no doctors. And we'll discuss where you've been later. Right now, we need to hit the road. Are you ready?"

"As ready as I'll ever be with no shoes."

"Fuck, I didn't realize." His eyebrows dipped, and the skin between them wrinkled. Kerrigan shouldn't have found that sexy, but everything about the large blond was a look she appreciated. His hair was longish, and he had several tattoos on his corded forearms. The attraction was a no-brainer, because the man could be on the cover of a magazine. What she couldn't understand was the pull. Like there was an invisible rope, and he was lassoing her to him. It was probably something akin to hero worship. That's all it could be. Her luck with men lately warned her against giving in to the attraction she felt bubbling inside every time he was near.

142

"It's okay. I might not be able to walk too fast because my feet are pretty torn up. But once we get to your motorcycle, it shouldn't be too bad."

"Damnit. Let me take a look."

When Warryck entered the tent and picked up one of Kerrigan's feet, she pulled it away. "No. They're gross."

"They're just feet, Sweetheart. And I kinda... Never mind. Don't worry about walking." Warryck dug around his bag and pulled out a pair of socks. As if he were tending to a child, he rolled them over her cut feet, taking care not to hurt her. "Let's get you out of the tent, and I'll carry you to the bike. We really need to get out of this area, and sooner rather than later."

"You don't need to carry me. I'm not a small woman."

Warryck frowned. "Are you saying I'm weak?"

Kerrigan huffed out a laugh. "Not at all." Taking a deep breath, she agreed. "Okay, let's do this." She had never been carried. Or had she? Something niggled the back of her brain. Something just out of reach she felt she should be remembering, but Kerrigan couldn't pin it down. One minute she was ready to be torn apart at the jaws of the dog chasing her, and the next thing she knew, she was being laid down on something soft.

"Here." Warryck held out a black leather jacket. "Let's get you wrapped up so the wind won't cut too deeply. The air is crisp on a bike, and if we didn't need to get you somewhere safe, I'd wait for you to dry out. But that's not a luxury we have right now."

When the jacket was wrapped around her, Kerrigan couldn't stop herself from taking in the smell of leather and man. After slipping the straps of the duffel over his shoulder, Warryck cradled one arm behind her back and placed the other under her knees, lifting her as if she weighed nothing. "See? I've got you." Kerrigan wrapped her arms around his neck. Warryck's mouth was so close to hers. Too close. The short beard that covered his lower face

143

looked soft. If she leaned forward just a couple inches, she could touch it with her lips. Warryck cleared his throat, and she looked up to find his blue eyes had darkened.

Shit. He probably had a girlfriend or wife at home. Looking away, she mumbled, "Sorry."

"Nothing to be sorry about, Sweetheart." Warryck took off away from camp, and Kerrigan looked back over his shoulder.

"What about the tent?"

"It's just a tent. I can get another one."

Before she knew it, they exited the trees and he was placing her atop the baddest motorcycle she'd ever seen. He bent over and flipped down a foot peg before going around to the other side and doing the same thing. When he stood back up, Warryck tucked her long hair under the jacket before zipping it up. He then placed a helmet on her head and fastened the chin strap. "That'll help hide all that gorgeous hair." Warryck looked her over. Clearing his throat again, he strapped the duffel around the back of the bike before stretching his right leg over the seat in front of her. He rocked the bike upright and looked back over his shoulder. "Your hands are probably hurting, but you'll need to wrap your arms around my waist and hang on. We'll be taking some curves, but I don't want you to try to lean into them. Just hang on to me, and let the bike do the work, okay?"

Kerrigan nodded. "Where's your helmet?"

"You're wearing it. I don't have an extra, because I never double anyone. Don't worry. I have a hard head." He smirked before turning away, but she hadn't missed the playfulness in his eyes. God, everything he did was sexy as hell.

Kerrigan did as he said and leaned forward to reach around his body, putting her snug against his back. Yes, her fingers throbbed, but the pain was dulled by the feel of his hard planes beneath her hands. She'd dated several men,

144

but none had been chiseled like he was. If this was another lifetime, she would dream of being his woman and beg to see him without a shirt. The bike rumbled to life beneath her ass, and the sensation brought something else to life. Warryck tightened her grip. "Hang on, Sweetheart." He eased the bike out of the clearing, carefully maneuvering the Harley until they were on the road. Warryck rolled on the throttle, and Kerrigan tightened her grip around his waist as he moved through the gears, accelerating until they were up to speed.

At first, she concentrated on doing as he said. It was hard to keep from leaning when they came to a curve, but she ignored the urge and just held on. Kerrigan pressed her chin to his shoulder, his long hair whipping with the wind. Turning her head to the side, she closed her eyes, allowing her body to just feel. The breeze across her face. The scents of rain and woods in her nostrils. The rumble of the bike between her legs. But the one thing that stuck out most was freedom. The man in front of her had given her that. How, she didn't know, but in that moment, flying down the road with nothing tethering her but her arms around Warryck's waist, she didn't care. For however long it took them to get to the hotel, she was free. Soaring.

The ride ended too quickly. Warryck geared down, slowing the bike enough to pull into the parking lot of the hotel. He pulled into a spot near the back of the building and cut the motor. When he turned and looked at her, a grin tugged at his lips. "You enjoyed that, didn't you?"

"How could you tell?"

"Because your face is still lit up." Warryck pushed the kickstand down, and the bike leaned to the side. Kerrigan tightened her arms, and she could feel Warryck's stomach bunching beneath her grip. "It's safe. I promise." He'd been laughing at her. Well, didn't she feel stupid?

Unhooking her fingers, Kerrigan sat there because she didn't know exactly how to get off the motorcycle without falling on her ass. She shouldn't have worried. Warryck slid his long right leg over the seat and held out his hand for her. She took it and allowed him to help her stand. Her legs were a little wobbly, but she still felt energized. Warryck unhooked the strap and set the helmet over the handlebar.

"Let's get inside and get you cleaned up." He unhooked his bag from the bike and placed his hand at the small of her back, ushering her to the door in front of the bike. Using an old-fashioned key, he unlocked the door and held it for her.

Kerrigan hesitated briefly before moving into the room. If he'd wanted to hurt her, he would have done so out in the woods where he could bury her body. *Dramatic much?* Once they were inside, the first thing she noticed was the single queen bed.

"Sorry about the one bed. I'll sleep on the floor. When I rented the room earlier, I only did so to get out of the rain. I didn't expect to find you."

"How *did* you find me?" That was a question she'd been running through her head on a loop.

Warryck gave her his back and set the duffel on the small table where the television was. When he turned back around, it was evident by the frown he was conflicted. "We have a lot to talk about, and I promise I'll answer your questions. But first, you need to get cleaned up. I'm going to run out and get you some new clothes if I can find a place that's open so I can take you to a doctor. I'll do that while you shower so you can have some privacy."

"I've already told you I don't want a doctor. If you can get some antibiotic cream and bandages, that should suffice." She held her hands out in front of her, assessing the damage. Her nails were broken, but they'd grow back out. Her ribs hurt, but she already knew from when Dalton beat her nothing could be done for them other than allowing them to heal on their own.

Warryck shoved his hands into his pockets. "Sweetheart, are you sure?"

Kerrigan didn't want to leave the hotel until her parents came to get her. "Yes. All a doctor will do is slap a bandage on my cuts and charge me a ton of money I don't have."

"Don't worry about the money. I'll cover it."

"No. You've done too much already. Please?" Warryck opened his mouth, but Kerrigan's stomach growled before he could argue further. Laughing, she said, "And, uh, maybe you could find food?"

Warryck grinned. "Anything you want. What would you like?"

"I didn't see any restaurants when we came through town. Then again, I wasn't really paying attention. I could really go for a cheeseburger with bacon."

"What would you like to drink?"

"Beer. A six pack, even. You don't know what you'll miss until you can't get it."

Warryck gave her a funny look. "We're definitely going to talk when I get back. Is there anything else you need?"

There was something, but there was no way she'd ask Warryck to grab a box of tampons for her. She'd just have to pray she didn't get her period until after her parents came to get her. "Nope. Medicine and food. And beer."

"I'll be back as quickly as possible. Don't open the door for anyone. If someone knocks, it won't be me."

"Got it. I'll probably be in the shower until you get back anyway, unless it runs out of hot water. It'll take me forever to get all this hair clean."

"You do have a lot of hair." He pushed a strand behind her ear before jerking his hand back and striding toward the door. He paused for a moment before he turned back. "Lock the door behind me." With that, he was gone. It seemed she wasn't the only one struggling with the attraction between them.

Kerrigan hadn't missed the way Warryck brushed her hair away from her face when he'd lain her down on the sleeping bag. Wait. Was that a memory or a dream?

Wracking her brain to remember the time between falling down and when she overheard Warryck outside the tent was evading her, no matter how hard she tried to recall what happened. It would make sense if it was a dream, but if it had happened, Warryck had shared a tender moment with her. Sighing, Kerrigan retreated into the bathroom to wash away the dirt and blood. She needed to focus on getting clean, not the way Warryck made her forget she should stay away from all men for the immediate future.

# Chapter **Nineteen**

WAR HATED LEAVING Kerrigan alone, but it couldn't be helped. If they were in a larger town, he could have had everything delivered. Instead of getting on his bike, he set out on foot. The walk would help to clear his head. It had taken every ounce of willpower not to kiss her. To beg her to let him take care of her. He'd already made the mistake of pushing her hair behind her ear. He didn't understand why his head was so muddled where she was concerned. Originally, he'd set out to rescue the woman. He'd succeeded, but now he wanted more than that. He wanted to get to know her. Find out why a woman as beautiful as she was would allow a dick like Dalton Watkins to lay his hands on her in anger. Why she was with the douchebag in the first place. It wasn't his business, and before he laid eyes on her in person, those things hadn't mattered. But once he saved her from the jaws of the dog and held her in his arms, everything changed. What he couldn't figure out was why.

*Because she is ours.*

"No, she's not. She has been through a traumatic ordeal. Yes, we saved her, but that doesn't mean we get to keep her." Warryck wasn't looking for a relationship. He had just started to figure out what he wanted to do with his future, and that didn't include a woman. He'd already had a wife.

*We deserve a good mate.*

149

Warryck bristled. "Harlow was—"

*—Greedy and selfish. You know this. We deserve someone who has our back and doesn't try to snuff out any part of who we are.*

"Tell me how you really feel." His Gryphon pushed against his mind. It was strange having it in his head so strongly after having silence for so long. It was right; Harlow had been selfish, but that didn't mean War was ready for a relationship.

*It's been too long.*

"Stop. Just…" Warryck pulled his phone out of his pocket and dialed his twin, needing to tell him he'd found Kerrigan and to have Ryker pull the other Hounds off the search.

"Hello, Brother."

"I found her."

"Kerrigan O'Shea?"

"Yes. It's a long story, but she was running for her life. She mentioned something about a cult."

"Motherfuck. If that's true, we need the family on this. Where are you?"

"I'm in New Woodland near Green Mountain. She's already contacted her mother, and I'm keeping her safe until her parents get here." War had known Maveryck would immediately want to bring in the Hounds as soon as the word cult left his mouth. It was one of the reasons he'd called his brother. Witnessing Kerrigan running for her life lit a fire inside War, one that hadn't been there in too long to remember. It also took his mind back to a different time when Harlow had been running for her life, too. He hadn't been able to save her, but Kerrigan… If he hadn't listened to his Gryphon when it urged him to leave the hotel, he would have been too late.

He now understood why his family did what they did in going after the Ministry. Was this the same group who'd taken Kerrigan? He needed to get back to her so they could have that particular conversation, but first, he had first aid supplies, food, and beer to purchase.

"Are you okay?"

"Yes. Why wouldn't I be?"

"Because this reeks of when Harlow was taken."

Damn. He should've known Mav would latch on to the past the same way he had.

"I'm fine. I've got to get some first aid supplies and food. When I know she's physically able, I'll ask her the details."

"I'm going to need all the information she can give you before calling Ryker."

"And I'll call you back as soon as I have it. She hasn't shared much, because I only found her a couple hours ago. I had the pleasure of meeting the ones who were after her. They were chasing her with a dog, for Zeus's sake!" War carded his fingers through his hair and huffed out a breath. "Once she's safe with her parents, I'm going to go back and find those motherfuckers and make them pay for every scratch and bruise on her."

"It seems you've found your purpose." Maveryck wasn't teasing War. No one knew him better, and his twin was right. He had found his purpose, even if it was a temporary one. Kerrigan would go back to her life, and he would help his family take down the bastards who had dared kidnap her and harm her. After that, War had a feeling he'd be entrenched in the family business sooner than he'd expected. His phone buzzed. He looked at the screen to find an unfamiliar number.

"It seems so. I have another call coming in, and it could be Kerrigan's parents. As soon as I have the information you need, I'll call you back." War switched over and answered.

"Hello?" Warryck looked at the phone to make sure it had connected then repeated, "Hello?"

"Uh, yes. This is Shawn O'Shea. My daughter called us from this number."

"Yes, Mr. O'Shea. I have Kerrigan, and she's safe."

"I'd like to talk to my daughter. I need to hear her voice." The man's words were barely audible. Kerrigan's mother was talking over him in the background.

"I'm not with her at the moment. I left the hotel to get some first aid supplies and food for her. I should be back with her in about twenty minutes. I'll have her call you then, if that's okay."

"First aid? What's wrong? Is she okay?"

"Just some scrapes, I promise."

"Who are you exactly? And how did you find my girl? She said she's in Vermont."

"My brother and I were at Harper's Point the night you and your wife came in looking for Kerrigan. We didn't want to get officially involved in case we couldn't find her. Didn't want to get your hopes up. Our family does this type of thing for a living, so my brother and I did a little digging. We were able to come up with a few clues as to the direction she'd been taken."

"How the feck did she end up in Vermont?"

"I'm not sure. I haven't had a chance to speak to Kerrigan about what transpired the night she disappeared. I'm sure she'll be able to fill you in once you get here. If you don't mind, though, I need to get the supplies and back to the hotel. I don't want to leave her alone any longer than I have to."

"Of course. Please, have her call. And, thank you, Mister... I don't even know your name."

"Warryck Lazlo. And no thanks are needed. I'm just glad we got our girl back in one piece." *Our girl?* "I'll have Kerrigan call back soon."

"We'll be waiting."

As he walked around town, Warryck thought about Kerrigan on his bike. Her arms encircling his waist and her front pressed against his back had been the best ride of his life. Harlow had ridden a few times when they first started dating, but only because he begged her. She never enjoyed it, and therefore Warryck didn't either. Kerrigan's smile when he helped remove the helmet made him want to put it back on her and take off to parts unknown. What would it be like to have a woman who enjoyed the open road as much as he did? His Gryphon's words came back to him. Having a partner again hadn't been on War's mind. Until now. Until Kerrigan.

But she wasn't his. He had to remember she was going back to Maine with her parents. Or maybe she'd go with them to South Carolina. Before she did, he needed to find out all he could about her abduction.

Even though it was a smaller town, there were some specialty stores still open. Warryck gathered everything they needed, plus a few items he couldn't resist getting her, including a new cell phone. When he returned, he knocked on the door using his boot, since he couldn't get to the key in his pocket. She didn't open the door, and War remembered telling her not to answer it if someone knocked, but he hadn't thought his hands would be so full. War kicked the door again. "Hey, it's me. My arms are full, and I can't reach the key."

A few seconds later, the door opened, and War about dropped everything he was holding. Kerrigan stood before him wrapped in a towel, her long, red hair hanging damp over her shoulders. He tracked each drop as it rolled down her creamy skin. Only when she stepped back, opening the door wider, did he come back to his senses. He needed to get away from her before she saw the erection straining against his jeans.

"Here, let me help." Kerrigan reached out to take the twelve pack from under his arm and the paper bag of food from his hand. The plastic bags containing first aid supplies and clothes were looped over his wrists. Kerrigan turned to set the food down, and War took advantage of the moment to adjust his cock so it wasn't pressed against his zipper. It

153

had been a long time since he'd encountered such a visceral need for a woman. Maybe it was because he needed to get laid. When Kerrigan broke into the pack of beer and pulled one out, War couldn't move. She popped the top off and turned the bottle up, drinking half down before coming up for air.

"Oh, god, how I've missed you," she murmured into the bottle before chugging the rest of it. She wiped her mouth with the back of her hand before letting out a long belch. Laughing, she looked over at him and shrugged. "Sorry. We were only allowed to drink water, juice, or milk."

He grinned. "That wasn't half bad." It was refreshing to see a woman get excited about something as simple as beer. He pulled the larger of the bags off his wrist and held it out to her, keeping his eyes firmly on her face. "I got you some clothes if you want to get dressed." As sexy as the towel was, War needed her to cover up. It was getting harder by the second not to stare at her shapely legs. It had taken him longer to shop than expected because he bought everything he thought she might need with the exception of underwear. He had guessed at her shoe size, but the black boots would be both practical as well as hot as fuck paired with jeans and a tee. Had he gone overboard for a woman he'd probably never see again? Yes, but he didn't care. Money was no problem, and he never spent it on himself anyway.

"Thanks. Anything'll be better than those dull scrubs I've had to wear. I'll just be a few." Kerrigan turned and retreated to the bathroom, and that's when he noticed the tattoo on her shoulder. He wanted to get a better look at it but decided that would put him in too close proximity to her bare skin. She returned half an hour later with her fingers wrapped in Band-Aids and the scrapes on her arms bandaged. Her hair was still damp, but she'd brushed the tangles out. "Thanks for the clothes. And those boots? They're so soft. I'll probably never wear anything on my feet but those ever again. How did you manage that so late?"

"I got lucky. There were a couple stores that were still open, which surprised me in a town this size. I'm glad you like the boots." Warryck couldn't wait to see her decked out in the leather jacket he'd bought as well. He would save that in case she decided to ride with him at some point.

"I'm starving," she announced, digging into the paper sack. "So, what's mine, and what's yours?"

"The burgers are the same, but I got fries and onion rings, so take your pick."

"Can we share?" She was adorable as she rubbed her hands together in anticipation.

Warryck chuckled. "Absolutely. I also got you a phone. Your dad called while I was out, and he's expecting you to call him back." He handed her his phone. "Here. You can use mine again, and I'll put yours on the charger."

"Thanks." Kerrigan called her parents while she divvied up the food. The call was short yet sweet, with Kerrigan assuring her parents she was fine. More than once she glanced his direction. Each time, she smiled before ducking her eyes. Once she hung up, she said, "They could take a redeye, but I convinced them to get a good night's sleep. They'll be here around nine in the morning. Now, where were we?" Kerrigan spread the food out on the bed. "Is this okay?"

No, it wasn't. Warryck was having a hard enough time behaving without sitting so close. "Of course." He sat as far away as he could and still reach the food. If she thought he was acting weird, she didn't let on. When Kerrigan took a bite of burger, she closed her eyes and let out a long moan that went straight to his cock. *Dear Zeus. Please give me strength.*

Warryck cleared his throat. "I'd like to talk."

"Sure. You're curious about what happened to me, and I want to hear how you tracked me from Maine to Vermont." After opening every pack of ketchup and

155

dividing it between their wrappers, she picked up a fry, dragged it through the ketchup, and popped it in her mouth. When she looked up, her eyes were wide. "Sorry. I should have asked if you like ketchup."

"Of course. It's my favorite condiment." He slathered an onion ring with it before shoving the whole thing in his mouth. She grinned and reached for a beer. She'd brought the carton over to the bedside table, and while chewing, opened a second one to wash down her food.

"Sorry. It's just been a while since I had decent food. I do have manners, but I seem to have lost them when I lost my freedom."

"I like seeing a woman eat with gusto. It's refreshing." Warryck wasn't intentionally thinking about Harlow, but he couldn't stop comparing Kerrigan to his wife. They were worlds apart in looks and mannerisms. The women he'd had sex with in past years had been nothing more than someone to relieve his aching balls. He'd never dated. Never taken a woman to a restaurant before he took her to bed. Harlow was the only experience he had to measure this one by.

"You said you overheard my parents. Can you tell me about that?"

War did, but he started with a little about himself and how he was just leaving his long-time profession to hit the road with his brother. He told her about choosing teaching over a private practice. He didn't go into too much detail about Lucy and Julian, but he did tell her he had family who had some pretty good computer skills. "Lucy, my daughter, spotted a sedan, the only other vehicle in the area the night you disappeared. She tracked it until it disappeared into the White Mountain forest. And when I say disappeared, that's exactly what I mean. It was never picked back up leaving. Mav and I searched the area for the car, but we never found it. At that point, we gave up."

Kerrigan's eyes shot up, but War held out his hand.

156

"I'm sorry, Sweetheart. We searched for almost a week. We decided to resume our ride while Lucy continued looking for any clues as to where the car might have gone."

"Then how did you find me?"

Warryck had to be careful. Sure, he could tell her the truth and then wipe her memory, but her parents would want to know the story as well. He hadn't figured out a lie that was believable, and he wasn't trying too hard to come up with one. He didn't want to lie to her or her parents. Something about her called to him on a deep level. His future was still up in the air, and now his Gryphon had convinced him to add Kerrigan to the mix of things to think about.

"Warryck?" Kerrigan reached out and touched his arm. "How did you find me?"

Her hand was cold from holding her beer, but it still sent warm tingles along his skin. He looked into her shimmering green eyes and told the truth. "It was a fluke."

# Chapter Twenty

KERRIGAN SWALLOWED HARD when War stared at her. She couldn't allow herself to get lost in the depths of his sparkling sapphire eyes. Couldn't think about the consideration he'd put into the clothes he'd chosen and the phone he'd picked up for her. And not just any clothes and any cell phone. The phone was top of the line. The jeans – which fit her like a glove – were a brand she only bought at the thrift store. Not that she couldn't afford them at full price, but Kerrigan had never been one to spend a hundred dollars for a pair of jeans when she could get the same thing gently worn when someone else tossed them aside for less than twenty bucks.

The black motorcycle boots, although half a size too big, were the softest leather she'd ever felt. There was no need to break them in. With her feet still sore from her ordeal of running through the woods, she'd opted to leave them off for the time being, but she couldn't wait to walk around in them.

At some point, Warryck had studied her body to gauge her size, and that sent a pulse to her core that she'd been tempted to do something about while in the bathroom. Surely, this man – this thoughtful, stunning man – was taken. He had a daughter, so there had to be a mother. And for some reason, that didn't sit well with her. Kerrigan didn't want to think about someone else having Warryck's attention. She casually glanced at his left hand when he took a bite of food. No ring. Maybe he was divorced.

Realizing he was silent, Kerrigan steadied her nerves and found her voice. "A fluke? Tell me about it."

His deep voice was hypnotic, and she had to really pay attention so she didn't have to ask him to repeat his story. "Mav and I continued on our ride, but Lucy kept digging. The only thing she found that could possibly make any sense was a large paneled truck that left the forest not long after the sedan entered. We thought either the car was hidden within, or you'd been passed off to the driver without us finding the original car. She tracked the truck here to Green Mountain. I wasn't lying when I told the men who were chasing you it's somewhere I camp every year. I set up my tent and was planning on searching the area when I heard the dog barking. I just happened to be in the right place at the right time. So, a fluke."

"Wow. I had given up hope of a higher power stepping in to help me, but maybe there's something to praying after all." Except, she hadn't prayed, had she?

"Your turn. I want to know all about what transpired that night. And start with Dalton. He's a piece of shit, by the way."

Kerrigan bristled. "You met Dalton?"

"Yes. Mav and I paid him a little visit to see if he had anything to do with your disappearance."

Kerrigan recounted what happened that night at the bar when Ambrose showed up, until the time "Stanley" stopped to help. Warryck actually growled when she got to the part where Dalton beat her. Not wanting to think more about that than she needed to, she pushed on. "When I woke up, I was at a place called The Sanctuary. I knew immediately it was something out of a bad dream." After walking Warryck through her time there, she added, "The weirdest part was finding the pictures. I think I was a substitute for an old girlfriend."

159

"That seems to be going around." Warryck gathered the trash from their meal and tossed it in the garbage can.

"What do you mean?"

"When we got to Dalton's, a redhead was trying to leave."

"So, he moved on when he thought I skipped town?"

"Sort of. Do you really want to hear this? You already know he's a dick."

"Why not? It's not like I'm going to run back to New Portland and see him around town. I've never been in a long-term relationship, but living alone does get lonely. So, when Dalton kept pursuing me, I thought I'd give it a shot. Lesson learned."

"What about Ambrose?"

"What about him? He and I are friends. Sure, there was some attraction, but it was pointless. He's married to the sea, and even though Harper's Point is always his first stop when he returns, it's only for a few days. So, there's nothing and no one for me in Maine."

"You're not going to let one man ruin you for the rest of us, are you?"

Kerrigan tilted her head to the side. "The rest of us? Why, Warryck, are you saying you're up for the task?" She laughed and waved her hand in the air. "I'm kidding. I know I'm just a job to you. Well, sort of. Your family sounds like a good one if they go off looking for wayward women without getting paid to do it." She reached into the cardboard box, retrieving another beer and holding it out to Warryck. After he took it, she grabbed one of her own. The food was keeping her from getting lightheaded. "Now, tell me about Dalton's other redhead."

The anger was back in the man's voice as he told Kerrigan about Tasha. When he explained how Dalton had a sort of shrine to Kerrigan in the closet, goosebumps rose on her skin. "We left him tied up for the police to find, and I'm not ashamed to say he wasn't without a bruise or two of his own."

Kerrigan wasn't one for violence, but the fact that this man who didn't know her got in some punches on her account made her warm and fuzzy. "Is it wrong of me to wish you'd given him more than a few bruises? I mean, he hit Tasha as well. He needs to be stopped."

"She was supposed to go to the police station when she left. If she did, he's probably in jail."

"I'd like to file my own report, but since I no longer have evidence, it'd be his word against mine."

"Yeah, and it's not like we can go to this Sanctuary and have them vouch for you. That's something else we need to talk about. When Maveryck gets here, he's going to want every bit of information you have on that place. If they took you there against your will, I'm betting you aren't the only one."

"I have no doubt. I do know there was one woman who tried to leave, but she wasn't as lucky as I was." Kerrigan touched her cheek, remembering where Mac's scar bisected her pretty face. "She fell in love with a man, but it wasn't allowed. Gideon, the leader, had to approve all couples, and one of the guards wanted Mac. She tried to run, like I did, but... I'm guessing by the scar on her face the dog got to her. Or maybe it was Lewis. I don't really know."

"What do you mean, he has to approve the couples?"

"It's such bullshit. He said he has to make sure the couples are compatible enough to sustain a long marriage. If they don't get along after a while, they are placed with someone different. Mac didn't want to be with the guard, so she ran."

"Maybe we can get Mac out of there once Maveryck gets here and we come up with a plan."

Kerrigan bit her bottom lip. She wanted to help Mac, but that would leave Sparrow to take her place. "There's a lot more to it than that. Sparrow, the young woman I told you lived at Gideon's with me? Mac is her sister. If Mac leaves, Sparrow will be given to Lewis."

"But I thought you said they have to be compatible or Gideon finds someone new for them."

"Like I said – bullshit. He lied. I think it's his sick way of being involved with all the couples. I even accused him of liking to watch."

Warryck coughed, and Kerrigan thought he might spit out the beer he'd just drank. After he swallowed, he was grinning. "And what did he say?"

Kerrigan shrugged, but the memory sent a shiver across her skin. "He turned it around and asked if I like to be watched." When Warryck narrowed his eyes, she rolled hers. "I don't, for your information." Unless it was by Warryck, then she wouldn't mind.

"That's good to know." Warryck winked at her, and Kerrigan tossed a wadded-up napkin at his face. Faster than should be possible, he caught it before it got close to him.

"Wow. That was—"

"I need to know everything about the compound. The layout. How many people are there. How many guards. Anything you can remember that will help us get in and take those bastards down. It'll take Maveryck a while to get here since he's riding over from Ohio, and you'll be gone with your parents by that time."

Kerrigan chewed on her lip. If she left with her parents, that meant giving up Warryck, and she wasn't ready to do that. But what choice did she have? She had just met him, so why was she ready to throw caution to the wind and stay with him? Not that he wanted her. She was probably nothing more than a job to him, or a charity case at the least. Besides that, other than the items he'd bought her, Kerrigan had nothing. All her furniture was locked away in a storage container, and she'd taken her personal items with her when she moved in with Dalton. There was no telling what he'd done with her things. She needed to go with her parents and get her life in order.

162

"Yeah, okay." Sighing, she stood from the bed and headed toward the window. Before she could take a step, a strong hand wrapped around her bicep.

"Hey, come here." Warryck pulled her to where she was standing between his spread legs. He slid his fingers down until they circled her wrist. "If you don't want to talk about it right now, we can give it a rest for a bit."

"It's not that. I..." Kerrigan couldn't think with his hand on her. She wanted to... What did she want? Him. Kerrigan wanted Warryck, and that made no sense. His sapphire eyes held her as captive as his grip did. She placed her free hand on his shoulder to keep from getting any closer. She'd never been the kind to put herself out there sexually, but Warryck had her wanting to close the distance and straddle his lap. She wanted to know what his lips felt like. What he looked like without his shirt on. What he would feel like when he rolled her so she was under him on the bed, making slow, passionate love. She'd spent months with Dalton in a loveless relationship, and months at the compound with only her memories to comfort her. Was it wrong to want to live in the moment? To actually feel something? To feel alive? Because Warryck made her heart beat wildly.

"You...? What do you want, Sweetheart?"

Feeling braver than she'd ever been in her life, Kerrigan leaned over and pressed her lips against his mouth. If he had a wife or girlfriend, he would stop her. Then again, maybe he wouldn't. She didn't know him well enough to know whether or not he was a cheater. Warryck growled low in his throat before slipping a hand behind her head and pulling her closer, keeping her lips where he obviously wanted them. He released her wrist and banded a strong arm around her waist, pulling her until she was where she'd wanted to be – straddling his muscular thighs.

When Warryck licked at her lips, she opened for him. He tasted of burger, onions, and beer. And something uniquely him. As their tongues danced together, it was passionate yet gentle. He didn't maul her the way Dalton had. Kerrigan had never been kissed with such tenderness and longing. Tugging on her hair, Warryck angled her head so he could kiss her deeper. She wound her arms behind his head, careful of her fingertips. She wanted to dig into the muscles underneath her palms, but that would have to wait until her nails weren't a mess.

She couldn't miss the erection growing longer and harder where she was pressed against his lap. Warryck nipped at her bottom lip before sucking on it. Her nipples hardened, and she pressed them to his chest, wiggling against his hard-on in the process. Warryck stood without warning and turned them, laying Kerrigan on the bed before stretching out over her, his hard cock nestled between her open legs. "I want to make you feel good, Kerrigan. We don't have to have sex, if you're not ready or it's too soon. There are other things we can do." Warryck hadn't moved against her. His strong arms were holding him above her, waiting for her answer, and the fact that he didn't just take what he wanted was sexy as hell.

"I know it's soon, but I need to feel alive. I need to know I'm really free, and I want you to do that for me." She knew she shouldn't want him. Should tell him no, but her body overrode her brain. If Kerrigan could only be with him until her parents arrived the next day, she didn't want to waste time talking. She would take what she could get and carry his memory with her. "Please."

Warryck ground his jean-clad erection against her core as he crushed their mouths together in a much harsher kiss. Yes! That was more like it. Kerrigan was on fire, and the only relief in sight was on top of her. "Warryck, please..." She tugged at his T-shirt, and Warryck rose onto his knees, grasping behind his neck and removing the garment before tossing it to the floor. Kerrigan licked her lips as she took in his wide chest. His abs were toned, and his Adonis belt cut a

164

perfect V, hidden partially by his jeans. She longed to trace its path with her tongue. With aching fingers, Kerrigan struggled to get the button loose, and Warryck replaced her hand with his and made quick work of undoing it then lowering the zipper.

While he was busy removing his pants, Kerrigan slipped out of her own T-shirt. He hadn't bought her new underwear, and the old-fashioned bra was embarrassing, so she removed it as well. When her chest lay bare before him, Warryck lowered his mouth to her neck, nuzzling and sucking at her skin. He licked a path down to one of her nipples, his beard teasing her flesh as he took the hardened bud between his teeth. Kerrigan arched her back to meet him, wrapping her leg around his thigh, begging him with her body to get closer. "I need you," she husked, grabbing his blond hair and holding his mouth to her breast.

Warryck pulled off, blowing cool air where his mouth had left her wet and aching. Reaching down between them, he worked to pull Kerrigan's jeans and panties down her legs, tossing them to the side. His erection stood long and hard, the head wide and glistening. He took it in hand, giving it a few strokes, and Kerrigan wanted it in her mouth. Rolling to her side, she angled her body so she could get close enough to drag her tongue through the moisture. She'd never enjoyed giving blowjobs, but she wanted nothing more than to please him. Warryck's dick jumped, and she grabbed hold to keep it where she wanted it.

"Sweetheart, you don't have to do that." His large hand pushed her hair off her face, keeping it out of the way, so she had better access. She didn't have to, but she wanted to. She'd never marveled at the dichotomy of something so rigid being encased in softness until now. Before, she'd wanted to get what she considered a chore over with as soon as possible, and that meant concentrating on maximum stimulation in the shortest amount of time. With Warryck, she wanted to lave and suck all night. She knew that was

165

impossible, but it didn't mean she wanted to rush bringing him to orgasm. She'd never had to worry about a gag reflex before, but with Warryck, he was longer than any man she'd been with, so she wrapped her hand around the base of his shaft in case he got carried away. If, by some miracle, she was to be with him for longer than this night, she could work on taking all of him then.

"Sweetheart... Fuck... Kerrigan... Oh fucking Zeus..." Warryck was obviously enjoying himself if he was cursing a fictional Greek god. Kerrigan sucked harder, using both her mouth and her fist, gripping him tighter with each stroke. Her saliva mixed with the precum leaking from his slit made the glide smooth.

"Fuck, that feels too good, Sweetheart. I'm gonna... Stop. Kerrigan..." Warryck pulled away, stepping far enough back she couldn't reach him. His chest was heaving, and there was a storm brewing in his eyes. He had a death grip on the base of his cock, staving off his impending orgasm. "Please tell me I can have you now."

"You can have me now." *And forever.* That last thought should have scared the shit out of her. It didn't, and that scared her more.

# Chapter *Twenty-One*

WARRYCK DUG INTO his jeans for his wallet, praying to all that was holy he had a condom. No way would he take her bare. Not that he thought she wasn't safe, but she'd been held captive for weeks, and he doubted she'd been on birth control. He already had one child he hadn't taken care of. No way he wanted another. At least, not like this. Not in the heat of passion with a woman he didn't know. When he found what he was looking for, he made quick work of opening the package and rolling it down his hard length, all while taking in Kerrigan's body. She was scratched and bruised, but she was a vision, lying on her back waiting for him. Crawling onto the bed between her legs, he slid his hands from her ankles up to her knees, pushing them wider.

The red curls between her legs were glistening, and that was enough for him to know she was ready. Warryck pushed the head of his cock between her folds, rubbing up and down through the slickness, teasing her clit. Kerrigan arched her back, her head falling to the side, exposing more of her pale neck. His Gryphon roared inside his head, encouraging him to fuck her hard. But this wasn't just fucking; it was a coming together of mind, body and soul. Warryck knew it was too soon. It had been a long time since he'd made love, and even with Harlow, it had mostly been young hormones coming into play. This beauty spread out before him called to his soul like the sunshine after a long, dreary, winter night. He bent down, taking her mouth in a sweet kiss while he pushed all the way in until he was flush with her mound. He didn't begin thrusting immediately, giving her time to adjust to being full.

Kerrigan's mouth had been heaven, and he almost waited too long to pull out of its warmth. He wanted to shoot his load down her throat. Onto her chest and her full tits. He wanted to paint her with his cum, marking her as his own. More than that, he wanted to fill her core with his seed. Not for the sake of making a child, but so she had something he'd only given one other person. He hated having the condom between them, but for now, it was necessary.

Warryck eased out of her tight walls until only the tip of his dick remained. He pushed back in, rolling his hips so his groin pressed against her clit. If she gave him the opportunity for round two, he was going to bury his face between her legs and eat her out until she shouted his name. Pulling away from her mouth, Warryck stared into eyes the color of a field of clover, full of emotions he was sure matched his own. He didn't want to let her go, and if he was reading her right, she wanted to stay with him. Putting that thought away for the moment, Warryck kept up a slower pace until Kerrigan's even breathing turned into short pants.

"Warryck, oh, god... Please... I need..." She wrapped her legs around his hips, digging her heels into the globes of his ass.

"What do you need, Sweetheart?" Warryck wanted this to be the best orgasm of her life.

"Faster. I need it... harder... I'm not going to break." Kerrigan's voice quivered as she met him thrust for thrust. "Oh, yes. I'm..." Kerrigan grabbed at his thighs then hissed. If she wasn't so close to coming, he would stop and check on her fingers. He counted on her orgasm to help her forget the pain for a few minutes at least. Giving her what she needed, Warryck amped up his thrusts, reaching deep

168

within while he ground his thumb against her clit. It didn't take long before Kerrigan was panting, her legs quivering as she found her release. Warryck lost all control when her walls clamped down on his cock.

"Fuck!" He threw his head back, squeezing his eyes and biting his lip to keep his sharp lion teeth from popping out as his balls drew up and his whole body shuddered with his own orgasm. A gentle laugh escaped his mouth as contentment wrapped around his heart. Yep, his heart. He opened his eyes to see Kerrigan smiling. He smiled back at her before releasing the grip he had on her legs and dropping down to press kisses to her nose, her forehead, her cheeks, and finally her lips. "God, you're perfect."

It was Kerrigan's turn to laugh then. "I assure you, I'm not. I mean, you've already heard me belch, but I'll take your blissed-out compliment for now."

Gripping the condom, he eased out and rolled from the bed. "Don't go anywhere."

"I don't think I could if I wanted to." Kerrigan tossed both hands to the pillows on either side of her head and let out a deep sigh, still grinning. Damn, she was good for his ego. And his dick.

Warryck disposed of the condom and stopped to look at his reflection in the bathroom mirror. He *was* blissed-out, and it had everything to do with Kerrigan. He couldn't remember sex being that good. Returning to the bed, he pulled the covers down on the side Kerrigan wasn't lying on. He then strode to the other side where he picked her up and scooted her over so he would be between her and the door. He slid in and pulled her close, wrapping both arms around her. Her hair was still damp, but he didn't care. He pushed it away from her face so he could drop kisses on her forehead and temple. It had been too long since he held someone after sex. Too long since he wanted the gentle touches and quiet reverence that went with making love and not fucking. He had no doubt he'd made love to Kerrigan, and he didn't understand why.

They needed to talk, but Kerrigan's breathing evened out quickly. She'd had a rough day, so he understood her falling asleep. Warryck didn't mind at all. It gave him the opportunity to hold her close while getting a grasp on his feelings. Or at least trying to. Being a psychologist, he had studied all about why people acted the way they did. While feelings were often blamed on the heart, emotions came from the brain, more specifically the hypothalamus. Knowing this didn't make it easier to understand why War felt so strongly about this particular woman he'd known only a handful of hours.

He had known love with Harlow. He had purposely married her. Planned on spending his life with her. They hadn't planned to have a baby so soon into their relationship, but Lucy happened, and in the beginning, War welcomed impending fatherhood. Harlow hadn't been perfect, but she had been perfect for him at the time. Had she not died, who knows if their marriage would have lasted. They would have raised Lucy together, but she still wouldn't have wanted their child to have anything to do with his family. Warryck wondered how Kerrigan would react to a family of bikers. As stunning as she was, the woman was a little rough around the edges. She'd have to be to enjoy a job slinging drinks every night. Dalton had beaten on her, but he hadn't beaten her. Kerrigan was strong enough to leave in the middle of the night with no money and a shitty car.

Granted, she had been fooled into going with the man named Stanley, but if her injuries were as bad as she said, Kerrigan was probably ready to pass out and feeling like she really didn't have a choice. Warryck couldn't wait to get his hands on the bastard. Him, Gideon, and that Lewis fucker. He knew Mav wouldn't go into the compound with no backup, and Warryck was determined to go with his twin and whoever else showed up to take down The Sanctuary.

170

*Like the last time.*

When his brothers had shown up at his graduation, War had been ready to ride off alone and figure out who tried to take Harlow. They had known, but instead of going after the cult members without him, they waited until after graduation so War could get his pound of flesh. Hayden and Kyllian had been too young, but Mav, Ryker, and several other Hounds were there waiting on him. To have his back when they took down the men who were responsible for Harlow's injuries. If she hadn't been a Gryphon, hadn't fought back against her attackers, she might have been lost to him in a different way.

It had taken more than a week to put their plan in place. That particular compound wasn't a large one, but it was still a well-oiled machine. People like Gideon Talbert and Obadiah Hutton, the leader of the cult who tried to take Harlow, weren't stupid. They were smart, calculating, and they spent years perfecting a sustainable environment where they could survive while living off the grid. They surrounded themselves with like-minded individuals who thought their ideals were the only way folks should live. Men were the lawmakers, while the women silently obeyed. Children were seen and not heard, and were raised to believe what their leader taught them.

Once they'd figured out the best way to get inside, it didn't take long for them to find Obadiah. He'd been in the pulpit, preaching his own brand of religion. There had been a few guards scattered around the perimeter, but they were no competition for the Hounds. Whether the males preferred their eagle or their lion, they were all stealthy predators, and the humans didn't stand a chance. Unlike Kerrigan, where she'd been tricked into going with Stanley under the guise of being taken to a doctor, Obadiah had sought Harlow himself. It was the last mistake the man ever made. Warryck had stormed into the church and dragged the man to a private room where he meted out the same

171

injuries Harlow had sustained. When the leader of the flock begged for mercy, War had shown none. He held up a photo of his late wife and asked, "Like you showed her mercy?"

The man's face morphed from recognition to fear in the span of a few seconds. "That's right, you fucker. She was my wife. The mother of my unborn child. You took her life, and now, I'm taking yours." Warryck released his Gryphon and tore the man to pieces. The original plan had been to simply take him from the compound and dispose of him elsewhere so the members of the cult couldn't go to the police, but War had lost his head.

The lion was more dominant than the eagle when emotions were involved. The eagle was good for hunting from the sky. More prone to thinking things through. The lion? It was a predator, but an impulsive one. When the Gryphon came out, Warryck was still there mentally, but the beast was in control for the most part. When Harlow died and Warryck shifted, he'd barely been able to come back to his human form. He didn't like not having control, and that had been the last time he'd allowed his inner being to fully form.

It was one of the reasons he didn't hang around and join his brothers in taking down the other cults they found and dismantled. His face was too recognizable. Now, twenty-four years later, he'd been off the grid long enough nobody should recognize him. He was in his mid-forties, but he had retained a more youthful appearance, as did all Gryphons.

It was why Sutton moved his family over the years so those they lived around wouldn't get suspicious of the fact that he and Rory didn't age the same way humans did. They were similar to the Gargoyles in that respect, but where the Gargoyles could live thousands of years if they chose, Gryphons only lived two or three centuries. War only knew these facts because he'd spent an evening talking with Lucy

172

about her shifter mate and his Clan.

Lucy was strong, and he thanked Zeus she was. She would have been even stronger had he allowed Rory to raise her. He was proud of his daughter. Proud of the woman she'd become. She was finally able to live her life the way she wanted, and that was how it should be. The same for any woman. They shouldn't have to be kept under a man's thumb just because some antiquated book dictated otherwise.

Strong women like Kerrigan didn't belong in a place like The Sanctuary. He grinned, thinking back to how she relished having a beer after all those weeks of doing without. How she enjoyed her cold cheeseburger like it was a lobster and steak dinner. He would love nothing more than to take her out to a five-star restaurant so she could eat whatever her heart desired. But, knowing as little about the woman as he did, War figured she be just as happy at the local steakhouse where she could drink beer from a bottle instead of wine from a goblet.

Maybe it was best if Kerrigan went with her parents. There was no way he would subject her to being around the ones who kidnapped her and kept her against her will. He could ride with the Hounds and see the job through first. Then, he'd go after her. If that's what she wanted. And then what? He couldn't plan a future with her until he knew how she felt. One night of good sex didn't a future create.

*She's ours.*

His Gryphon was practically purring.

Kerrigan shifted in his arms, snuggling in closer. It should feel odd holding a lover after sex, but it didn't. It felt right. Warryck couldn't remember being this content. Even with Harlow, they'd had so much going on in their lives with school and arguing about his family. He had loved his wife with his whole heart, but even then, he wasn't content. He'd been conflicted between choosing his wife over his family. Now he had a chance to rejoin his brothers, and he

173

would never let a woman come between him and them again. Not that he thought Kerrigan would, but that remained to be seen. He would let her go with her parents, and if they were meant to be together, they would find a way. Pulling her closer, he closed his eyes.

*Get up!*

War was startled from sleep when his Gryphon yelled in his head. The hotel room door flew open with force. The wood splintered, and before he could get his bearings, two men rushed into the room. Kerrigan yelled behind him, taking cover between the bed and the wall. Light glinted off the knife in the closer man's hand. With no thought to being discovered, the lion broke through and lunged, his sharp teeth clamping down on the hand holding the weapon. Blood flooded Warryck's mouth, but he didn't let go. He kept his large feline body atop the downed man while keeping an eye on the second intruder.

"Holy shit!" The second man backed out of the room and took off.

Warryck shifted back into human and punched the man he was sitting on top of, rendering him unconscious. Knowing the man would be out for a while, he yelled at Kerrigan, "Get in the bathroom and lock the door."

Eyes wide, she nodded and rushed to do as he told her. When she was safe, Warryck grabbed a pair of jeans off the floor and pulled them on before he took off out the door. The second man had already made it to his vehicle when War stepped outside. Calling on his shifter speed, he ran toward the car, reaching it before it was out of the parking lot. Wrenching the door open, Warryck jumped inside, his bare feet scraping the ground in the process. "If you don't want to die, pull this fucking car over." War recognized the man as one of those who'd been chasing Kerrigan through the woods. He wanted to kill the man for daring harm his woman, but his brain overrode his need for revenge on her part. He could use the man's knowledge of the cult when his

174

brothers arrived.

"What the hell are you?" the man yelled, his eyes wide and not on the road ahead. Warryck allowed his canines to extend, and the man slammed on the brakes. When the car was in park, Warryck hit the man in his temple, knocking him out.

"I'm your worst fucking nightmare."

# Chapter Twenty-Two

KERRIGAN SPLASHED WATER on her face. When laughter bubbled in her chest, she did it again before using the hand towel to dry off. There was no way she could have seen Warryck shift into a white lion then back to a human. She pinched herself hard. "Ow!" She was definitely awake. "Holy shit." Pacing the small space, she wrapped her arms around herself. "Holy fucking shit." Shaking her head, she stopped and pressed her ear to the door. This couldn't be her reality. Men simply did not turn into animals. Did they? No wonder he seemed so much sexier and, well, more everything. Because he was. In a word, War was a *beast*.

She had given her body to Warryck with hopes they might actually have a future after this nightmare was over. But the nightmare continued, one that now included a shifter of some sort. *If* she'd witnessed what her brain was trying to convince her she'd seen. No, she wouldn't run. Warryck had rescued her, not once, but twice. Somehow, she knew he was one of the good guys, even if he was less than human. Or maybe that was more than. She'd felt drawn to him in a way she'd never found herself wanting a man. Was that because he was able to manipulate her mind somehow? Just because he could transform into a lion – and god, what a fantastic beast that had been – didn't mean he had the ability to use mind control.

A low moan sounded from the other side of the door.

Warryck had knocked Lewis out, but if he was coming around, it wouldn't take much for him to get to Kerrigan behind the hollow door of the bathroom. Taking a chance, she slowly turned the knob and peeked into the room. Lewis was still on his stomach, but he was moving. As quietly as possible, she padded out to the bed and unplugged the lamp from the side table. Lewis's eyes opened, and Kerrigan rushed the large man, swinging the porcelain down with all her might, striking him in the temple. The lamp shattered, but it had done the job. She grabbed the knife from where it had fallen onto the floor, holding it in front of her in case he woke up again.

Voices gathered outside the room, and a woman poked her head in. "Holy shit! Are you okay?"

"Fine. He broke in, and I hit him over the head. I'm..." Kerrigan realized she was still naked and scrambled to her feet. "I just need to put some clothes on. Can you keep everyone back?"

"Yeah, sure." The woman stepped away from the entrance. "Do you want me to call the cops?" she asked while Kerrigan rushed to find her jeans and tee.

"That won't be necessary." Warryck's voice startled Kerrigan, and she jerked around, taking up the knife again.

"Whoa, Sweetheart." Warryck held his hands up. "Everything's gonna be okay." Before she could respond, he disappeared from the open door. His voice was a low rumble as he spoke to whoever was outside. When he returned, he glanced down at the floor. "What happened here?"

"Lewis was waking up, so I might have bashed him over the head with the lamp."

Warryck grinned at her. "That's my girl. Are you hurt though? Did you cut yourself?"

Kerrigan glanced down at her shaking hands. "Nope. Good as I was before." She looked back up and stared at the man in front of her. "What are you, and where did everyone go?"

"I promise I'll tell you everything, but we need to get out of here. If Lewis found us, it's safe to assume he called Gideon with our location. Can you gather our things while I get Lewis into the car?"

Kerrigan didn't move. She couldn't. Was she supposed to blindly follow without knowing what he was? She never saw Warryck move. The next thing Kerrigan knew, he had the knife out of her grip and had her wrapped in his arms, cradling her face with one of his large hands. "Sweetheart, I'm sorry I let them get this close to you, and I vow on everything that's holy, it won't happen again. I let my guard down, and for that, I'm deeply sorry. I should have hidden my bike."

Kerrigan relaxed against him until she felt the smooth skin of his back under her palms. Her body warmed from the inside out, and she mentally slapped herself. Now was not the time to get turned on. Nodding against his chest, she let out a deep breath. "How are we going to do this? If they found your bike once, won't someone spot it again?"

"I have someone on the way to pick it up. You and I are going to take Lewis and his buddy's car. We'll have to swap vehicles down the road, but for now, we need to go."

"Okay." Kerrigan had lost her mind. She patted his chest before pulling away and started gathering their things. When she turned to see what Warryck was doing, she caught him staring. "What?"

"You're one hell of a woman, Kerrigan O'Shea." War winked at her before he bent and lifted Lewis off the ground like he weighed nothing.

*Well, alrighty then.* She didn't respond that he was one hell of a man, because she didn't want to insult him if he didn't identify as such. She knew he was more than human, and for now, she was okay with that. She didn't have a choice. After all their belongings were packed in his duffel and the plastic bags from the stores, she slipped her feet into the black boots, sighing at the way they molded to her feet. Warryck returned from whatever he'd done with Lewis, slipping on his own boots. He took most of the bags from her. "You ready?"

"Yep. Let's blow this popsicle stand."

Warryck laughed deeply and kissed her on her forehead. "Let's."

Kerrigan followed Warryck outside where he tossed the bags into the backseat of the only car in the parking lot. "Where are the other cars?"

Warryck opened the passenger door for Kerrigan. When she was seated, he closed her up and strode to the other side. He was silent until he pulled out onto the road, heading in the opposite direction they'd come in from. "The desk clerk told them the inn was being closed because of a radon leak."

"Am I crazy? Did I hallucinate when you shifted into a lion? And why didn't the desk clerk warn us about a leak?"

Warryck flashed his eyes to her face before settling his gaze back to the road. "No, you aren't crazy. No, you weren't hallucinating, and I... I have the ability to alter a human's thoughts. It comes with being a Gryphon."

A gryphon? Kerrigan had seen pictures of the mythical creature. "But you shifted to a lion. I thought Gryphons were part lion, part eagle."

"We are. But we can call on both aspects of our inner self separately. When I rescued you from the dog, I was in the form of my eagle. When I told you before about how I found you, it wasn't the truth."

"Were you ever going to tell me?"

Warryck gripped the steering wheel tighter. "I don't know. You're taking this all rather well, but most humans can't accept there are beings walking among them who aren't human. I never planned to shift in front of you."

"Can you not control it?"

"Normally, yes. But my Gryphon is very protective of

179

you. I've only shifted one other time that I couldn't control it."

"When was that?"

Warryck swallowed hard. Kerrigan knew whatever the cause was a painful memory. She could feel the sadness rolling off him. "You don't have to answer. It's none of my business." Deep inside, she wanted to know, but not at his expense. "Tell me about altering thoughts. Have you done that with me?"

"Yes. I convinced you I was human when I rescued you. But I only manipulated those few minutes from the time I grabbed you to when I placed you inside the tent. I wanted you to be able to remember everything else."

"Are you going to make me forget what I've seen? You know, you being a sexy beast?"

Warryck barked out a laugh. "Damn, you're something else," he muttered around a grin. "I guess that all depends on you, really. Normally, the only ones who know of our existence are our mates. I figured you would go back with your parents and get on with your life. Hell, Sweetheart. We just met. I know we had a special night, but—" Warryck's cell phone rang, cutting off whatever excuse he was going to give her.

"Hey, Lucy. Is everything okay? Got it. They are?" Warryck listened a couple minutes, smiling at whatever she was saying. "Do not listen to Mav. He's trying to stir up shit." Warryck laughed, and the sound did something to Kerrigan. She wanted to make him laugh. Wanted to be the one to put a smile on his face. With her knowing the truth of what he was, Warryck was probably going to wipe her memories.

Kerrigan's heart sank. Yeah, last night was special, and she'd been ready to see if there could be more between them. She turned to stare out the window at the passing scenery. At least the part she could see illuminated by the car's headlights. Warryck was going to get on with his life

180

after she was back with her parents. Still, she didn't want to forget their time together. She didn't want that. At all. Last night had been the best she'd ever had. She'd been herself with him. Well, maybe not exactly herself, because she'd taken what she wanted without being shy about it.

"Got it. Thanks, Lucy, and again, thank Julian for mentoring you. I'll talk to you tomorrow." Warryck hung up and surprised her by reaching for her hand. "Seems like you get to meet the family. You up for that?"

"Your whole family?" Kerrigan was so not ready. She looked like crap, and she had never met someone's parents before. If the others were as intimidating as War, she was in trouble.

"Nah, just my older brother and Dad. They're bringing some of the Hounds with them."

"Hounds?"

"Oh, right. My Dad used to be the president of the Hounds of Zeus motorcycle club. Right about the time Lucy was born, he handed over the gavel to my oldest brother, Ryker. He used that name for the club because it's the name Zeus gave the Gryphons when he created us to watch over humans. So, everyone in the club is a Gryphon."

"Zeus? Like the Greek god?"

"Yes. I know humans think Zeus and his brothers and sisters were all a myth, but they weren't. Most myths come from some reality, and it just so happens Zeus is real."

"But how do you know? He's real, I mean." Kerrigan wouldn't have believed Gryphons were real if she hadn't seen Warryck shift into a lion, but Zeus?

"Do you believe in the Christian God?"

"I guess. I was raised in church, and I used to pray, so…" Kerrigan shrugged. She used to believe until the crap with Gideon happened.

"Why do you believe?"

"Because of the Bible."

"Which was written by man. The accounts of Zeus were

181

also written by man, so why would that be any harder to believe?"

He had a point. Kerrigan wasn't one prone to arguing, so she changed topics. "Tell me about Lucy."

Warryck sighed, and Kerrigan wondered why. The way he spoke to her on the phone didn't allude to problems between them. "Is that another subject I need to steer clear of?" She didn't mean to sound snippy, but she was beginning to think there was a lot to his past she might never know about.

"No. I'm sorry, but it's hard to think back on my past and not have regrets. I don't want that with you, Kerrigan. I don't want to start whatever this is between us filled with lies and half-truths. You need to know what you're in for if you're going to be with me, and that includes what came before Lucy."

Kerrigan squeezed Warryck's hand tighter, encouraging him to tell her everything. He might still intend to wipe her memory, but if she could handle what he was about to say, maybe there was a future for them after all.

"My wife, Harlow, wasn't a fan of motorcycles or the men who ride them. Her mother was killed overseas by a man riding a bike, and Harlow lumped all bikers into one pile, and not a good one. She'd already convinced me to go to college instead of joining my family in their MC. That didn't sit well with my family, but it was the choice I made. She got pregnant with Lucy, and about a month before she was due, a man named Obadiah Hutton tried to kidnap her. He was the leader of a branch of The Ministry. Have you heard of them?"

"Of course. I think Gideon might be part of that group, too. If not, he's at least got his own cult going on."

"Harlow was also a Gryphon. If not for that, she'd have probably been taken to their compound. She fought back, but her injuries were too severe. She gave birth to Lucy, but Harlow didn't make it."

182

"Oh, Warryck. I'm so sorry." How could he stand to look at her? She had to remind him of his wife with both of them being taken by cult leaders. She tried to pull her hand away from his, but Warryck gripped tighter, placing their joined hands on his thigh. He glanced down where their fingers were laced together with a frown before returning his eyes to the road.

"Anyway, before she died, Harlow made me promise not to let our daughter be raised in the MC world. I promised, and then I respected her dying wish. I asked her aunt and uncle to adopt Lucy and raise her as their own, but in return, I had to finish my college education. My mother barely talks to me, even though Lucy found out who she really was and is now part of our family. It took a while for the two of us to have any kind of relationship, but she forgave me, and now, I'm doing my best to be a good father. She's been through some shit in her life, but she's stronger for it. She worked for the GIA, but now she's with her ma... man and his family. There's a lot more to it than that, but it's a story for another day."

"Wait. You said she worked for the GIA. How old is she? Because you don't look old enough to have a grown daughter."

Warryck brought their joined hands up to his mouth and pressed a kiss to her knuckles. "She's twenty-four. Gryphons don't age the same way humans do. Once we reach maturity, the process slows down. I'm forty-four. My parents don't look much older than I do, so when you meet my father, don't be surprised."

"Warryck, I'm sorry if you rescuing me brings back sad memories for you. I can't imagine what you went through losing Harlow."

"It was a long time ago. At the time, I thought I was doing what was best for my daughter, because it was what her mother wanted. When I see her around my family now, though, I'm not so sure."

"So, you went on to become a psychology professor instead of opening an office and treating people. What did your students think of having a hot biker for a teacher? I bet you had students begging for extra credit."

Warryck laughed and shook his head. "I didn't ride my bike to campus. I was the epitome of the nerdy professor. Khakis and button-up shirts. I even have a hybrid SUV back home in my garage."

"Are you serious? I so cannot see you all geeked out. Besides, I like this leather look on you. You wear it well."

Warryck snuck a glance at her, grinning. "You're good for my ego, Sweetheart. I've missed dressing this way all the time. Like I said back at the tent, I go camping there at least once a year during spring break. Hitting the road on my bike is like a balm to my soul."

"I can see that. I only got to ride with you one time, but even that short trip was exhilarating."

"Would you like to do it again? Ride with me?"

"Let me think. Sit snuggled up to your back, my arms around your hard body, while the world passes by with no metal around us? Wind tangling my hair? Uh, yeah. I'd love it. Besides, some hot guy bought me these really kickass motorcycle boots."

"Then as soon as I take care of Gideon and his band of merry sheep, I'll make that happen."

Kerrigan couldn't wait.

# Chapter Twenty-Three

KERRIGAN WAS TOO good to be true. Warryck told her about his past, not because he wanted to test her, but to get it out there so she could see what kind of male he was. Or at least the kind he had been. He liked to think he had grown and matured since he left Lucy with Vera and Lucius. If he had it to do over, he would have raised her himself with his parents' help. "We're almost to the new hotel. Lucy booked it under her name. Gideon shouldn't be able to track me since he doesn't know my name, but if his men got the tag number off my bike, it's possible they have someone who could run it. She's trying to cover all our bases for us."

"She sounds like a good daughter."

"She is. She only booked one room. I hope that's okay." Mav had convinced Lucy to do that saying Warryck needed help in the dating department. Not that he and Kerrigan were dating, but if spending the rest of the night alone with her meant keeping her in his arms until morning, who was he to object?

"More than. I know we just met, but I like you. Oh, shit. I need to let my parents know we moved."

"About that. Lucy's mate has a jet and has offered it to you and your parents."

"He has his own plane?" Kerrigan's eyes were wide, and Warryck grinned at her.

"Uh, yeah. He might be a prince or something like

that." Warryck wouldn't share the fact that Tamian was a Gargoyle prince. Kerrigan was still getting used to there being Gryphons, plus it wasn't his place to share the truth of the other shifters.

"Damn. First Gryphons, then bikers, and now royalty. I feel like I woke up in another dimension. And I'm just an unemployed bartender."

"Is that something you always wanted to do?"

"Don't laugh, but when I was young, I wanted to be a ballerina. Turns out I have two left feet and no rhythm."

"I'm not laughing, because I'm not very graceful either. But, for what it's worth, I think you would look stunning in a tutu."

"Riiight. I'm not exactly the pencil-thin type, but I'm okay with that. You can't drink beer every night and keep a dancer's figure. Anyway, I got the job at Harper's Point in my second year of college. I really had no plans with what I wanted to do when I graduated, and I loved working behind the bar. It was a good fit for me, so I dropped out of school and stayed with Brooks. I hated leaving him the way I did, but at the time, I didn't think I had a choice."

"Would you go back there if you could?"

"I think I'd rather keep my options open."

Warryck wanted to pump his fist but decided to play it cool. They arrived at the hotel a few minutes later, and his heart thumped wildly for a different reason. It had been years since he'd spent any time with either his brother or father, yet here they were, ready to help him. They were waiting near the back of the lot, so he drove up and parked next to them. Ryker was grim as always, but Sutton was grinning like he had a secret.

After getting out, War went around and helped Kerrigan out of the car and placed a hand on her lower back. She didn't shy away from his touch. If anything, she leaned a little closer. Whether it was because she wanted to be near him or from getting her first look at Ryker, he didn't know.

Sutton closed the distance and wrapped War in a tight hug, pounding him on the back.

"War, it's good to see you, Son. And who's this beauty?" Sutton held out his hand to Kerrigan and brought her knuckles to his lips.

"Kerrigan, I'd like you to meet my father, Sutton. And this is my oldest brother, Ryker."

When Ryker pushed off his bike, his features softened. He shook Kerrigan's hand. "It's a pleasure to meet you. I'm sorry it's under these circumstances. When Maveryck called and told us what was going on, we headed out to help War." Ryker held out a set of keys and a plastic hotel room card. "I went ahead and signed you in so Kerrigan wouldn't have to wait to get into your room."

"Thanks, Ry. I'll just—" Thumping came from the trunk, and all four turned toward the car. "Ah, our guests are awake. Let me get Kerrigan settled in our room, and then we'll discuss next steps."

"I took the liberty of getting the room next to yours, Son. We'll wait for you in there." Sutton held out his arm for Kerrigan. "Shall we?"

Kerrigan looped her arm through Sutton's. "We shall." She looked over her shoulder at War and winked.

"Bags?" Ryker asked, gesturing toward the car.

"Yeah." War opened the car and pulled out their things, handing his duffel to Ryker before grabbing the rest of their bags. "Listen, Ry. Thanks for coming out to help. I know I'm not involved in this part of what the family does, but I'd like to be. I've been doing a lot of thinking now that I've had nothing but time, and I'm ready to do my part. Starting with this Gideon fucker. I want to make him pay for what he and those two put Kerrigan through." He kicked the side of the trunk hard enough to put a dent in it.

"Glad to hear it. I'm also glad you're making things right with Lucy."

"I'm trying. I have a lot of years to make up for, but she

187

and I have been talking a lot, and it seems to be going well."

Ryker strode across the parking lot without waiting for War. When he caught up with his brother, Ryker kept his face forward, but War didn't need to be looking at him to know his eyes were glacial when he spoke. "I'm glad to hear that as well, because that girl means the world to me, but if you ever hurt her again, you'll answer to me." Ryker used his own key card to enter the side entrance of the hotel.

War bristled at his words, but instead of getting into an argument, he kept his mouth shut. He already knew how Ryker felt about Lucy and the fact that the family felt he'd abandoned his daughter. War would just have to prove he was ready to put the past behind him and be the better son, brother, father, and Hound.

When they were both secure in the elevator, Ryker turned to him. "Nothing to say?"

"No. I've made my peace with Lucy, and I figure actions speak louder than words."

Ryker was only a few years older, but he made War feel like a teenager at times. More so than their father ever did. War always admired his oldest brother, especially when he'd suffered his own great loss early on. War handled Harlow's death on his own, never accepting help from anyone. He left Lucy with Vera and Lucius then lost himself in school. He didn't allow himself time to grieve. He found the bottom of a whiskey bottle a couple times, but that was it. Ryker endured his own suffering by taking to the road with Sutton, just the two of them on their bikes. He'd been a strong male before, but he seemed to mature overnight. War understood why Ryker latched on to Lucy, and he wasn't going to open old wounds just to get his digs in.

When they reached the door to the room, Sutton stepped out, grinning. "For all she's been through, that one's feisty. I like her."

"Yeah, she seems like she's got a good head on her

shoulders." War wasn't going to let on how much he liked Kerrigan. It was too soon for him to have such strong feelings for the female. Sutton would call bullshit, because he and Rory had fallen in love the first day they met and were married a week later. It was about five years before they had the girls as Rory still called War's six older sisters who were all in their eighties. Sutton kept trying for boys and gave up after three sets of female twins were born. It wasn't until Ryker came along unexpectedly almost fifty years ago that they decided to try for more boys, and Sutton got his wish. "So, what's the plan?"

Ryker pushed open the door to the room next to Kerrigan's. "First thing is to secure those two in the trunk. We need a place we can take them and interrogate them. What we don't get from them, we'll need Kerrigan to fill in for us. When are her parents arriving?"

"They're supposed to be on a flight out in the morning."

Ryker scrubbed a hand through his beard. "It's good they're coming to get her. We need to move on this compound as soon as possible, and we don't need her getting in the way."

"You don't think she could be useful?" Warryck wasn't ready to let her leave, but maybe his brother had a point.

"With information, yes. We're going in to take down a cult, not have a tea party."

Sutton set a hand on War's shoulder. "You'll need to focus on taking down Talbert and his guards. If Kerrigan's there, your mind will be on keeping her safe. It's nothing against her personally."

"Okay. I get that. Can you handle the guys in the trunk? It's been a long damn day for Kerrigan, and I'd rather wait and talk to her in the morning about the compound." War also wanted more alone time with her before her parents arrived.

"Don't you want to come with us?" Ryker asked, giving

War a knowing look.

"Only if I'm needed. If not, I'd like to stay with Kerrigan. Someone needs to watch over her in case Gideon happened to have us followed somehow. I didn't check his two goons for trackers or anything before I shoved them in the trunk."

"Shit. I guess we need to get on that. Sultan, King, and Judge stopped off to pick up your bike. They should be arriving soon. They won't bother you unless you need them." Ryker handed War a phone. "Here's a burner. All our numbers are already programmed into it. If you need them, call King first. If they run into trouble, they'll call you, so keep it close by. Pop, let's do this." Ryker strode toward the door and held it open for their father.

Sutton followed but turned before stepping into the hallway. "This shouldn't take long. If everything goes as it should, we won't bother you tonight when we return." He winked at War and set his hand on Ryker's back to get him moving. War didn't miss the way his brother narrowed his eyes. He wondered if Ryker was interested in Kerrigan, or if he just didn't want War to have her. Not that he had her. Ryker'd had just as much time to find a woman of his own, even though he'd vowed to never get involved again. If he did have his eye on Kerrigan? Tough shit.

Using the extra key card, War knocked on the door to his and Kerrigan's room before letting himself in. When he didn't hear her object, he pushed it open and froze. Kerrigan had on the leather jacket he'd bought for her and was admiring it in the mirror.

"Oh, hi." She blushed a pretty shade of pink. "I hope this was for me."

"It is yours. Do you like it?" War let the door close behind him, and he stepped into the room, tossing the card on the dresser. Kerrigan nodded, twirling around so he could see it from all sides. "Looks good on you."

"It fits perfect. Thank you."

190

"You're welcome. Sorry that took so long. Just making plans. Have you spoken to your parents again?" Warryck sat down on one of the queen beds and removed his boots.

"Yes. I let them know we moved hotels, but I didn't give them the reason. I went with the radon excuse. No need for them to worry any more than they already are. I need to warn you. My mother is probably going to lose her shit when she meets you. She'll cry on your shirt and offer to buy you an island or something. She's a wonderful mom, but she can get a little out there sometimes."

"You haven't met 'out there' until you meet my mother. If Rory likes you, she'll love you forever. If she doesn't? Just watch out for the sharp teeth."

Kerrigan narrowed her eyes. "Are you serious?"

Warryck stretched out on the bed, bunching the pillows behind his head. "I mean, she wouldn't really bite someone unless they were a threat to one of her kids. Momma lion and her cubs and all that."

Kerrigan removed the jacket and placed it over the back of the rolling desk chair. She crawled on top of the opposite bed and sat cross-legged facing War. "Tell me about her cubs. I'm an only child, so I have no idea what having siblings would be like."

War rolled over onto his side so he could see her better. "There's eleven of us. Three sets of female twins who are in their eighties. Dad wanted boys and kept trying, but finally gave up after Dahlia and Iris were born. Poppy and Holly are the oldest. Aster and Laurel are three years behind them, and Dahlia and Iris are two years behind them. About fifty years ago, Ryker happened. They weren't planning on having more kids, but once Dad got his first boy, he convinced Mom to keep going. Maveryck and I are four years younger than Ryker. Kyllian came along twelve years later, and Hayden's the baby at twenty-eight. The girls, Ryker, Mav and I were all born in Texas, but Kyllian and Hayden were born in New York. Since we don't age like humans, we have to move around before people get suspicious."

"Did you leave New York at some point?"

"No, but I did move away from the family when I began teaching. They've also moved to different parts of the state. Dad and Rory were ready to head south when Lucy found out she was adopted and got in touch. Rory wanted to stay close for her, but now that she's living with Tamian, I have a feeling they might be packing things up. My sisters all have children, and they have children, so it wouldn't surprise me to see our parents seek some of them out."

"It's all so strange, thinking about your dad, who's hot by the way, having great-grandkids."

"Hey, I'm supposed to be the only Lazlo you have eyes for."

Kerrigan picked up a pillow and tossed it at War. "You're too easy."

"I'll show you easy." War dove off his bed and tackled Kerrigan, pinning her beneath him. Securing her hands over her head with one of his hands, he tickled her until she gasped. He'd completely forgotten about her injuries. "Shit!" War rolled to his side and sat up, running his hands through his hair.

Kerrigan placed a hand between his shoulders. "Hey, it's okay. You didn't hurt me." Kissing the side of his neck, she set her chin on his shoulder. When he turned his head to apologize, Kerrigan pressed their lips together. Not wanting to hurt her further, he kept his hands in his lap, but she had different ideas. With their tongues tangled together, Kerrigan straddled his lap.

# Chapter Twenty-Four

GIDEON PACED THE small area of his office, sliding his fingers through his hair for the hundredth time since Kerrigan escaped. He glanced at the living room where Sparrow was tied to a chair, tears streaming down her face. Deep down, he knew she had nothing to do with Kerrigan running away, but she was McKenzie's sister, and she had also tried to leave The Sanctuary. Coincidence or not, he couldn't trust her. Lewis had filled him in about the two women taking a walk to the area around the barn. Either Sparrow or Mac must have mentioned Mac's attempt at running, since they were the same trails Kerrigan had used.

Kerrigan had lied to him when she said she wanted to be with him, and that knowledge pissed him right the fuck off. He should have known better. She was just like the other redhead in his life. Both beautiful, lying snakes. Fuck! When he got his hands on Kerrigan, and he would get her back, he would teach her the same lesson he'd taught Juliette.

"Gideon."

The voice was lethal. Making sure his face was indifferent, he turned and faced his older brother.

"Josiah, what brings you here?"

His brother's laugh was deep. Sinister. "Are you really going to pretend like you don't know? Like I don't have the pulse of every one of my compounds?"

It took all Gideon's self-control not to flinch. The Sanctuary was Gideon's, but Josiah liked to think all compounds in the Northeast were under his command. They both knew who was in charge. Just because Josiah was married to Abraham's oldest daughter, it gave him the impression he had more control than the other leaders. Still, Gideon knew to tread lightly.

"I have no illusions where you're concerned, Brother. But this situation is under control."

"Is that what you think? If so, you're less competent than you believe, because Lewis and Steven are now in the hands of a biker gang. The same gang who helped your female escape."

"What?" Gideon raised his hand to rake it through his already disheveled hair. Again. "How could you know that?"

"Because I know how to do my fucking job!" Josiah strode closer, getting in Gideon's face, snarling. "Lewis might be your guard, but he's loyal to the Ministry first and foremost. He called me when he and Steven were on their way to retrieve that which you lost. He knows what can happen if the wrong people find out about us. He knows how important it is to keep the sheep in line."

"And did Lewis also tell you he was the one who was supposed to be watching Kerrigan? That I wasn't even here when she escaped? I was meeting with the elders. A meeting Abraham himself called. A meeting you weren't invited to. So, why were you in the area?" Gideon knew his brother kept close tabs on all their properties, but he should have been hundreds of miles away, not close enough to arrive within hours of Kerrigan running.

"Abraham sent me here as soon as he learned you'd moved the redhead into your home. He didn't trust you to turn her after what happened with Juliette. Seems he was right."

Gideon couldn't dispute his brother's words. He had

194

moved Kerrigan in sooner than he should have, but he mistakenly thought he could sway her if she was given an opportunity to see him in his home environment. He had grossly miscalculated the woman's acting abilities. *Give her a fucking Oscar.*

"So, who are these bikers?" In Steven's foray into the world, using his Stanley Carson alias, he had the task of bringing new members to The Sanctuary. Normally, it was the homeless closer to the compound. He'd been visiting a cousin in Maine who was asking about starting his own compound when Steven happened upon Kerrigan O'Shea. He'd watched the woman for over a week, knowing she was someone Gideon would be interested in, since she so closely resembled Juliette. While watching Kerrigan, Steven never encountered a group of bikers anywhere around Kerrigan, only her bully of a boyfriend. As luck would have it, Dalton Watkins was an idiot who drove Kerrigan from their home, and Steven happened to be in the right place at the right time. Like Juliette, Kerrigan was stunning with her red hair and bright, green eyes. And more so than Juliette, Kerrigan had a mind of her own, which led them to where they were now.

"They call themselves the Hounds of Zeus. How they ended up with Kerrigan is a mystery. I've yet to uncover their relationship to the woman, or how one of them happened to be camping right outside your compound. The fact that someone was so close to your location just proves you aren't capable of keeping The Sanctuary free from outside influences. Until Abraham finds someone suitable, I will be taking over. You are to move into one of the cabins, and I will be staying here with your little bird."

A startled gasp escaped from behind the gag in Sparrow's mouth. When Gideon looked at the girl, she was shaking her head no. Gideon knew if she was left alone with his brother, the young girl would be ruined. Those who thought they knew Gideon thought he had no heart, but

195

when it came to that young woman, he'd brought her into his home to protect her from Lewis. Sure, he had given the sister to his guard, but Mac was nothing like Sparrow. Mac was worldly and brash. A rebel among the sheep. Sparrow was as innocent as the day was long. Damn Kerrigan O'Shea for bringing this shitstorm to his door!

"Until Abraham shows up and removes me as head of my compound, I'll remain in charge. I'll also handle this mess with Kerrigan. Just tell me where they are keeping her, and I'll get her back. I'm not worried about Lewis or Steven. Neither one of them would betray the Ministry, no matter how bad the torture is."

Josiah pulled to his full height. He was only a couple inches taller than Gideon, but the malevolence made him seem bigger. "Do you dare dispute my authority?"

"Yes, I dare. I've overseen The Sanctuary for almost twenty years. Grown it into the success it is today. I've never let the Ministry down, and I don't intend to allow this small infraction to mar my reputation."

"Success? You call farming only enough food for your flock and raising a pitiful head of cattle a success? You have only enough guards to protect the perimeter, and you even failed at that. Your job is to raise soldiers, Gideon, not play God while pimping out the women." Gideon flinched, and Josiah sneered. "Didn't think I knew about that, did you? You're supposed to approve couples who will bring forth sturdy offspring, not allow your guards to have their choice of whomever catches their eye. That McKenzie bitch is nothing more than a piece of trash. You should have let the dog finish her off!"

Another sob broke from Sparrow's throat. Josiah finally turned his attention to the girl. "If you know what's good for you, you'll admit to helping Kerrigan escape. If you decide to keep up this innocent charade, well, let's just say you won't be useful. Liars aren't suitable choices for the men who are looking for a wife. If you have nothing to offer

196

a husband other than treachery, you're no use to The Sanctuary."

Sparrow's eyes pled with Gideon to help her, but Josiah stepped into Gideon's line of sight. "You have twenty-four hours to retrieve Kerrigan O'Shea. If you do not return with her or dispose of her properly within that time, you will step down as leader. If you refuse, Abraham has given me permission to do with you as I see fit."

"And you'll what? Kill your own brother? Should I start calling you Cane?" Josiah swung a meaty fist towards Gideon's face. He ducked, but not quickly enough. He should have been expecting it. As boys, they had gotten into more brawls than he could recount, and he'd always held his own. But this man was fueled with something Gideon hadn't allowed himself to fall victim to. Sometimes, he felt close to losing his soul, but he still held a shred of humanity within. His older brother? Not an ounce was to be found. Gideon wiped the blood from his split lip. "Give me the information you have so I can get Kerrigan back."

Josiah stared at Gideon for a beat then told him where the bikers were holding her. "Like I said, you have twenty-four hours." He turned on his heel and left the office. Josiah stopped beside Sparrow and trailed a fingertip through the tears on her cheek. "Such a pity."

Only when the front door closed did Gideon move. He stepped into his bathroom and wet a washcloth. When he returned to where Sparrow was sitting, he removed the gag from her mouth and gently wiped her face.

"G-Gideon. I p-promise. I would n-never betray you."

Gideon tipped Sparrow's face up. "I would hope not, but I can't trust you. For the time being, you'll be moved to the inner chamber. Once I've retrieved our wayward lamb, I'll give more thought as to where you'll stay." He knew she didn't have the same inner strength Kerrigan did, but he couldn't worry about that. She'd either think on the truth and confess her sins when he returned, or she'd find a way to survive the isolation.

Turning to one of the guards who had remained silent while Josiah visited, Gideon instructed the man to take Sparrow. He allowed the girl to grab a pillow and blanket off her bed, but that was all. Gideon waited until they were gone to head over to the main building. He was going to cancel both women's and men's Bible study, something he only did when he had to travel for meetings. It was probably a good thing, because his mind wouldn't be on teaching the flock the same message he regurgitated every day just in a different way. After he made the announcement, one of his guards, Baker, met him in his sanctuary office to let him know Lewis and Steven had returned. Gideon followed Baker back to his house where he found his two men sitting on the sofa with another guard standing watch. When they saw him, both men jumped to their feet. Both men looked like hell.

"What happened?"

Lewis shook his head and shoved his hands in his pockets. "We got to the hotel room where that biker was keeping Kerrigan, but they'd already gone, and some big guy was in the room instead. He didn't appreciate me busting in the door."

"And? What about the bikers who took you?"

"What?" Steven and Lewis looked at each other. "We weren't taken. We came back here when we got away from the guy in the hotel."

"Don't lie to me! Josiah told me you were taken. So where did they take you, and why did they let you go?"

Steven frowned and scratched his head. "No, that's not right. There were no bikers. Gideon, we — oomph." Steven doubled over when Gideon punched him in the stomach. Panting, he raised his eyes to Gideon's. "I swear to you. There were no bikers. Tell him, Lewis."

Lewis backed up a step and held his hands up. "He's telling the truth. We..." Lewis narrowed his eyes and

198

cocked his head to the side. "It's all a little sketchy, to be honest. The bike was at the hotel parked in front of the room. I saw the biker go in. They must have slipped out somehow, because when we got to the door, it was some random man."

"Did you search the room? They could have been hiding in the bathroom." Gideon was barely containing his temper. He'd sent his most trusted men to retrieve Kerrigan, and they failed. Now they were telling him the bikers didn't get hold of them. What were they playing at? Or was it Josiah who'd been lying? That made more sense. His brother would do anything to undermine Gideon's authority where his men were concerned.

Both men looked at one another then shook their heads. Something was going on with them. He didn't feel they were lying to him, but their actions didn't speak of the truth, either. "Baker, sit on these two. Don't let them out of your sight. I don't want them leaving this house until I return."

"Yes, Brother Gideon."

Gideon closed himself in his office and opened his computer where he did a quick search of these Hounds his brother mentioned as well as the area where he said they were keeping Kerrigan. He needed more information than his brother had given. When he felt he had as much intel as he was going to glean from the internet, Gideon headed out to do the job his men had failed to do.

Josiah might think Gideon wasn't a good leader for the Ministry, but his brother was wrong. Gideon had known the day might come when Josiah tried to step on his toes, and he was glad for the secrets he'd kept from both Josiah and Abraham.

# Chapter Twenty-Five

KERRIGAN MAY OR may not have tried listening through the wall when Warryck was in the next room. Their words were muffled, so she had no clue what was said. Instead of sitting around worrying about it, she unpacked the bags, folding all the clothes and putting them in the dresser drawers even though they were only staying one night. She ignored the urge to strip out of her own T-shirt and put on one of Warryck's.

*War.*

That's what his brother and father called him. She could see that. War was the biker who flew in and saved her from Gideon. Warryck was better suited to the buttoned-up college professor. War was the one who made her fly apart when he made love to her. Warryck was the sweet man who bought her boots and a leather jacket. War was the sexy-as-hell male she would ride behind on his badass Harley. And she would ride with him again. She just had to convince him she wanted to stay. But what if that wasn't what he wanted? Just because he'd given her the best orgasm of her life didn't mean he wanted to keep her around.

When War tackled her on the bed, she was caught off guard, but she liked the playful side of him. She'd been ready for another round of toe-curling sex until he tickled her. He thought he hurt her, but she hated being tickled. Straddling his lap, she placed her hands on his face, running

200

her bandaged fingers through his short beard. She'd always liked facial hair, and his was soft. Not giving him time to think, Kerrigan leaned in for a kiss. She didn't brush her lips across his. No, she went in with the passion she wanted in return.

War gripped her hips when she started rocking against his erection. He broke the kiss and pressed their foreheads together. "As much as I want this, I don't know when Dad and Ryker will be back. I doubt they'll need to talk to us this late, but I don't want to embarrass you if they catch us in the middle of sex."

"I understand." Kerrigan pushed off his lap, already embarrassed. "I'm tired, anyway, so I'm just going to get some sleep." Moving over to the opposite bed, she pulled back the covers and got underneath them, not bothering to remove her clothes. She didn't want to strip and make a further fool of herself.

War flipped the covers off her. "You are not sleeping in your clothes. If you don't want me in the same bed, that's fine, but sleeping in jeans isn't comfortable." War turned around and stripped out of his own clothes, leaving on his tee and boxer briefs. God, the man's ass was a piece of art. Perfectly round. His thighs and calves were muscular, dusted with light blond hair. She'd had those legs under her, over her, and she had to look away before he caught her ogling. Pushing her own jeans down, she tossed them to the end of the bed where she could grab them should his dad and brother return.

Kerrigan rolled over to her side, facing away from the man who did things to her body by merely being in the same room. If she couldn't have him, she didn't want to have to look at him. Closing her eyes, she took a deep breath, willing sleep to come. The bed dipped, and War picked her up.

"What are you doing?"

He gently placed her on the bed farthest from the door

and pushed her hair off her face. "I need to be between you and the door." His eyes were the same dark storms she'd noticed when he was turned on. Maybe he did want her and had been telling the truth. Being around him made her forget where she'd been this time the day before. He was there to protect her, and she was throwing herself at him. *Idiot.*

"Oh, okay. Goodnight."

After a few seconds, the lamp between the beds clicked off. The only light was filtering through the gap in the hotel drapes. "Goodnight." His voice sounded conflicted, but that was probably her imagination. Or wishful thinking.

Kerrigan closed her eyes, but every move War made in the other bed, every sigh, called to her. She shouldn't want him. They'd talked a little, but she still didn't truly know what type of man he was. But he wasn't a man, and that should have her running the other way. Knowing he was something other than human was exciting. Kerrigan had seen the lion, and now, she wanted to see the rest of him. There was no way she would ask him to shift for her. That seemed a little too personal. *More personal than having sex?* Yes. Sex was something two people did when they had an itch to scratch. It didn't have to mean something deep. Yet, she'd felt a connection and something more when they'd made love. He'd been attentive and gentle while taking her body to heights she never thought possible. Kerrigan wanted that closeness again, even without the sex. She didn't want to sleep by herself. Couldn't he keep her safe in the same bed? "War?"

"Yeah, Sweetheart?"

"Will you hold me? At least until I fall asleep?"

Within seconds, War was beneath the covers, spooning his larger body around hers. Not trusting herself to keep her ass from brushing his crotch, she turned over and used his shoulder for a pillow. "Is this okay?"

"Perfect." War moved her hair off her shoulder and

kissed her forehead. Kerrigan settled quickly and closed her eyes.

War surprised Kerrigan a few minutes later when he softly said, "Tell me about your tattoo."

"My middle name is Roisin after my grandmother on my mom's side. It means 'little rose.' She came with my parents when they moved from Ireland and lived with us until she passed away when I was eight."

"Can I see it?"

"Sure." Kerrigan sat up and pulled her shirt off one arm while War turned on the lamp. His fingers ghosted over the ink, and she shivered.

"Does the stem say sláinte?"

"Yes. Since I was a bartender, I thought the Irish toast was fitting."

"It's beautiful." War pressed a kiss to her skin before helping her put her shirt back on. "Thank you for showing me."

"You're welcome. I would ask about all your ink, but that would take a while, and I'm pretty wiped. Besides, if I look at them, I'm probably going to want to lick them." Kerrigan ducked her head, her cheeks heating at the admission. She did want to lick every one of War's tattoos, not just learn if they had special meanings.

War chuckled and pushed her hair over her shoulder, kissing her neck. "You can check them all out later." He turned the lamp off, and they settled back into their former positions, with him holding her close. His breathing evened out after a few minutes, and Kerrigan drifted off soon after.

The hotel room door closing followed by muffled voices woke Kerrigan. Sitting up, she pushed her hair back from her face and looked around. Finding herself alone, she stood and stretched. Figuring her time with War was coming to an end, she grabbed her jeans and slid them up her legs. Her body ached, and a bath would probably help, but she didn't have the energy. What she wanted was a pot of coffee. She didn't have any money, but surely War wouldn't mind paying for a little room service.

She'd just picked up the phone when the door opened, and War returned holding a bag and a tray with two to-go cups. "Morning. Dad brought us breakfast."

Kerrigan went straight to the table where War set the items down and grabbed one of the cups. She didn't care if it was black. She needed the jolt of caffeine. "Ahhh." When she looked up, War was smiling at her. He turned his attention to the bag and pulled out several breakfast sandwiches before dumping cream and sugar onto the table. Kerrigan doctored her coffee with cream and returned the lid to the cup.

"He wasn't sure what you liked, so there's several options."

"I'm not picky." And she wasn't. Kerrigan ate just about anything. Sure, she loved a good steak or lobster dinner, but she didn't need those things to be happy. Her parents hadn't been rich, but neither were they poor when she was growing up. Her dad was careful with his spending, and Kerrigan had learned how to get by on not having a six-figure income as well. She would have had a good bit of savings if Dalton hadn't stolen it from her. After taking a bite of sausage, egg, and cheese on sourdough, Kerrigan chewed while thoughts of her future flitted through her head. Her parents would be arriving in a couple hours, and she wasn't sure how she felt about seeing them.

"We need to talk." War finished his coffee then tossed the empty cup in the waste can. Leaning against the dresser, he crossed his arms over his broad chest. The bite of food she swallowed threatened to stick in her throat. She washed it down with a long drink of coffee.

"Okay." She wiped her hands on a napkin, not daring to take another bite.

"Ryker got a lot of information from Lewis and his buddy. Since your parents will be here in a couple hours,

204

Ryker wants to talk to you about what was said. Mav is still on the road and won't be here before you leave."

"I'm not sure what more there is other than what I already told you, but I'll talk to him."

"I want you to know I'm going to take Talbert down. He won't be kidnapping anyone else."

Kerrigan was thankful for that, but she was worried about Mac. "What will happen to the people who live there?"

"Since I've not been involved in these operations before, I'll let Ryker answer your questions. I'll go tell him you'll be ready to talk in thirty minutes. That enough time for you to finish eating?" War pushed her sandwich toward her, but she'd lost her appetite.

"We can go now. I'd just as soon get it over with."

"Sweetheart, I'm sorry if this upsets you." War pulled her into his arms and hugged her close. She allowed him to comfort her, even though he was wrong about why she was upset. She didn't understand why she felt so attached to him when they'd just met. Yes, she was grateful he saved her. But it was more than that.

Pulling away, she plastered on a smile. "I'm fine. Let's just get this over with."

Kerrigan was nervous. She trusted War, and she felt his father was a nice man, but Ryker scared the crap out of her. War used a key card and let them into the other room. Ryker was leaning against the dresser with his arms crossed over his chest. If she had met him on the street, she'd have avoided eye contact and walked away as fast as possible. When he turned his stormy gaze toward her, she almost ran back to her room. With War behind her, she couldn't retreat. Kerrigan stepped closer to the wall so he could pass by her. Instead of doing so, he placed a hand at the small of her back and remained by her side. It was only a small bit of comfort, but it was enough to keep her calm.

"We had a little chat with Lewis and Steven. Both men

assured us nobody is held at The Sanctuary against their will. Steven said he found you when you were all but unconscious and were asking for a doctor."

Kerrigan stiffened at the accusatory tone. "I was in a great deal of pain, yes, but I wasn't unconscious. He mentioned his brother was a doctor, but when I woke, I had no idea where I was, but later found out I was hundreds of miles away. That definitely hadn't been part of the plan. When I asked to leave, Gideon told me I was free to go, but I would receive no help. That I had to find my own way out. When I attempted exactly that, they sent their dog after me. Same as with McKenzie, only she wasn't lucky enough to have a Gryphon waiting for her. I didn't talk to very many people, so I have no idea if there's anyone else who was taken there against their will."

Warryck took a step closer to Kerrigan, but she shifted away. She wanted his comfort but not at the risk of him alienating his brother. He had plans to become part of their world again, and she wouldn't come between them. For an hour, Kerrigan told the three Gryphons all she knew about the compound. Ryker asked her the same question several times, and she was getting tired of it. War had interceded on her behalf, but she cut him off each time. When Ryker asked her another question she'd already answered, she opened her mouth to snap at him, but her phone rang, saving him from her redheaded temper. "That's my parents." She excused herself and left the room, retreating to her own.

"Dad?" she answered as she pushed open the door, letting it slam behind her.

"Hey, honey. We're in the lobby. We just need your room number."

Kerrigan leaned against the wall, sliding down to settle on her ass, pulling her knees up. She told her dad where to find her, and she hung up. Maybe it was better if she went with her parents. War had enough on his plate without worrying about her getting in the way of his family. It was obvious Ryker didn't believe her, and she couldn't stand to be around the man any longer.

Pushing to her feet, Kerrigan set about packing her clothes. When her parents knocked, she let them in. She was immediately crushed between their arms. She let them have their moment to realize she was really okay. "I'm fine, I promise. Let me get my things, and we'll go."

"But we don't have a return flight scheduled. We didn't know how long you needed to stay, and besides. We want to meet the man who saved you." Kerrigan's mom pushed her hair back from her face, searching the way she did when she was worried.

"He's next door, but you can meet him in a minute. If it's okay with you, I'd like for us to rent a car and drive back."

"Honey, it's a sixteen-hour drive to South Carolina. Unless you were planning on returning to Maine, we thought you'd want to come stay with us." Kerrigan's dad took her hand and led her to the bed. Sitting them both down, he turned her face toward him. "What's going on?"

"It's been a really long morning."

"But it's only a little after nine." Her mother sat down on her other side. "Kerri, what's wrong?"

"I…"

# Chapter Twenty-Six

"WHAT THE FUCK was that?" War swung his arm backward toward the door Kerrigan had just gone through as he glared at his older brother.

Ryker pushed away from the dresser and ran a hand through his long beard. "That was me getting all the information we needed to raid the fucking compound. Don't come in here, acting like you know how to interrogate someone."

"Interrogate? Jesus H. Christ. Kerrigan isn't some suspect. She's the victim here." Warryck tightened his hands into fists, ready to knock some sense into his brother. He wished Mav was there. His twin would have gone easier on Kerrigan while still getting useful information. Ryker was hardened by his past, and he gave no fucks whether anyone liked him or not. What happened... Oh, fuck. Kerrigan was a tall redhead, just like—

"It's clear you have feelings for Kerrigan, but Ryker was doing his job." Up until that point, Sutton had kept quiet, but he stepped between the brothers, turning to face Warryck. "Yes, he might be a little brusque, but his methods are effective. We needed to make sure she remembered everything correctly. When we take down these bastards, we need to have all the information, and sometimes asking a question more than once gets a different answer. We have to make sure we know what and who we're dealing with.

Heading into a heavily guarded compound is different than going into one of these places where they're all Kumbaya and shit. We don't dismantle every cult we come across, even if we don't agree with their ways. If they aren't harming anyone, we leave them alone. It's the ones who are raising armies we focus on."

"Did you get enough information to take this one down, or am I going after Gideon on my own?"

Ryker smirked, and War took a step closer. "What's your problem with me?"

The bastard had the audacity to shrug. "You've been a college professor for twenty years, yet two weeks on the road, and you think you're ready for what we do."

"Yeah, it's been twenty years, but don't forget, I have done this before." War had killed a human, the one who caused Harlow's death, and he still had no regrets over it.

Sutton placed a hand on War's shoulder. "I know you're a Gryphon, Son, and we haven't forgotten what happened with Obadiah Hutton, but you can't go off half-cocked or alone. We're going to take them down, but we will do it once we have a solid plan in place. Neither Lewis nor Steven would admit to The Sanctuary being part of the Ministry. It doesn't mean they aren't. The two could be in the dark as to who Gideon answers to. The fact that they didn't come after you with guns doesn't mean they don't have them at the compound. We have to do a little recon to see exactly what we're dealing with. It's not just grown men. There are women and children, and we have to make sure they're safe. Go check on your woman, and after she and her parents leave, we'll regroup." War didn't correct his father about Kerrigan being his. She wasn't, even though he wanted her to be.

He let himself into the room next door. "Kerrigan?" Her parents were already there, so he paused at the edge of the room. "You must be Shawn and Enya. I'm Warryck Lazlo."

Both her parents jumped to their feet. Her dad held out

his hand, pumping War's grip heartily, but her mom pulled him into a hug. Kerrigan hadn't been kidding about her mother smothering him with gratitude.

"Thank you, Mr. Lazlo. Thank you so much for finding our girl."

Warryck hugged her back, looking over her head at Kerrigan. Kerrigan rose from the bed and put something into a bag that was already mostly packed. Shit. He knew she was pissed, but he'd hoped for more time with her.

When Enya released him, War stepped up beside Kerrigan and grabbed her hand before she could gather her bags. "I'm sorry about Ryker. He was an ass, but he said it was only because he needed to make sure you remembered everything exactly as it happened."

"No, I get it. So, I guess this is it?"

"Are you leaving now? What about the flight home? I didn't call Lucy."

"I think we're going to drive. I want to spend some time with my parents."

War reached up to cup her face, but hesitated, not wanting to upset her parents by touching their daughter. "I... Can I call you? After this is over?"

"Yeah. I'd like to know what happens with everyone. Especially Mac. I doubt Sparrow is going to want to leave her parents, but I know Mac would like to get out of there and start a new life. Maybe she and I can start a cult survivor's group." Of course, Kerrigan would want to know what happened, but that was all. She wasn't interested in seeing him. Ignoring her parents, Kerrigan pulled War down and kissed his cheek. "Thank you for everything. I wish... Just take care of yourself. Okay?"

She wished what? Warryck wished they were alone so he could tell her how he felt. Explain, or at least try to, how he wanted her in his life when this was over. "I will. And you do the same. Maybe..." War couldn't finish his thought with her parents in the room. "Call me if you need anything.

Anything at all." War wrapped his arms around Kerrigan and held her tight, pressing a kiss to her temple. When he released her, War looked into her eyes, conveying the feelings he didn't dare speak. Tears peppered her eyes, and he turned toward her parents before he broke down and tossed her over his shoulder, taking her far away.

Her parents were staring at him, but he plastered on a fake smile. "It was a pleasure to meet you both." They returned the sentiment, and War let himself out of the room. Instead of going next door to face his family, he left the hotel. He couldn't watch Kerrigan get into the car with her parents and drive away. He still couldn't understand how he could come to care so much for the woman in such a short time.

War wanted to get away. He needed time to clear his head. He was torn about going back inside and begging Kerrigan to stay, but he knew he had to let her go with her parents. If he was going to prove his ability to become part of his family's world, she would be too distracting. And, by Zeus, he *was* going to prove himself to Ryker. He wasn't worried about his dad. Sutton would have his back like he always had. Even when War let Lucius and Vera adopt Lucy, Sutton had been the buffer between War and Rory. He often wondered if Harlow had lived if he himself would have been a buffer between her and their daughter.

Three bikes rumbled into the parking lot, and a Hound he vaguely remembered rolled up on War's bike. King pulled up to War and turned off the motor. "You've kept her in great condition."

"I ride every chance I get. I might not be part of the MC, but I prefer two wheels over four."

"You ever think about joining us?" One of the other Hounds – Sultan, with his shaved head, dark beard, and mirrored sunglasses – joined King, running his hands across the smooth skin of his head after removing his helmet.

"Yeah. Now that I'm no longer teaching, I want to get

211

more involved with the family, and that includes the club." Warryck didn't know how Kerrigan would feel about that, but if they had a chance at a future, it would have to be on his terms this time. He'd spent too much time away from his family, and he wouldn't accept a woman not willing to be part of their world. Kerrigan had enjoyed riding on the back of his bike, but that didn't mean she would want everything that went with being a biker's woman or a woman who could agree with the types of jobs the Hounds took. Still, it was a deal breaker, because he had enough regrets from his first marriage. *Marriage? Slow your roll, asshole.*

King handed the key over. "Ryot asked us to meet him and your Pop in their room to discuss plans for going after Gideon. Are you in?"

Thoughts of getting away for a bit were replaced with another type of need. War wasn't going to let the Hounds go after Kerrigan's captor without him, and he wasn't going to let his brother steamroll him either. Yes, Ryot – Ryker – was in charge, but this was his revenge for Kerrigan, much like going after Obadiah had been his revenge for Harlow. He rolled his shoulders and kept his feelings about Ryker to himself. As Ryot, his brother was these Gryphons' leader, and they wouldn't stand for War to badmouth him, even if he was a Lazlo. He had to remember that they were a different type of family. One War wasn't a part of. At least not yet.

"I'm in. I just needed a bit of fresh air and to let Kerrigan and her parents have some privacy." That wasn't necessarily a lie, but they didn't need to know why he couldn't breathe at the thought of Kerrigan leaving. He followed King, Sultan, and a Hound who introduced himself as Judge, back into the hotel. Kerrigan and her parents were stepping out of the elevator. When she saw War, she gave him a sad smile. War itched to pull her into one last embrace, but he entered the lift with the Hounds. He didn't miss the wide eyes of her parents when they sized up the three large males with him. Shawn put a hand on Kerrigan's back, urging her toward the front door.

"She yours?" Judge asked as the elevator moved upward.

"I hope so. We've both got a lot of things to work out, but..." War didn't know how to explain it, nor was he sure he wanted to. He didn't know these Gryphons, and he wasn't ready to share with anyone other than Maveryck.

"She know about our kind?" Judge pushed his sunglasses to rest atop his thick, dark hair.

"Yes. She saw me shift into my lion when those cult fuckers busted through the door. And before you ask, no. I didn't wipe her memory. If she's going to be part of my world, I need to trust her."

King clapped War on the shoulder. "I get that. I did the same thing when I met my woman. Shifted when she was in trouble. She peed her pants then burst out laughing. The first time she threatened to put catnip in my food, I knew she was a keeper."

Judge barked out a laugh. "If I had to eat Millie's cooking every day, I'd be begging for catnip."

"Shut up, you fucker. Her cooking's not that bad." King pushed the other male, and Sultan coughed to hide his own laugh. King punched his shoulder, too. "You're both jealous you don't have someone as pretty as my Millie to go home to every night. So what if she's not a good cook? She's sweeter than any woman I ever met, and she gave me two beautiful babies."

The other two men smiled at their friend, and both agreed his wife was a good woman. War wanted that for himself. Not just the woman, but the camaraderie with others of his kind. He'd spent too many years pretending to be human while keeping most of his fellow professors at arm's length.

When the elevator doors opened, War led them to Ryker's room. He didn't bother knocking. He used the spare

213

key card to let them in.

"Did our two captives make it back to The Sanctuary?" Ryker asked.

King stepped farther into the room and took a seat on the sofa. "Yes. We did a little snooping while we were there. The good news is the children are relegated to one area of the compound. There were twelve guards stationed around the perimeter, but from what we could tell, they aren't armed. Not visibly. The two men drove the car into a large building which looked like storage of some kind. They were taken by four guards to a house that is secluded from the other smaller living quarters. A man fitting Talbert's description left what we assumed was their church and walked to the house, accompanied by one guard. He remained in the house a few minutes before he came back out alone. He left the compound and headed this direction. When he was about two miles out, he pulled into the parking lot of a strip mall without getting out. Then, fifteen minutes later, he turned and headed back the way he came."

"Are you sure it was Talbert?" Sutton asked.

"Unless he has a brother, pretty sure. We were in eagle form when we were scouting, so we didn't get any pictures. It's tame as far as compounds go. There were a few men walking from one building to another, but like most of the ones we've gone into before, it was quiet. When Talbert left the church, all the women soon followed and went their separate ways. None of them were speaking to one another."

"Kerrigan said they have separate Bible study every day before they go do their assigned jobs. What exactly did you convince Lewis and Steven to say upon their return?" War asked. Ryker mentioned altering their memories, but he didn't share what he "pushed" into their minds.

"I didn't want them spouting nonsensical things, so I merely suggested they tell Gideon they found Kerrigan's room, but she was already gone. I scrubbed the parts where

214

you shifted into your lion and knocked them out, as well as being interrogated. Everything that happened from the time they busted open the door to when they were put in their car is gone."

"How are they going to explain the wounds they received?"

"I told them someone had rented the room Kerrigan had been in, and the rather large man didn't take too kindly to being surprised. Their stories will be the same. Gideon may or may not believe them, thus causing discord among his ranks."

A loud banging startled them all when the door flew open. Mav and Kyllian strode in the room, both grinning.

"We're here, bitches. Let the party begin." Mav hooked his arm around War's neck and smacked a kiss on his cheek. War grinned back. He'd never been so happy to see his twin in all his life.

Ryker frowned, crossing his arms over his chest. "How'd you get in here?"

Mav waved a keycard in the air and wiggled his eyebrows. "I just used my charm on the desk clerk."

"I thought the desk clerk was a young man," Sultan said.

"No one, male or female, is immune to all this." Mav waved a hand down his body. "Now, what'd we miss?"

# Chapter Twenty-Seven

KERRIGAN WAS QUIET in the back seat. Her parents had already asked a million and one questions about where she'd been and everything that happened before and after she'd been kidnapped. She rehashed all the details except for her private time with War. Her parents weren't blind, and they didn't miss the tender way War held her before he said goodbye. She didn't miss it either.

There was so much emotion in his eyes, and she'd barely kept herself from begging him to let her stay with him. She'd wanted more time to talk. To get to know him better. To convince him to give her a chance. She didn't know if he wanted a future with her or if their time had been nothing more than heat of the moment and close proximity. Kerrigan had never been so inexplicably drawn to a man the way she was War. Technically, she was just getting over her relationship with Dalton, but she didn't think she was on the rebound. Not from that at least.

"Kerri?" Her mother was turned around looking at her.

"I'm sorry. What?"

"Dad asked if you're hungry. We didn't have breakfast. We drove straight from the airport to come get you."

"I could eat. Warryck's dad brought sandwiches earlier, but I didn't get a chance to finish before his brother wanted to talk." It was a good thing her parents hadn't seen Sutton Lazlo. Kerrigan couldn't explain how the man looked the same age as his sons. Well, she could explain it, but they would think she'd lost her mind. Besides that, she would never betray Warryck's trust in telling the truth of what he was. Even if she never saw him again, his secret would die along with her. And that would be many years before he did. War had explained how Gryphons lived longer than normal lives where their human partners didn't. That made her sad, but War had admitted he would rather have a few years of epic love than to never know what it was like.

Her dad parked in front of a diner, and she followed her parents inside. After they placed their order, Kerrigan excused herself to the restroom, which was located down a narrow hallway at the back of the building. As she reached for the doorknob, a hand covered her mouth, and a strong arm wrapped around her body. Kerrigan tried to scream, but her voice was muffled. She struggled, twisting her face, trying to get loose so she could scream.

"Come with me, or your parents will disappear for good." Kerrigan knew that voice, even if it was barely more than a growl. His breath was hot against her face, but it was nothing like Warryck's when he was talking to her. *Warryck.* Gideon pressed his hand tighter, his fingertips digging into her already painful ribs. She nodded behind his hand, because what choice did she have? He was stronger than her, and she would do anything to keep her parents safe. She should have known Gideon wouldn't just let her go without a fight. "If you make any noise at all, I'll call my men, and your parents are dead. Got it?" Kerrigan whimpered and nodded again. It pissed her off she was showing weakness, but he was using her parents as leverage.

Gideon kept his arm around her as he pushed her out the back door and behind the building where his car was waiting. He looked around before forcing her into the trunk. Kerrigan curled into a ball as the lid slammed closed, blocking out the light. A few seconds later, the engine roared to life, and the car started moving.

Damnit! Not again. There was no way she was going to let Gideon take her back to his compound, but what if he really did have someone watching her parents? If only she could get word to War. Her cell phone! It was in her back pocket. Kerrigan was surprised Gideon hadn't searched her before shoving her into the trunk. Kerrigan put her phone on silent and thanked all the gods, including Zeus, she had a signal. She sent War a text telling him what happened and begged him to find her. Again.

Her phone vibrated almost immediately.

Warryck: *Hey, Sweetheart. Hold on. I'm coming for you.*

Kerrigan: *Please send someone to the diner for my parents.*

Warryck: *We'll keep them safe. If Gideon pulls you from the trunk before we get there, try to hide your phone so we can track the signal.*

Kerrigan: *I will. War…*

Warryck: *I know, Sweetheart. I'm sorry I let you leave. When I get you back, I'm never letting you out of my sight again.*

Kerrigan gasped. He wanted her. War, the big, badass Gryphon wanted her! Now she had to stay alive long enough for them to be together. The car hit a bump, and Kerrigan's head was knocked against the side panel. "Damnit." Kerrigan rubbed her temple. At least it wasn't bleeding. Her phone vibrated.

Warryck: *Lucy has a lock on your phone. Hang tight. I'm on my way.*

Kerrigan wanted to tell him she didn't have a choice, but she responded with an OK instead. Had her parents noticed she was missing yet? It had only been minutes since she'd left them sitting at the table. She should probably text them, but whoever War had going to look after them would tell them what happened. "Please, Zeus. Don't let them get hurt," she whispered.

Kerrigan braced her arms and legs against the back and sides of the car, doing her best to not get beat all to hell. She had no idea where Gideon was taking her. If he took her back to the compound, she had a feeling she'd end up in the inner chamber again, never to see the light of day. That was better than the alternative, though. She was too young to die. Had too much living to do, especially if War had meant what he said about keeping her with him. God, she hoped he meant it. As much as she loved her parents, she wanted to find out what a future with the Gryphon looked like. War was looking forward to his future with his family, but maybe they could figure out both their futures together.

The steady hum would have been soothing if she weren't in the trunk, kidnapped, and most likely on her way to another hidden compound. Kerrigan figured they were on an interstate when they passed louder engines she imagined were eighteen wheelers. If she could get their attention somehow, one of them might call the cops on her behalf. Using the flashlight of her phone, Kerrigan found the lights were secure behind a solid panel. She attempted to loosen the plastic bolts, but her fingers were still too sore to get a good grip.

Shifting around wasn't easy, but Kerrigan scooted as far back in the trunk as possible and searched for any type of weapon. The spare tire was supposed to be hidden in a compartment beneath her along with a lug wrench, but she couldn't pry the mat up far enough to get at either. When she flopped down onto her back, the light of her phone flashed over the trunk release. She had no idea if the release worked when the vehicle was moving, but it was worth a shot.

Kerrigan pulled on the plastic tab, and the lid opened a fraction instead of flying up like she'd wanted. She pulled the tab again, but the lid remained in the same position. Kerrigan maneuvered until she could stick her fingers through the small gap, wiggling them. She didn't know if there was a car directly behind them. If not, she was risking a lot by pissing Gideon off when he eventually pulled over.

The car hit a dip in the road, and the trunk closed down on her fingers. "Ow, shit!" Kerrigan jerked her hand back inside and cradled it against her chest.

Her phone beeped, and she searched for it with the hand that wasn't throbbing. Instead of an incoming text, it was her low-battery indicator. *Great.* If Warryck didn't hurry, his daughter was going to lose Kerrigan's location. The time showed they had been driving over an hour when she felt the car swerve then slow down. She hit the button on the side of the phone to dim the light, then she placed it face down as far back as she could, thankful it didn't have a colorful case on it.

The car came to a stop, and Kerrigan contemplated fighting Gideon when he opened the trunk. She had on the biker boots War had bought her, and she knew they would hurt if she managed to land a kick to his face, but if she was too slow or missed, it would only piss him off more than he already was. As she waited, Gideon's voice echoed through the car. His words were heated, and when she didn't hear another person, she figured he was on the phone. She wanted to text War and ask where he was or if he still had her on his radar, but she didn't want to risk Gideon finding the phone. So, she waited.

"You just thought you were smart." The trunk slammed shut before it was popped open all the way. Kerrigan tried to throw her hands up, but Gideon smacked them away and grabbed Kerrigan by her hair, dragging her from the car. He kept his fist secure in her long tresses, pulling her upright so she was in front of him. Gideon laughed in her face, but his eyes were filled with rage. "Ah, my sweet Juliette."

*Juliette?*

"You're more trouble than you're worth. Now, let's see." Gideon kept one hand in her hair while the other roamed over her body. "Where is it?" he yelled, spit landing on her cheek.

"Where's what? Gideon, you're hurting me. Please

220

stop."

"I'm going to hurt you worse if you don't tell me where your phone is." He twisted his fist in her hair, and tears leaked from her eyes.

"In there." She pointed at the car. If Lucy was as good as Warryck said, the girl would have a lock on their location. All Kerrigan had to do was stall until he could get to her.

Gideon shoved her, and Kerrigan lost her footing, landing hard on her hands and knees. She looked around, finding they were in the parking lot of what appeared to be an abandoned warehouse. There was no one around she could see, and her only options were to stay there and see what he had in store for her or to run. In her mind, she only had one choice. She slowly climbed to her feet while Gideon's back was turned. When he rose from the trunk, he had her phone in his hand. He dropped it to the ground and stomped it several times, smashing it into small pieces. Kerrigan took advantage of his attention being elsewhere and took off running.

"Stop!"

Kerrigan didn't stop. He would have to catch her. Which he probably could if he —

A shot rang out, and chunks of asphalt exploded around her feet.

"I said stop, Kerrigan! Don't think I won't shoot you."

Oh, she absolutely thought he would shoot her if she continued running, so she jerked to a halt, her chest heaving. When she turned around, her captor had the gun aimed at her.

"We could have been good together, you and I." He started walking toward her. "I would have given you the world. We would have been married, and you would have ruled The Sanctuary alongside me. But now, now I have to turn my community over to someone who will not be as kind as I have been." When he reached her side, he grabbed her arm and dragged her back toward the building. "This is all your fault, Kerrigan. Remember that when —"

A low rumble caught their attention. Gideon cursed, turning toward the sound. The rumble crested into a loud vibration as the group of Harleys rounded the warehouse, echoing off the metal structure. *Yes!* War was there.

If Gideon didn't have a gun trained on her, the sight of the Hounds would have thrilled her.

"Let her go, Talbert!" Ryker yelled from his bike as he removed his helmet and set it on one of the handlebars, the others doing the same.

"Not a step closer, or she dies." Gideon moved the gun from her side to her temple.

"Ryker, no," she pled. She didn't want him or any of his family to die for her. But where was Warryck? She recognized most of the men from when they'd entered the hotel with War. One of the others resembled War a great deal. Was that his twin?

"This is what's going to happen. She and I are going to get in the car, and you're going to let us leave. You are not going to follow. If you do, I'll shoot her."

The man who resembled War let out a roar that could only come from a large cat. The others followed suit, and it was enough to startle Gideon. He turned the gun toward the men. "What the hell?" Gideon muttered.

A sound unlike anything she'd ever heard echoed all around just as a shadow fell over Kerrigan from above, and a large beak snapped onto Gideon's wrist. Her captor let out a strangled cry, releasing his hold on her hair.

When she stumbled away, Kerrigan gasped. She'd tried to imagine what War would look like as his Gryphon, but her imagination hadn't done him justice. Standing over eight feet, War – somehow, she knew it was him – was magnificent. His eagle had Gideon's wrist in his sharp beak while his talons were wrapped around Gideon's neck, raising him off the ground. Gideon dropped the gun, and

War released the hold he had on the man's arm.

"War, don't kill the fucker," his lookalike yelled.

Warryck, the Gryphon, squawked at his brother. Kerrigan didn't have to be an eagle to understand Warryck's "fuck that."

"Yeah, I know he deserves it, but we need him alive. For now." The man closed the distance, picking up Gideon's gun along the way, using some type of cloth to keep his fingerprints from covering Gideon's. When he got close, he looked up at War. "Take care of your woman. We've got this."

The Gryphon craned his neck around, staring down at Kerrigan.

Kerrigan smiled and waved. "Hey there, big guy. I'm fine, but I could really use a hug."

War tossed Gideon away from Kerrigan with so much force he skidded a good twenty feet. In the blink of an eye, the Gryphon was gone, and War stood naked before her. If the others noticed or cared he didn't have clothes on, they ignored it and them. Warryck dragged her into his arms, nearly crushing her. He pressed his lips into her hair and inhaled. "Never again," he muttered against her temple. Kerrigan hugged him back as tightly as possible, never wanting to let go.

"War." The guy she assumed was a brother set his hand on War's shoulder, holding a set of clothes in the other. "You need to get dressed."

"Thanks, Mav." So, this was his twin, Maveryck. War took the offered clothes and quickly dressed in his usual jeans and tee. He was pulling his boots on when Maveryck approached her.

"Hi, Kerrigan. I'm Maveryck, this one's better-looking twin." He gave her a wink, and she couldn't help but roll her eyes. "Ah, so it's like that, is it?" His teasing tone put her at ease. "Seriously, though. Are you okay?"

Answering Maveryck, she looked up at Warryck when

she spoke. "I'm good. A few bumps from hitting the inside of the trunk, but it could have been a lot worse. What's going to happen to Gideon?" Kerrigan looked over to where the man was being hauled to his feet by a couple Hounds.

"Eventually, he'll go to jail for kidnapping and aggravated assault."

"You have no idea who you're messing with!" Gideon yelled. "Juliette, tell them!"

"What the fuck?" Ryker, who had been holding one of Gideon's arms, jerked him around, grabbing both of his biceps. "What did you call her?"

"Kerrigan. I meant Kerrigan. She —"

"Tell me about Juliette." Ryker's hands became talons, digging into Gideon's flesh. Nobody stepped in to stop him. The other Hounds had gone quiet for some reason. Kerrigan had also frozen at the deadly tone in his voice. She stepped closer to War, reaching for his hand, and he threaded their fingers together.

"Juliette was the name of Ryker's wife. She disappeared, and a few months later, he received word she'd died in a fire," War whispered. "He never received proof, though. What's worse is she was pregnant when she disappeared."

"Sh-she w-was my w-wife. Please... I... She died."

"And you just happened to mistake Kerrigan for your dead wife? Why is that?"

"Because Kerrigan looks like her." So that explained the photos, unless Gideon had a thing for all redheads.

Sutton stepped forward, placing his hand on Ryker's arm. "Son, you need to back away."

"No, Pop. I need fucking answers." He shook off his father's hand, returning his gaze to Gideon. "You have one chance to save your wretched life, and that's by telling me the truth. Right now. Where did you meet Juliette?"

"She..." Gideon shook his head. "I went to a party at my brother's house. Ju-Juliette was there. She was... the

224

entertainment. Not by choice. I hated what he was doing to her, but I couldn't tell him that, or he'd have made her life worse. I... I convinced him to let me have her once... once the party was over. I saved her."

"Where did your brother get her?"

"He said... he said he saw her out dancing, and he figured no one would miss a whore."

Ryker's lion roared from deep within his chest, and blood dripped from where his talons were digging into Gideon's arms. If this Juliette was Ryker's missing wife, Kerrigan couldn't blame him for his anger.

Ryker pulled Gideon closer until their faces were inches apart. "And what happened to the baby?"

"Sh-she gave her up for adoption."

Ryker released one of Gideon's arms and wrapped his talon around Gideon's neck, puncturing the skin.

"Ryker, no! As your Alpha, I demand you let him go." Sutton's voice echoed off the building, and all the Hounds froze, including Ryker.

# Chapter Twenty-Eight

WHAT A SHITSHOW. War grabbed Kerrigan, keeping her far away from Ryker and Gideon. His brother's rage was a tangible beast, swirling through the air, clawing at everyone around them. Between the bombshell Gideon had dropped on Ryker and him basically admitting he and his brother weren't the saints they claimed to be before their flocks, Warryck couldn't blame Ryker for his actions.

Kerrigan let War hold her back, but she didn't stop yelling about how Gideon was a hypocrite, cursing him. Sutton had pulled the Alpha card on Ryker, something War couldn't ever remember him doing. Ever. He was content to let all his kids make their own decisions and learn from the consequences if they weren't the right choice. War had wanted to kill Gideon himself, but Sutton had his reasons for keeping the man alive. Otherwise, he would have let Ryker tear him apart.

Hearing the man admit his brother had been the one to take Juliette all those years ago had been a shock to them all, but none more than Ryker. He'd spent over twenty years wondering what happened to his woman for her to be killed along with their unborn child in a fire. Now he knew, but it probably wasn't going to give him the closure he needed. Knowing Josiah Talbert kidnapped her then used her for private parties would set Ryker on a course for revenge.

"Where is your brother?" Sutton was in Gideon's face.

226

It was hard to hear the question over Ryker's threats and Kerrigan's accusations.

"Last time I saw him was this morning at my home. He doesn't share his plans with me, so I have no idea where he was going."

"Where does he live?"

"H-he'll kill me if he finds out I talked."

"And I'll kill you if you don't. You've seen what we are. We can rip you to shreds and scatter the pieces far and wide where no one will ever know what happened to you. You can take your chances with your brother, or..." Sutton let the rest of the threat go unspoken.

Gideon shook his head, looking at all the Hounds surrounding him. His eyes landed on Kerrigan, and War stepped in front of her. The man had caused her enough grief. "Talk. Now." War was ready to get Kerrigan away from Gideon and decide whether or not to wipe her memory. He didn't want to, but Sutton wouldn't allow her to be witness to Gideon's death without insisting she had no memory of it.

Kerrigan eased around War and slid her arm around his waist. "If he refuses to talk, you can probably wait a few days for Josiah to return to the compound. Gideon has meetings there at least once a week, and I'd lay bets his brother is in attendance. Also, I think his precious flock should know what kind of man has been leading them all this time. In fact, you should probably use your, you know" — Kerrigan tapped her temple — "on him before taking him back. Let them decide for themselves whether or not to hang around before his brother comes back and takes over."

"Those at The Sanctuary aren't capable of living without someone leading them. They rely on me to purchase the things we can't make ourselves. You can't just turn them back into society. They'd never make it." Gideon sighed. "I admit Kerrigan was there against her wishes, but other than that, I haven't broken any laws."

227

"No? What about Mac? You tracked her like an animal all because she fell in love. You kept her there against her will, too. Tell me, Gideon. What happened to Elijah? Did you let your dog go after him? Where is he?" Kerrigan was shaking, so War wrapped his arms around her, trying to calm her down.

"He was taken to Josiah's compound to live."

"Forgive me if I don't believe you."

Sutton stepped closer to Gideon. "We're going to need the address to see for ourselves. If we find this Elijah safe and sound, that'll be one less mark against you."

"I've done nothing wrong."

Ryker tightened his grip. "If you consider kidnapping and imprisonment nothing, then our definition of wrong is worlds apart."

"Whatever. I'm dead either way."

"Are you refusing to give up your brother's location?" Sutton asked. Gideon shrugged, and Sutton told Ryker, "First, we're taking him back so his followers can hear his sins, then he's all yours."

"You can't make me talk, and they'll never believe you."

"Tell me, Gideon. What did Lewis and Steven tell you happened at the hotel?"

"What does that have to do with anything?"

"It has everything to do with what's going to happen next. Did they tell you Kerrigan took one of them out with a lamp before she got away? Or did they say someone else was already in the room when they got there?" Sutton crossed his arms over his chest, smirking.

"What... how...?"

"That's what I thought. Ryker, tie him up and stick him in the back seat. We're going to pay a little visit to his people before his brother comes back. After we finish there, we'll go check on the Elijah kid."

"I'm going with you," Kerrigan demanded, ready to

228

fight War if he refused. He wouldn't take that away from her. She deserved to follow this thing through to the end, and he wasn't about to let her out of his sight.

"Of course, Sweetheart, but you need to call your folks and let them know you're okay."

"Gideon crushed my phone."

War handed her his phone and placed a kiss on her forehead. While she called her parents, War and Mav walked over to where their father and Ryker were in a heated argument. His adrenaline had waned, somewhat. When he got the call from Kerrigan's father that she'd disappeared from the diner, he'd lost his shit. It had taken several of the Hounds to hold him back from leaving without a plan. He knew then his feelings for Kerrigan were real, and he wanted her in his life for as long as she'd have him. When she sent him the text saying Gideon had taken her again, first he vowed to get her back. Then he swore he would tell her how he felt, regardless of how little time they'd known each other.

War was going to have to do something nice for his daughter. If it wasn't for her sitting behind a desk in New Atlanta, he never would have found Kerrigan in the first place. Probably never would have met her and fallen... War glanced back at Kerrigan and caught her staring at his ass while talking on the phone. She looked up, and when he smirked, she shrugged. God, she was perfect.

With Lucy's help, he and the Hounds tracked down the car Gideon was driving. If the man had known he was surrounded by Gryphons, War doubted he'd have pulled over. Men like Talbert thought they were untouchable. When he saw the gun pointed at Kerrigan's head, his Gryphon had taken over. Sure, he had the element of surprise on his side, but he was a little pissed at his animal for doing something so rash. The gun could have gone off. It didn't, and they saved Kerrigan, but still. War had argued, but in the end, it hadn't mattered.

*We saved our female.*

"Shut up."

Mav looked at him. "You say something?"

"Just arguing with my Gryphon."

"Yeah, I hate when mine gets mouthy. Thinks it's in charge. Fucker."

*I am in charge.*

"Whatever."

"Did you hear what I said?"

"Huh?" War looked back at Mav who was laughing at him.

"No worries. I get it. This thing with Kerrigan is new, and if she were mine, I'd be distracted too. I asked if you were going to take her with us to the compound."

"Yes. She knows about the layout, and she wants to go."

"And you don't want to let her out of your sight."

"There's that. I never should have let her go off with her parents as long as Gideon was still out there."

"What's your plan when this is all over? Before I left to do the job in Ohio, you talked like you were ready to come back to the family. Has that changed?" Mav looked over War's shoulder at Kerrigan.

"That hasn't changed. I just hope I can convince Kerrigan to come with me."

"I hope so too. Love is a good look on you."

War didn't correct his twin. He had loved Harlow, and his feelings for Kerrigan were just as strong if not stronger. He didn't care how short a time he'd known her. He knew what he felt was love, and the way she looked at him said she felt something for him as well. If it wasn't love on her part, War would give her time.

When she walked back to where he was standing, Kerrigan was frowning. "My parents are really upset that I'm planning on going with you to The Sanctuary. They want to come get me and continue with our original plan to

230

go to South Carolina."

"Are they going to wait for you?" War held his breath, waiting on her answer.

"That depends. I was hoping you and I could spend some time together, but I don't want to intrude on your time with Maveryck."

"I like the idea of you on the back of my bike. Taking off and just going wherever the roads lead. Would you like that?"

"I really would. I've spent most of my life in New Portland. Now that I'm out of a job, it's the perfect time for a vacation with a sexy man and his motorcycle. Maybe we can head south and spend a few days at the beach so my parents get used to us being together." War placed his palm behind Kerrigan's hair and tipped her head up, placing his lips on hers.

"Sorry to interrupt." Mav stepped closer when they pulled apart. "Sutton wants to head to the compound now before Gideon's brother figures out something's wrong. If you want to drive Kerrigan in the car, one of the Hounds can ride your bike."

"Can we take your bike, please?" Kerrigan asked War, grinning.

"Whatever you want, Sweetheart."

Mav whistled low and nudged War with his elbow. "Kerrigan, do you have a sister?"

"Sorry, no."

"Figures. Well, if you get tired of the serious twin, let me know."

War shoved Maveryck away. "Shut up, you pest."

Maveryck threw his head back, laughing. He winked at Kerrigan after sobering. "Let's ride."

When they approached War's Harley, King walked over. "Why don't you take my bike? I've got a backrest for when Millie rides with me, and it will be safer as well as more comfortable for Kerrigan." War swallowed hard and nodded. Most bikers didn't allow someone else on their ride, but War was quickly learning the Hounds were different. They treated each other like family. "Thanks, King. I would appreciate that." They swapped keys, and War grabbed his helmet while the other male did the same. He set it on Kerrigan's head and secured the chin strap. "Our first order of business after this mess is over is to get you a helmet. Then we will go shopping for clothes and whatever else you need." War had plenty of money, and he planned on giving Kerrigan anything her heart desired. The smile spreading across her face warmed him from the inside out.

War should have included himself in the discussion the Hounds had about how they would handle things once they arrived at the compound, but he'd been too invested in everything Kerrigan. He tried to concentrate on what would happen when they arrived, but her arms around his waist and her chin on his shoulder were too much of a distraction. He settled his left hand on her knee, and she leaned in closer. The ride took well over an hour, and he'd never enjoyed a trip as much as he did that one.

War had always prided himself on being responsible, and as Maveryck joked, serious. He wasn't always like that. Before Harlow, War had been just as fun-loving and carefree as his twin. He couldn't blame the change in his demeanor on his wife's death, though. He'd changed before that. War wanted to get back to the way he'd been before. As he rode with the Hounds, a temporary member of their group, he felt something shift inside. He wanted this. To be part of both their MC as well as the other work they did. And he wanted to do it with Kerrigan by his side.

When the Hounds pulled over to park their bikes, Maveryck rolled to a stop beside them. "Most of us are going to walk in so the guards in the area aren't aware there are so many of us. Sutton and Ryker are going to drive Gideon inside. Kerrigan, you can ride with them so you don't have to walk."

She turned to War. "Will you come with me?"

"Like you could stop me." They angled off the bike, and he held Kerrigan's hand as they strode to the car where his father and brother were waiting.

# Chapter Twenty-Nine

KERRIGAN WAS NERVOUS. She trusted Warryck to keep her safe, but being back inside the compound was the last place she wanted to be. But she'd willingly returned if for no reason than to save Mac. Before she and War joined Ryker and their dad in the car, Sutton explained how they "convinced" Gideon to cooperate. The only memories of his they erased were the ones where War shifted into his Gryphon and Ryker used his talons. At some point, they had cleaned his wounds well enough they weren't immediately noticeable. The plan was for Gideon to walk into the compound, gather his followers in the building where he held Bible study, and admit to his sins. All of them.

When they arrived, several guards met them at the large building next to the barn. There were no roads or drives leading farther into the compound, so it only made sense to stop there.

"What's going on?" The guards had surrounded their vehicle, and the largest of the group held open the door for Gideon when Ryker stood aside to let him out of the back seat.

"I need to have a meeting with everyone. Gather all the men and women into the sanctuary. The workers watching the children can remain where they are. The kids don't need to be bothered." Gideon looked like hell, and his guards were staring instead of moving. "Now, James. I'll explain everything, but I don't have a lot of time. Oh, and make sure to bring Sparrow from the inner chamber."

The guards held back, but the one he addressed as James inclined his head then motioned for the others to follow. Gideon set out on the same path she and Sparrow had walked. "This path leads to his house, not the sanctuary."

Gideon turned and snarled, "I need to change clothes, if that's okay with you."

Ryker grabbed hold of Gideon's bicep. "It's not okay. Once you confess to your flock the kind of man you are, they're not going to care if your shirt is ripped or not. Besides, when we're done here, you'll be wearing prison garb."

Gideon jerked his arm free and turned toward the path the guards had taken. Ryker looked at Kerrigan, and she nodded. In her mind's eye, she could picture the layout of the buildings, and the direction they were headed should lead them to the center of everything. When they got through the trees, men and women were leaving their jobs and walking quietly to the sanctuary. If they thought it odd Gideon had called them all together, they weren't talking about it amongst themselves. Some greeted Gideon, and he responded to those who dared to say hello. When they noticed Kerrigan and the others following behind, people pointed and whispered.

War leaned over and whispered, "This isn't creepy at all." He was looking around, and Kerrigan remembered she had the same thought when she first saw how everyone was dressed, moving around like a heard of sheep. Kerrigan searched the masses for McKenzie. She wanted to talk to the younger woman and give her a head's up, but she didn't see her anywhere.

While the men and women entered the building from the front, Gideon stepped through a door at the back and stopped just inside. "What are you waiting on?" Ryker shoved him forward. If looks could kill, Ryker would have been incinerated, but the large Hound ignored Gideon and continued marching him toward the door leading to the sanctuary. The front pews were filled with couples, and behind them, single women filled the rows on the left, while the single men took those on the right. Those who had already seen the Hounds and Kerrigan stared, but those who hadn't whispered and pointed. Gideon had allowed talking before he brought the congregation to order during Bible study, so it wasn't surprising the building was filled with quiet murmurings.

When Gideon stepped to his podium, the crowd immediately hushed. Sutton and Ryker flanked him on either side, while Kerrigan and War stayed a few feet back. She didn't miss the way people stared at her. Kerrigan supposed she did look a shock in her jeans, boots, and leather jacket. It wasn't cold out, but she loved the coat so much since it was a present from Warryck she refused to take it off. Besides, she felt like a badass dressed like a biker chick, even without any makeup on her face.

Before he began speaking, Gideon looked over his shoulder to where Kerrigan was standing with War. He glanced down at their joined hands, frowning. Shaking his head, he turned his attention to the congregation. "You're probably all wondering why I called you together. I want to start off by saying it has been the greatest joy of my life, leading this community. When I built The Sanctuary all those years ago, I was a sinner with a narrow mind. My father and brother had started their own communities, and I was determined to follow in their footsteps. Over the years, I became a different man. A better man. At least I had in my own eyes. But like all men, I fall short daily. And not so long ago, I fell far." Gideon wiped his brow with his knuckles and cleared his throat.

"Those of you who were here from the beginning know

236

I had a wife. I took her from a life of depravation and brought her here to live, where I did my best to turn her from her sinful ways to a life filled with God's word and what he wanted from all the women He created. When she told me she was already married, I didn't believe her. I thought it was her way of..." Gideon stopped speaking when Ryker growled at him. "Long story short, I was lost when Juliette died. I thought I could continue with my work here, leading all of you to happy, fulfilling lives. I brought women to my home in hopes I'd find a suitable replacement to stand by my side, but that never happened. Then, Brother Steven showed up with Kerrigan O'Shea, and I thought God was giving me a second chance at my own happiness. I know some of you recognized the resemblance between Kerrigan and Juliette. I was sinful and selfish. I kept Kerrigan here against her wishes." Gideon turned to face her. "I'm sorry, Kerrigan. I should have let you go the first time you asked it of me."

Kerrigan narrowed her eyes at the man. She had heard Gideon speak during Bible study. She'd heard him in his home when he held meetings. She knew he was a gifted orator, and she knew he was lying through his teeth. He was only sorry he got caught. Kerrigan crossed her arms over her chest and cocked her head to the side. The man was playing to the sympathies of the congregation, and she was having none of it.

"You're sorry? Are you sorry you sent your dog to hunt me down? The same way you did McKenzie? Are you sorry you kidnapped me a second time, tossed me in the trunk of your car, and held me at gunpoint threatening my life? Tell the good folks all about that, Gideon."

"I... No, I..." The congregation grew louder, drowning out Gideon's words.

"Tell them, Gideon!" Kerrigan shouted. When she had their attention, she continued. "Tell them about your brother's parties. About how the two of you are the same

237

types of men you preach against. Tell them the truth!" War wrapped his arms around her from behind.

Gideon's face turned red, his eyes full of hate. He took a step toward Kerrigan, but Ryker stepped between them at the same time War pushed her behind his larger body.

"She's telling the truth!" Everyone turned as McKenzie stood and yelled over the din of excitement. "His dog did this to my face," she cried, pointing at the scar. "He made me give my baby up for adoption just because I was in love with Elijah and wanted nothing to do with Lewis. I didn't even get to see her after she was born. What kind of monster does that?"

A woman in the front row stood. Her husband tried to pull her back down, but she jerked away. "McKenzie? Oh, honey." The woman jogged back to where Mac was shaking in the aisle between the pews and wrapped her arms around her. "Why didn't you tell me?"

"Because he wouldn't let me! Wouldn't let me see anyone. I was hidden away from everyone for months. I spent every day by myself. Gideon brought in a doctor once a month to check on me, and after I gave birth, I was alone again. I could have fucking died, and no one would have known!"

"You bastard!" the woman yelled. "You promised. You promised she'd be safe here if we did what you asked. How could you do that to your own flesh and blood?"

"Because she's not mine!" Gideon yelled. "She's a whore, the same as her mother was!"

"Momma, what's going on? What are you talking about?" Sparrow had joined McKenzie and their mother in the middle of the room. Kerrigan hadn't noticed the girl walk up.

"That... that man up there is a liar and a snake. He promised he'd keep your sister safe if we adopted her. Told us she was his, he couldn't raise her after her mother died. Was Juliette even McKenzie's mother?" she asked

238

Gideon.

Several things happened at one time. McKenzie passed out. The man who'd been sitting with Mac's mom rushed the stage, yelling at Gideon. The guards started toward the front of the building from where they had been standing around the room, but the Hounds who had been waiting outside, stormed into the sanctuary, stopping them from getting to Gideon. Sutton and War were holding Ryker back from killing Gideon or shifting, Kerrigan didn't know which. Mac's dad – her adoptive dad – tackled Gideon and punched him. Gideon got the man in a head lock, and they wrestled each other until they rolled off the stage. A Hound Kerrigan hadn't seen before separated the two of them and grabbed Gideon by the collar, lifting him off the floor.

An ear-piercing whistle rent the air, and the room went quiet. Sutton stepped up to the podium. "Everyone be quiet and sit down. Now." Kerrigan thought he might have been using his shifter voice, because she sat down on the floor without meaning to. Sutton took the few steps between them to reach her and held out a hand. Sutton gave her a cheeky grin as he pulled her to her feet, keeping her close. When he looked back out over the congregation, his grin was gone, and in its place was the face of a man who had something important to say. "As you can see, your leader isn't the man he claims to be. I'm sure there are some of you who won't want to leave, seeing as this has been your home for a long time. No one can make you leave unless we find out your whole community was complicit in the kidnapping of Kerrigan O'Shea, or you've been conducting illegal acts here at The Sanctuary. For those of you who wish to move away, my family and I will do everything in our power to help you."

"Why would you do that?" a man in the front row asked.

"Because it's the right thing. No one should have to live somewhere because they're forced to do so. I'm not going to try and convince you this community is a bad place to live given the right leadership. Gideon and the men who helped kidnap Kerrigan and kept her here against her will are going to be turned over to the police. An investigation will be opened, and your lives will be chaotic while that happens."

"Don't listen to this outsider! None of you can run The Sanctuary. You don't have the money or the knowhow. Your home will fall into ruin the minute I leave here. Umph!" The Hound holding onto Gideon twisted his arm behind his back and whispered something in his ear. Gideon's eyes grew wide, but he kept his mouth shut afterwards.

"Our family doesn't claim to know how to keep a community like this afloat. We don't come in and try to take over. Our concern is only for those living here against your wishes. If you want to leave, meet us outside. We will arrange for you a place to stay as well as transport for your belongings. If you decide you want to remain here, we wish you nothing but the best."

It didn't surprise Kerrigan when only a handful of people moved from where they were seated. McKenzie had regained consciousness by that point, and she said something to her mother before making her way to where Kerrigan was standing. "Can I just say I'm glad you didn't listen to me about staying out of the woods?"

"How did you know I took off through the woods?" Kerrigan smiled at Mac, wanting to reach out for the other woman, but held back. She couldn't imagine being put on the spot in front of the whole community. "I didn't think people were allowed to talk around here."

"Oh, you know. That rule's only for us troublemakers. Lewis told the other guards who told their wives who... You get the picture. He said, and I quote, 'Kerrigan was amazing.' At least that's how I heard it. By the time it got through the hundreds of people and down the line to me, he could have said something about carrots being amazons."

Kerrigan laughed, but she could tell Mac was using humor to stifle the pain. "Did you know you were adopted?"

Mac looked to where her parents were standing with Sparrow. "Yeah. I don't remember anything before them. I've asked about my biological parents often, but they said they couldn't tell me. Guess now I know why."

"I'm sorry about Juliette. But..." Kerrigan wasn't sure whether to open that certain can of Ryker worms. What if this wasn't his Juliette? "I need to do something right quick. Will you wait here for me?"

"Yeah, sure. I need to figure out where I'm going to go now." Mac looked glanced at her parents again, but she didn't make a move to go speak with them.

"I'll be right back. I promise." Kerrigan squeezed Mac's shoulder before approaching Ryker. "There were some pictures in Gideon's nightstand, and I'm pretty sure they're of his Juliette. They're sort of, well, the woman in the photo is tied up. I don't know if you want to—"

"Let's go," Ryker barked, grabbing Kerrigan's bicep.

"Take your fucking hand off her." War stepped in front of them, his hands clenched at his sides. Kerrigan had seen that look on War's face. The one that meant he was about zero-point-five seconds away from shifting.

"I need answers, and she might have them." Ryker was shaking, but he did release her arm.

Kerrigan reached for War's hand, and he laced their fingers together. She turned to Ryker, offering a soft smile. "Come on. I want to give both you and Mac some closure."

It didn't take long to walk to Gideon's house. The door wasn't locked, so that was one less thing to worry about. She had no doubt Ryker would have kicked it in, and they didn't need anyone coming around to interrupt. War and Ryker followed her to the bedroom, and she didn't make them wait. Kerrigan opened the drawer and found the photos along with her credit cards. When she held the pictures against her chest, Ryker held out his hand.

"You've already warned me."

Kerrigan sighed and handed the stack to him. As he flipped through each one slowly, his face went from hard to soft to sad.

"It's her." Ryker shoved the photos into the pocket of his leather coat. "Which means..."

"Mac is your daughter." War placed a hand on his brother's shoulder. "Your daughter is alive."

"But she's not mine. Not anymore."

"Yes, I am." They all turned to find McKenzie standing in the doorway. "Unless you're ashamed of me, too."

Ryker pushed past War and took her hands in his larger, scarred ones. "Why would I be ashamed of you? As far as I know, all you did was fall in love."

"Will you tell me about her?" Mac shuddered out a sob. "Please?"

War motioned for Kerrigan to follow him so they could give Ryker and Mac some privacy. When they reached the kitchen, she leaned against the counter, staring at her credit cards.

"What do you have?" War asked.

"My credit cards. Gideon took them along with my driver's license when I got here. I found them when I first saw the photos of Juliette. I hate to even check with the companies. I bet Dalton maxed them out while I was missing."

"If he did, I'll pay the balance." War took them from her and shoved them in his pocket.

Kerrigan didn't want that. War had already spent too much money on her. "You don't have to do that."

"I know I don't, Sweetheart, but I want to."

Kerrigan already knew she was in love with War, but his generosity was another thing that drew her to him. She'd never had that, and she wanted it. Kerrigan wanted War in

242

her life.

"I have a question. If Ryker is Mac's father, does that make her a Gryphon too? I'm just wondering, because if she has the ability to shift, wouldn't she have been able to get away from the dog?"

"Not all offspring are shifters if one of the parents is human. Since Juliette was human, Mac had a fifty-fifty shot at being Gryphon."

"So..." Kerrigan wasn't going there. War already had a child, and Kerrigan didn't need to think about things she probably would never have. Instead she asked, "What happens now?"

"I'm guessing it's like my father said. They'll call the cops in to deal with Gideon. You'll need to give your statement about everything that happened. If it goes to trial, you'll probably have to testify, but I'll be right there with you the whole time. Like I said earlier, I'm not letting you out of my sight."

"And like I said, I'm good with that." Kerrigan pushed War back against the counter and settled between his legs. "Kiss me." She had nothing tangible to offer, but she could give him her whole heart.

War dug his fist into her hair and slanted his mouth over hers. Kerrigan wrapped her arms around his neck while teasing his lips with her tongue. War took the hint and deepened the kiss, dragging her closer with a hand on her hip. Passion flowed through their connection, and War's cock grew hard against her thigh. Kerrigan wanted him naked and inside her.

"War," she panted against his mouth.

"I know, Sweetheart. Me, too."

Someone cleared their throat behind her, and War pressed his forehead against hers, growling low.

"Sorry to interrupt, but the cops are on their way. Plus, we need to help round up those who want to leave." Ryker stood with his arm around Mac's shoulder. Both their eyes

243

were rimmed in red, but they were smiling. It was a good look for them. The smiles, not the bloodshot eyes.

Kerrigan stepped away from Warryck, going to Mac. "Are you okay?"

"I will be."

# Chapter Thirty

HOLDING KERRIGAN'S HAND, Warryck stood in awe of his father. Ryker might be the President of the MC, but Sutton was in charge when it came to dealing with the police as well as getting the members of The Sanctuary somewhere to stay while they figured out next steps. He'd always looked up to his dad, but seeing him in action solidified War's need to return to the family and help any way he could.

"Your dad's something else," Kerrigan whispered, her eyes glued to Sutton as he spoke to the local cops who had Gideon, Lewis, and Steven in the back of different patrol cars.

"So is my mom. But where Dad takes control of a situation with a calm demeanor and grace, Rory is this balls-to-the-wall tornado who sweeps in and nobody knows what's hit them."

"She's going to hate me, isn't she?"

"Why would you think that?"

Kerrigan bit her bottom lip. "Because you already told me she didn't like the way Harlow came between you and your family."

"Sweetheart, I'm not sure I follow. I thought you were okay with what I explained to you about the Hounds and what my family does." War had been honest about how they sometimes took jobs as mercenaries, but he figured if she disagreed with that aspect of things, he'd wipe her memory.

"Oh, I'm fine with it. In fact, I think I'd like to help when you go in and take down the Ministry. Having firsthand knowledge of what goes on behind compound walls could be useful."

"And I agree. I'm still not seeing how Rory wouldn't find that a plus."

"I guess I figured now that you've agreed to work with your family and given how we met, she'd think less of me."

War smiled and tipped Kerrigan's face up so he knew she was listening. "She's going to love you. All Rory wants is for all her kids to be happy. I think she knew deep down I wasn't with Harlow. Don't get me wrong. I loved Harlow, but if there's one thing I learned from watching my parents, it's that love is more than two people being together. It takes compromise. I think we both know how it is to be in a relationship where one partner gave more than the other, and I just can't see you being a selfish person. I'm sure at some point we won't see eye to eye on things, and I haven't been in a relationship in almost twenty-five years. I'm bound to screw things up. But I care deeply about you, and I'll do anything to make this work."

"Won't your mom be mad you're going to spend time with my parents first?"

"Mom is in Texas with a couple of my sisters, but I think once she returns, she's going to focus all her attention on her new granddaughter." War pointed to where Ryker was standing with Mac. "Rory's good about making up for lost time. When you meet Lucy, she'll tell you all about that."

"I can't wait to meet her. From what you told me, she had a big hand in you finding me. I need to thank her."

"I know I've already asked you this, but are you okay with me being something besides human?" War would let Lucy decide whether or not to tell Kerrigan about Tamian being a Gargoyle, but only if she was really good with the

246

knowledge of shifters.

"Are you kidding me? You're so sexy in human form, but when you shift? Holy smokes, you're something else. I am so okay with it." Sutton got their attention, and War led Kerrigan over to where the deputy was waiting to take her statement.

"I would ask what has you looking like that" — Sutton pointed to War's face — "but I know the feeling. I still look that way when your mom walks into the room."

"I know it's sudden, but it feels right."

"When you know, you know. I don't mean to be insensitive, but you never smiled like this around Harlow."

"I loved Harlow with all my heart, but it was young love, and with Kerrigan, it's different. God, Dad. It hit me before I even met her. I had this pull to search for her as soon as I saw her photo. But when Mav and I couldn't find her, I gave up. If it wasn't for Lucy continuing to dig and my Gryphon prodding me to return to the campground, I might not have ever met her."

"But you did, so don't be too hard on yourself. Everything happened as it was supposed to, when it was supposed to. If Mav hadn't taken the job in Ohio, you wouldn't have returned to Green Mountain when you did. Kerrigan loves you. Take that knowledge and go forward. She's good for you, and she's going to fit right in with our family."

"Yeah, she's already looking forward to helping with the Ministry. Besides that, she looks hot on the back of my bike."

"You're not wrong there." Sutton nudged War.

"Hey, old man. Eyes off my woman."

"What? I'm old but not dead." Sutton laughed softly, but soon after, he sighed, his eyes bright with unshed tears. "Not only did you find a good female, but you brought your brother some closure. It's been a long time since I've seen him without a haunted look on his face. He's kept himself

247

guarded all this time, so maybe now that he knows she's really gone, he can move on." As if he knew they were talking about him, Ryker looked their way and inclined his head. War hoped his father was right.

Warryck stood patiently while Kerrigan gave her statement and graciously answered their questions. He stood close as she and Mac talked briefly about Mac's future getting to know Ryker, and Kerrigan promised to check on her once she'd gotten settled. She'd tried to find Sparrow, but the younger woman and her parents were nowhere to be found. His female had a good heart, and he was proud to not only know her, but to know she was his. He couldn't wait to begin their new life together.

War and Kerrigan stopped off in New York before heading south. Hayden was the Hounds' go-to mechanic for their bikes. Even though adding a backrest wasn't technically a mechanical issue, War didn't want anyone besides his younger brother to do the work. Introducing Kerrigan to more of his family felt good, especially when they instantly fell in love with her. Just like Mav had, Kyllian asked if she had a sister. Kerrigan took it in stride, but War could tell it made her feel good about herself even if her cheeks blushed a delicate pink. After Hayden finished up with the bike, the four of them enjoyed pizza and beer while they talked about Gideon and The Sanctuary.

After spending a few hours with his brother, he and Kerrigan headed out on the road. They weren't in a hurry to get to South Carolina, but War was eager to get his female alone. Having her on the back of his bike was a blessing and a curse. She not only looked good all decked out in the leather he'd bought her, but she felt amazing snuggled up against his back as they rode. Too amazing, and it was all War could do not to pull off every exit leading to a hotel.

They rode several hours until his need to be inside her overrode every other thought. Kerrigan never complained about needing to stretch her legs or having to pee. She was

248

the perfect riding partner. After checking into one of the nicer chain hotels, they settled into their room. Even though they had already had sex, War was nervous.

"Are you hungry?" he asked as he placed their bags on the floor beside the dresser. When she didn't answer, War turned around and stood immobilized. Kerrigan had already tossed her jacket aside, removed her boots, and now she was sliding her jeans down her long legs, taking her panties off at the same time. Biting her bottom lip, she nodded at him with heated eyes.

"Starving."

Seeing her bare skin, War found he was starving as well. Fully clothed, he stalked the few steps it took to reach her and slid to his knees. He couldn't wait to be inside Kerrigan, but first, he needed a taste. Gently, he pushed her back against the bed, and when she was sitting, he picked up one of her feet and massaged her arch while sucking on her toes. Kerrigan gasped. "Is this okay?" She nodded, so he continued exploring each toe before switching feet. After getting his fill, he urged her thighs apart and licked her from her pretty pucker up to her clit, savoring her essence.

War made love to her pussy with his mouth, working his fingers in tandem with his tongue. Kerrigan grabbed his hair, squeezing tighter the closer she got to release. Her harsh breaths alternated muttered curses as she released the hold she had on his head and grabbed onto the comforter. "War." His name sounded like both a curse and a plea. He took his time, licking her folds and sucking on her clit while his fingers explored inside. She was so wet and tight. He ignored his own need and concentrated on driving Kerrigan to the brink, over and over, until her legs were trembling.

"I can't... War... Oh, please let me come," she begged.

When War stood to remove his clothes, Kerrigan jerked her head up. "Where did you go?" He had never seen her angry, not with him, but leaving her at the edge without taking her over had his pretty redhead steaming.

"I'm coming right back." He made quick work of undressing, desperate to be inside his female. He would let her come, but it would be around his cock. Kerrigan's face was still etched with exasperation as she reached between her legs and circled her clit with her fingers.

War grabbed her hand and pulled it away, licking her glistening fingertips. "None of that, Sweetheart. I'll get you there, I promise. But it's going to be while I'm inside you."

After rolling on a condom, he scooted her up the bed so she was lying on the pillows. Her thighs opened for him, and he didn't make either of them wait. Sliding into her wet core, War knew he was home. Their bodies fit perfectly. Bracing himself on his forearms, War kept his eyes locked to hers so she could see how much he loved her. His Gryphon urged him to take her harder, but War kept his pace slow and sensual. There would be time for down and dirty later. She had been through some trying days, and War wanted to erase the bad with nothing but good.

He wanted to tell her exactly how he felt, but he would wait until the time was perfect. He was afraid she would think it was the sex talking and not his heart.

"War, I…" Kerrigan arched her back, gaining more friction against her clit as he stroked her core faster. Thrashing her head side to side, she scraped her still-jagged nails down his back. She was marking him, and he wanted to do the same to her. Gryphons didn't have fated mates, but sinking their sharp teeth into a partner's neck was something reserved for that special one.

*Do it. Make her ours.*

War let his lion's sharp canines drop from his gums. When Kerrigan saw them, her eyes widened, and her breathing hitched.

"Do it. Mark me."

When Kerrigan gave permission for something War had never done, his Gryphon roared inside his head, and he dropped his mouth to her neck, puncturing the skin until her blood seeped into his mouth. He'd tasted the blood of animals when he hunted, but that had been for sustenance. This was a claiming, and in that moment, War's spirit aligned with Kerrigan's. She cried out as her body tightened around his cock, and War shot his seed into the condom as he came harder than he ever had in his life. He retracted his canines and licked at the blood, the wounds closing instantly. He slowed his movements, his cock throbbing through the aftershocks.

"Holy shit, that was intense." Kerrigan raised her head, pressing kisses to his neck, nipping at his beard with her lips. When he caught his breath, he took her mouth, teasing her tongue with his own. Kerrigan wrapped her legs around his hips, deepening the kiss. His cock was lengthening, and he cursed the need for protection.

"Shit, Sweetheart. Let me get rid of this condom."

"I need to get back on the pill, because this" – she motioned at him pulling out – "isn't going to cut it."

War huffed out a laugh. "I agree. But until then, it's a good thing I bought the large box." After tossing the spent rubber into the waste can, War grabbed several wrappers out of the box and tossed them beside Kerrigan on the bed. By the time they fell asleep, exhausted and sated, they'd used them all.

War woke with a tangle of red curls in his face and a handful of Kerrigan's ass under his palm. He released a contented sigh thinking how much his life had already changed in the course of a few weeks. His uncertain future when he left the university was now clear, and he got to proceed forward with this amazing woman by his side.

Another lovemaking session later, followed by her giving him head in the shower, they ate breakfast in the hotel restaurant before hitting the road again. They arrived at the beach in time to witness the sun setting on the horizon, oranges mixing with yellows and pinks. War had

251

watched plenty of sunsets over the years, but never had one moved him as this one did. Standing barefoot in the sand with Kerrigan's back pressed to his front, War felt peace like never before. Her hands, which were healing nicely, stroked his arms as she leaned her head back against his shoulder. War kissed her temple and inhaled deeply. Her scent was already ingrained into his senses, but he knew he'd never get enough.

"What do you think of a sunset wedding?"

Kerrigan stiffened, and War's heart stuttered. He knew it was fast, but he also knew she was it for him, and he didn't want to waste one minute more. Turning her in his arms, he took her face in his hands. "Sweetheart, when I set out on the road with Maveryck, I had no plans other than to go where my bike led. I had no purpose. And then I overheard your parents when they came into Harper's Point, and it hit me. Somehow, I knew you were mine the moment I heard you were missing and saw your photo. I had no choice but to find you. I lost my heart to you then, and you became my purpose. I love you, Kerrigan O'Shea, and I want you to become my wife. Not today, but whenever you're ready. I can't promise our life will be easy, but I can promise to love you with everything I am."

Kerrigan slid her hands up his shoulders and threaded them through his hair, pushing the long strands away from his face. "And I love you. I never thought I would find someone who looks at me the way you do or touches me so gently yet so passionately. You've also given me a purpose, and I look forward to a future with you. So yes, Warryck Lazlo, I will be your wife."

War picked Kerrigan up, kissing her while he spun them around in the sand. When he placed her on her feet, she frowned.

"What's wrong?"

"Does this mean I'll be your ol' lady?"

War chuckled and pulled her back into his arms.

"You'll be the wife of a Hound, but you'll never be an ol' lady. You'll be my life. My everything."

Kerrigan looked up at him, her eyes shining with tears. "I'm ready. For everything."

They spent the next few days with Shawn and Enya. War enjoyed getting to know them while letting them get to know him, as well as seeing how much he loved their daughter. They spent hours on the patio, drinking beer and sharing stories of Kerrigan as a child and their time in Ireland before relocating to the States. War shared as much about his family as he could without admitting the darker parts they wouldn't understand. By the time they were ready to head back to New York, War had asked Shawn's permission to marry his daughter. If their emotions hadn't been so high, it would have been comical when the older man threatened War that if he hurt Kerrigan he'd have to answer to Shawn. Kerrigan's father was tall, but War had about seventy pounds of muscle on the man. War promised he'd take care of Kerrigan and love her with everything he had.

# Chapter Thirty-One

*Two Weeks Later*

LUCY'S HOUSE WAS full of Hounds, and there was a welcome home party in full swing for Warryck, Kerrigan, and Mac. Rory had offered to host them at home, but Lucy insisted there was more room in the large three-story house she'd inherited from her adoptive parents. After stopping off in New Atlanta to visit his daughter and her mate, War was even happier than he'd been when he and Kerrigan left South Carolina. The two most important females in his life hit it off immediately, and he got to know Tamian St. Claire as well as a few of the Gargoyles of the Stone Society Clan.

When War explained his intent to move back to upstate New York to be closer to the family, Lucy offered her house to him and Kerrigan until they could find their own home. He graciously accepted after talking it over with Kerrigan. Tamian also offered to fly them on his private jet, but Kerrigan wanted to continue their trip on the Harley.

Lucy and Tamian surprised them by being there when they arrived a week later. Being surrounded by his family was more wonderful than War could have imagined. Kerrigan and Mac bonded over being new to the family, and Lucy helped Mac navigate the waters of being a granddaughter and niece to the loud group of Lazlos.

Ryker and Mac spent a lot of time catching up, and part of that was introducing her to Rory and the other brothers.

"I love you, Son."

War turned at his mother's voice. Rory was smiling as she watched Kerrigan and Mac shooting pool against Kyllian and Hayden. "I'm sorry I let our differences get in the way all these years. There's not a lot I regret in my life, but that I do."

"No, Mom. It's all on me. It took me finding Kerrigan to realize how I let Harlow manipulate my decisions. Like I told Dad, I loved my wife, but if she had been the right one, she would never have asked me to make the choices she did."

"True, but then we wouldn't have Lucy. And you wouldn't have come to this point in your life where you found Kerrigan who in turn led Ryker to McKenzie. Seeing a smile on his face is worth you and me spending a few years apart." Leave it to Rory to find the good in the bad.

Sutton walked into the room with Maveryck at his side, both stopping to speak quietly to Ryker. When he nodded at whatever they said, Sutton whistled to get everyone's attention.

"Everyone, gather around." When the room was quiet, he stepped over to where War was standing. "I truly believe everything happens for a reason, when it's supposed to happen. War, in traveling your own path, you've brought us Kerrigan and Mac. Ladies, welcome to the family. I started the MC knowing one day, all my sons would sit at the Hounds' table. It took longer than expected, but now, I have the honor of seeing that happen." Maveryck stepped forward and handed their dad a black, leather vest. Sutton held it up, showing the full Hounds of Zeus rocker on the back. "I know you said you wanted to start as a prospect, but we took a vote. Not just your immediate family, but every member of the MC unanimously decided you're already worthy to wear the kutte." Sutton held the vest out, and War allowed his father to slide it up his arms.

War had to clear his throat a couple of times to get his words out. "I will wear this with pride and do my best to always deserve it."

Cheers went up around the room, and all the Hounds stepped up to congratulate him and welcome him to the club. War never thought a piece of clothing could make a difference in how he felt, but wearing the symbol the rest of his brothers did instilled a sense of pride he only felt when he was with Kerrigan. He had ridden alongside the Hounds when they rescued Kerrigan from Gideon, but he'd felt like an imposter. Now, he was truly one of them and couldn't wait to hit the road as a fully-patched member.

Kerrigan brushed her fingertips over the patch with his name on it. Where the others had biker names, War was still War, but he was okay with that. "And I thought you couldn't get any sexier. Do you think you could wear this and nothing else for me later?"

War grinned at his female. "I think that can be arranged."

While in South Carolina, Kerrigan had called Brooks and told him she was safe. The cop who had come in to Harper's Point to talk to her parents had kept Ambrose apprised, and in turn the fisherman had kept Brooks in the loop. War asked Kerrigan if she wanted to file charges, knowing she wouldn't. There was no evidence of what Dalton had done to her, and she said she just wanted to leave that part of her past where it belonged, so she asked Brooks to let both Ambrose and the cop know she was safe.

The party resumed, and when Kerrigan went back to her pool game, Ryker asked War to step outside. He worried for a moment his older brother was going to lecture him or tell him the decision hadn't really been unanimous. Standing on the patio, Ryker's face was unreadable, but that was nothing new.

256

"While you were on the road with Kerrigan, I had the chance to speak to Donald and Amy, Mac's adoptive parents. They told me what happened to Juliette."

That wasn't what War had been expecting Ryker to say. "And? Do you want to talk about it?"

"I've had a lot of years to cope with her being gone, but to finally know the truth... You'd think knowing would make it easier, but honestly? The night she disappeared I was on the road with the Hounds. We didn't get done with our job until about three in the morning, and by that time I figured she'd already be in bed. When I was on a job, I didn't call and check in every day, but I should have. She was just such an independent woman, and I never worried about her. By the time I got home and figured out she hadn't been there, it was too late. I called the friends she'd gone out dancing with, and I even went by the club. Her friends thought she'd called a cab, and the club's cameras didn't show her leaving with anyone. She just walked right out the front door.

"Maybe she went outside for some fresh air and Josiah grabbed her then. I won't know for sure until I talk to the fucker, because I am going to talk to him when I go look for Elijah. Anyway, when Gideon found out Juliette was pregnant, he'd already fallen for her. He kept her locked at his compound the same way he did Kerrigan. He had just started The Sanctuary, and he wanted Juliette to run it with him, but if the followers knew she'd had someone else's kid, they wouldn't have bought into the bullshit he was preaching. He hid her away, and once she had the baby, he got his cousin to adopt her. They'd always had a rough time making ends meet, and Gideon agreed to help pay their bills if they'd take Mac. Eventually, Donald lost his job, and he moved his family to the compound.

"By that time, Juliette had already tried to run away twice, and the last time..." Ryker scrubbed a hand down his face, pulling on his beard. "The last time, she managed to get her hands on a car, and one of the guards chased her. You saw the roads leading into the compound. She lost control on one of the curves, and the car flipped end over end. It burst into flames when the gas tank was punctured. So that part wasn't a lie."

"Fucking hell, Ry. I'm so sorry."

"Yeah, me too. I probably shouldn't tell you this, but I'm going to kill the bastard. I'm going to find Josiah and make his death more horrible than hers."

"I'm there. Whatever you need."

Ryker reached out and rearranged War's kutte, even though it didn't need it. "This looks good on you."

"Kerrigan thinks it's sexy." War wiggled his eyebrows, and Ryker barked out a laugh.

"Thank you, War. For finding Kerrigan and in turn Mac."

"So, things are good with the two of you?"

"Yeah. She doesn't want anything to do with Donald and Amy. She knew she was adopted, but when she found out how Juliette was taken and her parents went along with the adoption knowing that, she just can't forgive them for it. She wants to keep in touch with Sparrow if it's something her sister wants. Mac's a grown woman, but she's still my kid, and I'm going to do everything I can to help her find her way. I'm also going to see if I can find out who adopted her baby. I have a granddaughter out there somewhere."

"Lucy can probably help you with that, and I'm here if you need me. You're a good male, Ry. The best I know besides Dad."

"You're not so bad yourself. I might have misjudged you."

"No, you didn't. I let Harlow influence my decisions, and they were the wrong ones."

"Well, that's all behind us now. You've got a good one this time."

258

"I sure do. And I better get back to her before Hayden tries to convince her he's the better Lazlo."

War found Kerrigan and Lucy hanging out in the kitchen, mixing margaritas. Kerrigan was explaining the best way to make them without using a mix. Tamian was sitting at the counter. The Gargoyle was never far from Lucy, and War could understand that. He hated when he wasn't in the same room with Kerrigan. He took the stool next to the male, and both sat quietly while their females chatted away about the use of fresh limes over concentrate.

Maveryck and Kyllian came into the kitchen, arguing. Mav shoved their younger brother. "Forget it. The last time I let you talk me into a bet, I came home with my —" As soon as Mav noticed the females, he shut up.

Kyllian laughed, and Maveryck's face turned red. There wasn't much that embarrassed his twin, so War really wanted to know what he was about to say. "Come on, Kyllian. I'll take you on," Ryker said from behind them.

Kyllian narrowed his eyes at their older brother, but then he smiled and wrapped his arm around Ryker's shoulders. "You got it, Ry. So, what are we going to bet? Mav's a fan of piercings."

"I'm gonna kill him and tell Rory he ran away," Mav muttered as he grabbed the pitcher of margaritas and took off with the whole batch.

"Uncle Mav, you bring that back here," Lucy yelled as she took off after him. Tamian rolled his eyes and got up to follow them, leaving War and Kerrigan alone.

"So, welcome to the family." War pulled her into his arms and pressed their lips together. "Ready to run yet?"

"Are you kidding? After being raised an only child, this is heaven."

War kissed her more deeply this time. Catcalls came from the next room, and he broke the kiss, smiling against her lips. "You sure are, Sweetheart."

The End

.

# A Note from the Author

Thank you for reading Waging War. I really hope you enjoyed this first book in my new MC series. Starting a series is always exciting, but it's also daunting. You have to build the world and introduce the characters, giving insight to what's brought them to this point as well as what's to come without overwhelming the reader. I hope I have achieved this. Maveryck's story is next, and boy is it a doozy. I almost wrote it first, but the world-building needed to happen in War's book. With Maveryck, you'll get more of the mercenary side of the Hounds, as well as more of the bikers. If you enjoyed War and Kerrigan, I hope you'll leave a review wherever you purchased the book. Reviews and word of mouth are an author's greatest form of advertising.

# About the Author

Multi-genre author Faith Gibson began writing in high school, and through the years, penned many stories and poems. As her dreams continued getting crazier than the one before, she decided to keep a dream journal. Many of these nighttime escapades have led to a line, a chapter, or even a complete story.

"Love is love, and there's not enough love in the world." This belief she holds strongly, and it's the prevailing theme in her works, all of which come with a happy ending.

Faith believes her purpose in life is to entertain the masses, even if it's one person at a time. Living just outside of Nashville, Tennessee, with the love of her life and her pit bull pup, when she's not hard at work writing her next adventure, she can often be found playing trivia while enjoying craft beer, listening to live music, or off on an adventure of her own.

Connect with Faith via the following social media sites:

https://www.facebook.com/faithgibsonauthor

https://www.twitter.com/authorfgibson

Sign up for her newsletter:

http://faithgibsonauthor.com/newsletter/

# Other Works by Faith Gibson

## The Stone Society Series

*Rafael*

*Gregor*

*Dante*

*Frey*

*Nikolas*

*Jasper*

*Sixx*

*Sin*

*Jonas – A Stone Society Novella*

*Julian*

*Urijah*

*Dane – A Stone Society Novella*

*Tamian*

## The Music Within Series

*Deliver Me*

*Release Me*

*Finding Me*

*Finding Us – a Music Within short story*

**Tap Dancing with the Devil** – *Standalone MF Suspense*

**The Samuel Dexter Books**

*The Ghost in the Mirror*

*The Ghost in the Water*

*The Ghost in the Desert – Prequel Short Story*

**The Guardians of Truth –** YA Fantasy (writing as Andi Copeland)

*Oracle*
*Seeker*

.

Printed by Amazon Italia Logistica S.r.l.
Torrazza Piemonte (TO), Italy